I0673525

SPENCER SPARKLES

ISBN 978-1-7642211-0-8 (paperback)

ISBN 978-1-7642211-1-5 (e-book)

For all of you
who believe in
magic.

1. In bed.

You've seen this in so many movies when the main character was fast asleep, curled up in bed and then the alarm went off. Time to start the day, that was what the sound represented. Get out of bed and have a good day, that was what the sound represented. Get dressed and make yourself pretty to feel good and to enchant the world, that was what the sound represented.

What the sound represented for me was dread. Dread of starting the day because it was really cosy in bed and my world in here was warm and peaceful. Dread of getting out of bed because I knew there was a chance the day could be challenging, unbearable. Dread of getting dressed because there was a chance people will give me a hard time over my clothing choices.

"Spencer!" I heard my mum call from downstairs. Not with any kind of force but with kindness and warmth in her voice. My mum was a very loving mum. And I appreciated all that she was doing for me. Especially because I knew she hasn't had it easy herself. She had her challenges too with the divorce from my dad. I didn't even remember all that much about him. I remembered that they fought a lot, I remembered he threatened her a lot, I remembered he drank a lot. I also remembered that he came into my room a lot to steal my pocket money. That was enough to remember. I was only 6, maybe 7, when they separated and consequently divorced. Since then, it has been just me and my mum. She's done the best she could to keep us financially stable, to provide food on the table each and every day, and even to make sure we had a holiday each year. When I was little, we would always go to the coast for a beachside holiday. Always the same little town, always the same quaint guesthouse that was just across the road from the beach. It was a little summer paradise for me, for us. I didn't know if we could really afford it but it was a priority for her, and she managed to make it happen one way or another.

She taught me early how to make basic food, like pasta and instant soups. She also made sure I was involved in the household chores, how to wash the dishes, how to vacuum or how to do the laundry. I didn't like it. Another dread moment. But looking back, it made me grow up that tiny bit quicker. It gave me a certain power of independence, a certain power of knowledge, and a certain power of belonging - a power I didn't feel much when I left the house. But when I came home from school, I felt that power of belonging and the power of home.

I thought about that often. My mum. My childhood. My experiences. My dreams. My fears. My home. My … bed. My haven of safety and comfort. The sound of the alarm though forced me to snap out of it, to stop reminiscing and instead, to get the party started. Even though I knew the day would be anything but a party. Reluctantly, I threw open my blanket in an attempt to motivate myself to move out of the cosy bed. But the motivation didn't kick in immediately - as it never did - and I lay there for a while longer. The blanket shovelled next to me. A little chill entered my body. I just lay there for a bit, trying to get my bearings. Breathe in. Breathe out.

The smell of toast was entering my nose. Breathe in. Breathe out. Okay, on the count of three. One, two, three. And… Let's go. "Uhhh!" I grunted as I got up. Lethargically. The smell of toast still lingered in my nostrils. It intensified when I opened my door and ultimately led me downstairs to the kitchen while thinking, "I hope mum bought the strawberry jam I like."

2. On the bus.

I was walking to the bus stop while looking down on the ground, inspecting my semi-baggy jeans. They were ripped but not fashionably in the way that the cool kids wore them. They had holes in various random areas. The most prominent one being just beneath the zipper. It was not too obvious with my sweatshirt over it, but one could notice when I sat down and had my legs slightly apart. I was conscious of it, I was worried, I was anxious. But the bus was going to be there in a few minutes, I couldn't go back to change. And even if I could have - my only other pair was in the wash. So here I was. Walking to the bus stop with holes in my pants, hoping for the best.

At least nobody was going to be able to see my blue-dotted pink socks. I really liked them. They were a present from Aunt Ruth for Christmas. I was actually a bit surprised that Aunt Ruth got those for me and not inconspicuous, plain ones. "You're a colourful person, so you should have colourful socks to match that," she said. I didn't know what she even meant by 'colourful person'. I wasn't colourful, I was boring really. And why did socks of all things match that personality? But I was not complaining. I was happy it was socks she gave me and not a sweater or hoodie with those colours. While they were both my favourite colours, I probably wouldn't have worn a sweater out to school. Too attention-drawing when all I wanted was for everyone to leave me alone and not bother me with their unwelcoming, harassing comments. So the socks were actually a good way for me to have a cheeky little secret on my feet that lifted my spirits, gave me some sort of oomph and made me feel more whole, more me, even if it was hidden.

The bus arrived, slightly delayed like most days. Eddie, the bus driver, greeted me with a big smile, exposing his huge, sparkly white teeth. "Good morning, Spencer, come on in. Did you have a nice weekend?" he asked as I entered the bus. "Yes," I answered briefly, hardly acknowledging him. I always felt bad about that. He was such a nice guy, a ray of sunshine, and he did make my school days so much better. He always listened to the local radio station Fun FM while whistling along to any kind of song he may or may not have known. Sometimes, I found his upbeat energy confronting, so early in the morning, but then I caught myself with a concealed smile on my face, observing his happy disposition.

He must have been in his 30s, mostly in tight blue jeans, well-worn sneakers, a casual collared shirt and a cap that said 'Bald' on it. One time, I asked him if he wore the cap because of what the cap said, because of baldness underneath. His reply was funny and unexpected. He said, "Bald is a German word and means 'soon'. I got it from a second-hand store and it spoke to me." I didn't know how to react to that and just left it at that. But since then, whenever I saw Eddie in his washed out black cap, I thought, "Soon". Soon, the day was going to be over and I could go back home, back to my room, back to my space of comfort, away from all these people. Soon, I was going to be free. Soon, it was going to get better.

I walked past Eddie quickly, in the hope of finding a spare seat somewhere without anyone noticing me, without any obstacles. But what was I thinking. I should have known better. The group of people who were already on the bus, those people were my obstacles. "Hey, Penny is here," Robbie bellowed from the back of the bus. Robbie was a strong and muscular guy for his age. He didn't look 15 at all. He looked way older. I have always jokingly entertained the thought that he was hiding his true identity and was in fact a grown-ass man that still had to finish school. While Robbie may have been mature-looking, buff and popular, he was not the smartest. Which was why it was astounding to me that he had so many followers - both in school and on social media. His

Insta name was 'Rubber Rob'. I suspected he chose it because he thought rubber was difficult to fight, hard to destruct, and the name simply made him look tough. His posts were cringingly eye-roll-worthy. Pictures of him and his big brother Toby on a Harley Davidson in matching leather gear and helmets. Reels of him on the scariest thrill ride I knew, the Death Drop, with Robbie posing, unfazed and emotionless. Obviously, this struck a chord for many people, it spoke to them, it resonated. They thought it was cool. But for me, nah, I was not interested but rather repulsed by it.

"Penny!" he yelled again. Penny - he came up with that name, and everyone else joined in to call me this. Ugh. Penny. Apparently, Penny was a common, lovingly created nickname for Spencers. In my case, however, it was not a nickname of endearment but rather ridicule. An expression to show their dislike, an expression to show their opinion of me. An expression of how they saw him. As this skinny kid, hiding himself in semi-baggy pants with hidden holes and hidden secrets. Well, they didn't know about the holes in my pants, or any of my secrets really. Sure, they thought I was different, odd even. But they did not know anything about me or my secrets. One secret in particular that I had not openly disclosed, yet a secret that didn't seem to be a secret after all. Maybe it wasn't much of a secret, rather than the unspoken - but perhaps obvious - truth of my personality that had many people call me 'Penny'.

"Hey, leave him alone, Robbie," I heard Eddie call out from the front. He had a stern look on his face, looking through the mirror. A look you didn't see often with him. I appreciated the sentiment, but the fact that Eddie was interfering made me feel even more of an outsider. They probably thought I couldn't defend myself and needed help from an adult. Well, they were not entirely wrong. I didn't defend myself much. I just tried to ignore them, let it all be and hoped it would be over soon. Soon. There it was again. Soon. The supposedly German logo on Eddie's cap kept on giving.

I spotted a seat next to Adrian. Adrian was a quiet boy, usually with his nose in either his phone or a book. I've often thought that maybe we could be friends, be allies, be two peas in a pod. But Adrian always seemed quite standoffish. In some ways, I felt connected to him because of how quiet and detached he seemed to be. But then again, I didn't feel connected at all because the cool kids didn't pick on him. Why? Why was that? Of course, I didn't want him to be picked on, but I still wondered... why? Why me and not him? Why not both of us? Why not neither of us? Why couldn't I just sit on the bus, unbothered by the likes of Rubber Rob and his minions. I called them minions because they were basically all the same. Zac, Mike and Benji formed the core of Robbie's gang and went along with whatever Robbie was saying or doing. They were not necessarily as nasty as him but the fact that they stuck with him made them just the same.

I looked over to Adrian as I sat down. "Hey Adrian," I muttered. I saw him peek over to check who sat down beside him but that was about all of the reaction I got. He continued to immerse himself in the world of social media, scrolling through uncountable posts at lightning speed. "Alright then," I thought and shrugged.

As I heard Robbie and the others behind us laugh and talk nonsense, the bus rolled on. I closed my eyes. I wanted to block out where I was and just focus on my own little fantasy world. I imagined lush forests and excited birds flying like acrobats. I often had dreams about flying actually. Very often, in fact. I thought about that often. Why did I dream of flying so much? My subconscious seemed to gravitate towards it. Was that normal? Upon analysing my dreams, I realised that there was probably a connection between my overall situation and my dreams. My situation transpired to my dreams. The desire to break free from burdening circumstances, the wish for liberation from stress and anxiety, the longing for escape to a happier me.

The bus stopped abruptly and pulled me away from my fantasy world, erasing the calming image of forests and birds. We were there. We were at school. "Ugh!" I thought, as I dragged myself outside.

3. Sonya.

As I walked down the front stairs of the bus, I could already see Sonya. Sonya was my best friend, my only friend. I have known her since kindergarten, where we clicked immediately while playing hide-and-seek with the rest of the group... The first thing I had noticed about the kindergarten grounds was this massive tree in one of the corners of the playground. It looked like an ordinary tree. It was right in front of the fence with hardly any space in between. So to most people, it would have just looked like a tree. Just another tree. Nothing more, nothing less, nothing special. But if you looked closer, more carefully, you saw that the tree stem was half-hollow. And there was a tiny gap between the tree and the fence, just enough for a three-year-old child to get in - granted, with a little effort but successfully in the end. So when we had to look for a place to hide, I naturally made my way there. It was the perfect hideaway. When I got there, I was surprised by the sight of Sonya. I thought I was the only one who had spotted the hollow tree. I looked at her and she looked at me, we both smirked in silent excitement. She reached out her hand to help me through that tiny gap between the tree and the fence. Then, we just stood there. Close together. Still. Quiet. We didn't say a word but our eyes said everything: "I got you."

It made me realise... You could find treasure in everything, and sometimes in the most unexpected places. Like this tree. Not only was the tree a hidden treasure in itself but also what I found inside was a treasure. A friend. A like-minded person. A peer. I walked past the kindergarten pretty often. The tree was still there. So every time I passed it, it put a smile on my face, thinking of that special moment. The moment when Sonya and I met.

She was very chill, and very gothic. She was just locking up her bike at the ranks as I walked towards her. She turned around, her face slightly whitened as usual with the contrast of black eyeliner and black lipstick. Her black fringe was centred between two easy-to-manage pigtails. She waved at me, exposing her painted fingernails. Black, of course. While her look was everything that I was not, I really liked it. It suited her. And it went so well with her confidence that she was not afraid to use and show.

"Hey rat," she said, "how's the morning been so far?" She always called me 'rat'. Certainly a change to 'Penny'. Rat. A peculiar choice for a nickname, one might think. But she didn't call me that for nothing. It was not a coincidence. She actually had a collection of rats at her house. Three of them. Grey-furred, pink-eared rats. Alvin, Simon and Theodore. Yes, like the chipmunks. Those were her pets. I used to get offended when she first called me 'rat' because I had always considered them filthy. But Sonya enlightened me and told me that rats are actually quite clean and good about grooming. And more than that, they are intelligent and curious. She would say, "They bond with other rats and also with humans, they have so much love to give. And would you look at those cute faces... Come on, Spencer! How could I not see you as one of my rats?!" She had her own way of showing affection, and I liked that about her. I got her, I understood her. I knew she loved me just as much as she loved her rats. And just as much as I loved her.

"Just the usual. Robbie being Robbie," I sighed. "And we didn't have any strawberry jam this morning," I added with a mock straight face, casually joking about my breakfast experience, trying to deflect from my main feelings. Apparently, my facial expression was so convincing that Sonya stopped for a moment, wondering if I was being serious or not. And then she realised. "Uh yeah, I can see how annoying both of those things are, especially the jam," she said. We both giggled lightly. "As for Robbie," she continued, once recovered from the giggles, "he has nothing else to do than to bully other people. Just ignore him, he's not worth it." I knew she was right but it wasn't easy to do. "I'm trying," I said as I sighed again.

Despite the joke I made, Sonya could see that I was upset. "I should be used to it by now," I kept thinking to myself. But should I? Should anyone be used to being bullied? Should anyone just let it happen? Should anyone allow another person to make them feel like garbage? I knew what the answer was but I had no idea how to fight it.

Sonya put her arm around me as we walked towards the school entrance.

4. At school.

The first two lessons of the day were English. We were doing the first "Harry Potter" book. I was pleasantly surprised when Mrs Anderson announced that we would be reading this, it was a welcome relief after last term's Shakespeare lessons. Although I actually did like Shakespeare, the language could get a little tiring. Sure, the terminology in "Harry Potter" could also be challenging at first, but it was quite easy to get the hang of it. And it certainly was a lot more fun than Shakespeare. I have always liked fantasy stories, especially combined with magic, so I was excited to read this book.

When I was a boy, I watched episodes of "I Dream of Jeannie" over and over, a show about a genie and her beloved master. I thought the show had a certain charm, and I adored the funny stories and Jeannie's ability to alter reality, to make it the way she wanted it to be. I often pretended to put spells on people or do any other of Jeannie's tricks. There was one day when my mum was going to work in her red 1980's Audi. I went behind the car and stood just in front of the exhaust. When she started the car and left, I imagined that the exhaust smoke was my genie smoke that would carry me out of my bottle. I realised later that it wasn't the healthiest scenario but I had so much fun, pretending to be Jeannie in her pink costume. Looking back now, maybe that was why I liked the colour pink so much?

"Good morning, class. Happy Monday," Mrs Anderson greeted us with an enthusiastic smile. She was my favourite teacher. She was understanding, kind and positive with an obvious love for teaching. Hence the enthusiastic smile. While she was always in good spirits no matter what, full of beans and motivation with everything we did in her class, I felt a slight difference in her demeanour. Her smile, her body language was even more upbeat. My guess was that she was just as excited about a magical fantasy book as I was. No doubt, it was a nice change.

"Let's start by getting to know the characters of the book," Mrs Anderson said while rubbing her hands to signalise that she was ready to get into this. I heard whispering from the opposite side of my seat. It was Robbie and Zac. They put their heads together, speaking to each other, laughing, their eyes locking in agreement. They both kept gawking at me and couldn't seem to hold their giggles. They pointed at me, at my pants. "Oh no, the zipper hole," I thought. "They can see the hole in my pants. Damn it." I crossed my legs to try and and hide the hole but they had already seen it. It was too late, the damage was done. Not just to my pants but to my day ahead. A hole in my day.

When the lesson was over, I walked out to the corridor to go to the bathroom. Robbie and Zac were following me. "Hey Penny, I guess you don't even have to bother with the zipper. You can just use the hole in your pants to pee out of." I kept walking without acknowledging them, I was way too embarrassed. I heard them going on about it. "Penny has an easy access glory hole in his pants," they shouted while pointing at me. Everyone looked at me, they started to laugh. Louder and louder. It was like the walls were closing in on me, that the walls would eventually crush me. With such a force of violence that I couldn't do anything about it.

I kept on walking, faster and faster, looking down to avoid the stares of everybody in my path. I reached the bathroom and escaped into one of the cubicles. I locked the door and sat on the toilet with relief. My eyes started to water. Why were they so cruel? What had I ever done to them to be treated like this? The tears made my vision blurry. The sheer fact of knowing that I was crying made me want to cry even more. The tears kept coming, like a never-ending waterfall. I felt sorry for myself, helpless, violated, powerless.

I looked at my pants, the hole seemed to have gotten bigger, probably from walking to the bathroom too quickly, with larger steps than usual that led to stretching the material and therefore ripping it even more. "Pull yourself together, don't show them that they get to you," I told myself. Then I heard a knock on the cubicle door. "Spence, are you okay?" It was Sonya. She didn't care about coming into the boys' bathroom. "I've seen many horror movies in my life," she once said. "What can be scarier than that. Definitely not a selection of underdeveloped male genitalia." I loved Sonya for her bluntness.

"Come on, rat, open the door." Sonya softly tapped on the cubicle door. I turned the lever of the lock, and the door slowly opened. Sonya's face peeked through, it comforted me right away. Her lips pressed together, her eyes open wide and her left eyebrow raised into her whitened forehead. I came out and walked towards her, she gave me a hug. It felt good. It always did. It made everything a bit more bearable. At least I had her, at least someone who was on my side.

She grabbed her shoulder bag and pulled out a packet of cigarettes. She knew I wouldn't want one, so she didn't even ask me. She took one cigarette and went to the window. She opened it wide. The view from this bathroom was actually amazing. You could see the church with its tower and bells, the line of merchant houses at the town square as well as a huge park with a lake. The view was wasted on this bathroom but at the same time, it was a hidden gem of the school. Not only could I come here to hide but I could also take in the views while trying to catch my breath. Just another hidden secret, another hidden treasure, it seemed.

Sonya lit the cigarette and took a satisfying puff, exhaling with pleasure. "They're losers, you know that, right?" she said while some excess smoke tried to escape her mouth. "They're full of their own insecurities and they are trying to compensate by putting the focus on you. They think hurting you is a form of power that deserves applause and gratitude. Just punch them in the face, rat. Just punch them." She said this in her usual dry manner but it came out so unexpectedly, I had to laugh. Her face cracked. Her stern look dissolved and we found ourselves laughing out loud together. The thought of seeing Robbie's face if I did that, it just made me laugh.

Sonya took another drag. Then, she pointed the cigarette at her body and moved it towards it. "What are you doing?" I looked at her in disbelief as she burnt a hole in her black cotton pants underneath the zipper. "Why did you do that?" She smiled, the cigarette in her mouth ready for another puff, while saying, "Your hole is my hole. Your pain is my pain." I glanced at her with adoration and hugged her abruptly. She stretched out her index finger and pointed it at me. It was a thing we did sometimes. Ever since we met in the secret hollow tree in kindergarten, in fact. It was like a mutual understanding. A sign of being there for each other. A sign of being honest with each other. A sign of our bond. A fingertip touch. Or 'FTT', as we called it. I looked over at Sonya and stretched out my index finger. I gently touched the tip of hers as we simultaneously said, "FTT!".

"And also, any hole is a goal, right?" Sonya said while shrugging and throwing up her hands. It almost looked like a cheerleader's move which made it even funnier because she just didn't have that typical cheerleader look. I didn't even know how to respond, it was so random. But funny. Any hole is a goal. "Haha," I smirked.

"Goal. Ah, damn it." I checked my phone and realised I was late for sports class. "I gotta go, Son. I'll see you at lunch." I rushed out, and even though I was stressed for being late, I couldn't help but still smile at Sonya's hole pun.

5. Sports.

I sprinted downstairs and towards the gymnasium. The class always waited in front of the gym entrance for our sports teacher, Mr Moore. And then we would go in together. When I got to the entrance, nobody was waiting there anymore, so they must have already gone inside. With haste, I walked into the changing room where I saw clothes and bags lying around everywhere. It looked like a pigsty. Quite appropriate actually. I found a spot where I could put my stuff and get changed into a plain t-shirt, drawstring shorts and white sneakers that looked like Reeboks but they were just a cheap knockoff.

I entered the gym hall. I always hated the smell. It was a mixture of sweaty feet and anxiety. Well, it just gave *me* anxiety. I hated sports lessons. Not always though. I was quite into them in primary school when the whole class participated in the same sports lesson, both boys and girls. I enjoyed the mix of gender and the mix of vibes that came with it. It made me feel more relaxed and uninhibited. It was mainly the presence of the girls. I always felt more comfortable with them. They always seemed to have a more kind approach to things. Sure, they could be bitchy but at a less cruel rate compared to boys. At least in my experience. I was devastated when we started year 7 and we had to have separate sports classes, one for boys and one for girls. The girls were my allies, maybe not my friends but allies who welcomed me with open arms, no matter how I dressed or how I acted. I never had that with other boys, they were always obnoxiously loud among each other in an unspoken contest to show who had more alpha male attributes than the other. They always had the need to prove something while girls just seemed to have fun together. Simply fun. Sure, the boys seemed to have their fun too but when they had fun, it usually meant that I didn't. I was just different like that.

I saw Robbie, Zac and the other boys of my class jog around in circles. "Good," I thought. "They are still in warm-up. Maybe I can just sneak in and Mr Moore won't notice." Mr Moore was standing at the other far end of the hall. He was dressed in his usual grey jogging pants and wide t-shirt. When I entered, he looked up at the roof with his oversized, old-school glasses which complemented his round face well. His dark blonde and slightly curled hair always had good volume. His appearance reminded me of both a porn star and a serial killer. Maybe it was that 1970s vibe he was still projecting.

I took a deep breath and waited until Adrian passed me. It seemed a good entry point to join the circle, inconspicuous to link yourself with the other quiet boy in the class. "Good plan, well done, Spencer," I said to myself. I jogged along in relief. For about 5 seconds. Until Mr Moore said "Well, well, well, who have we here. Spencer Wise. Nice of you to make an appearance." His sarcasm was overwhelmingly obvious. He always used my full name. Never with the other kids. Never with Adrian, never with Robbie, Zac or Benji. But with me, it was always Spencer Wise.

Wise. My last name unsurprisingly gave my fellow classmates more reason to make fun of me, and it encouraged them even more to call me 'Penny'. Penny Wise. Pennywise. Like the scary clown in Stephen King's "It". My red wavy hair didn't help the case. While I clearly wasn't scary like that clown, they believed it was a clever connection to emphasise on their opinion that I was a weirdo, a freak. So Mr Moore calling me this at every given opportunity definitely wasn't helping. He hoped to put his point across that he disliked my behaviour, that he disliked me. He didn't like how I participated in his lessons, or rather how I didn't participate in his lessons.

I had often skipped sports lessons because they gave me a huge amount of anxiety. Just the thought of going to those lessons made me break out in sweat. It was the thought of doing something that I didn't want to do, that I was forced to do. Okay, I knew, of course, that a lot of kids didn't like specific lessons and they still had to do them but sports was different for me. I never really understood why this was a mandatory class to attend. Sure, kids needed a balance, both physically and mentally, but if kids like me experienced a physical and mental imbalance because of it, that should be reason enough to consider an exception, or at least a talk about what could be done to make it work.

Last year was especially bad for me. So bad that I faked illnesses with my local doctor. I became a regular in his practice. At first, I would tell him that I had stomach cramps or headaches, so he would write me a note for school that I wasn't fit to go in that day, and sometimes more than just a day. It was pretty obvious that I would miss school on days where we had sports lessons. But nobody really asked me about it either. Well, except Mr Moore. "You missed my class again last week," he would say on occasions when I did try to pull myself together and attend, regardless of my mental state. I knew I had to attend in order to pass the class because unfortunately, sports was a graded subject.

For me, that could have made all the difference. Sure, maybe I didn't like sports - or at least not the kind of sports we did there - but if I had known that it didn't matter how I performed but just needed to attend, that would have taken the weight off my shoulders. I most likely still wouldn't have had a lot of motivation due to the behaviour of the others, but it would have been something.

I considered going to the principal to state my case. But then I realised that I would have gone basically against the whole school system. I would have questioned how things were done. Which was not a bad thing, but I felt it was too much to bare. So I kept going to the sports classes where possible but with a lot of misses. One day when I walked into the gym with all the others, Mr Moore stopped me and said, "Oh by the way, you will not be passing my class this year." When I asked why, he just said that I was absent too many times. Despite the fact that I had medical documentation for my absence, he didn't accept that and went ahead to have me fail that year. This cemented the path for him to see me as an outsider.

Initially, I always thought of teachers as a crucial part of the school system, as the people who taught you things that you will or will never need in life later on, as the people who were supposed to guide you, make you feel safe and seen, make you feel accepted. So when I first encountered Mr Moore's disposition towards me, I immediately felt guilt. Guilt because it was my fault that he didn't like me, it was my fault that he spoke to me in this way. Because I didn't embody his apparent beliefs that boys were supposed to be tough - and good at sports. And how were my classmates going to accept and include me if my own sports teacher didn't? He was supposed to be an example to encourage others to be the same. Instead, he put fuel in the fire that everyone seemed to thrive on.

It was like when witches were burnt hundreds of years ago. Everyone cheered as the witches went up in flames and perished. People feared witches so much that they were happy and relieved to be rid of them. But to me, there was one obvious question: How did everyone fear the witches while nobody questioned and feared the people who burnt them? The viciousness and cruelty, the anger and hatred. How did nobody fear those people instead?

As my heart sank into my shorts, I softly said, "I'm sorry." One could hardly hear what I said. I was out of breath. Out of breath not from the few seconds of jogging but out of breath because of Mr Moore's verbal kick in my gut. While he fuelled the fire of dislike for the others, he fuelled the fire of anxiety for me. I just wanted to fit in, or even just be unnoticed. But I was faced with more anxiety instead. "Everybody," Mr Moore loudly said, "get a basketball and continue to warm up on the left basket section. Everybody but Spencer Wise. Spencer Wise, you do 5 extra laps of jogging."

"Great!" I thought. "Now I can feel the humiliation even more." And that I did… every time I passed the boys in their basketball section. Every time I passed, they stopped for a second and glared at me with spitefulness. Everyone including Mr Moore. The boys and Mr Moore exchanged looks of agreement and joy. To them, Mr Moore was a hero. A legend. Maybe even a father figure. "Well," I thought, "if this was the only kind of father figure out there, then they can have it." The boys were throwing baskets after baskets, cheering each other on, laughing and roaring. "Good job, boys!" Mr Moore commented.

After a while, I finished the 5 laps and stood next to the others. Mr Moore grabbed his whistle and put only the very top part of it in his mouth. He blew and squeezed out a screeching sound that made us all stand still and listen, eyes on Mr Moore. Like in the military. "Okay boys, what do you want to play today?" He didn't have to wait long for an answer. "Soccer, soccer, soccer!" they chanted, everyone but me. The chanting rumbled through the air for several seconds, as if they were possessed, it was almost unbearable, until Mr Moore concluded, "Let's play soccer then. Zac, Robbie, you're both team captains. Please select your teammates."

Ugh, another dread. Picking teammates. Another humiliation because surprise, surprise. I always got picked last. It was usually down to Adrian and me. There was always a moment of suspense because on many occasions, I have wondered if they would pick me before Adrian. But they never did. Today was no exception. "Adrian," Zac yelled. Adrian ran across to his team which tapped him on the shoulder as a greeting that symbolised both a welcome for Adrian and a message of "Glad we didn't get Spencer" for me. "So that means, team Robbie. You get Spencer Wise," Mr Moore wrapped up the selection process, and Robbie and his mates moaned. "You can go and be the goalkeeper."

I was happy to be the goalkeeper actually. I knew nothing about soccer. I was never interested in it. And it was never explained to me properly by Mr Moore. You'd think that anything you were supposed to do and learn should come with an explanation. But something as simple as soccer didn't count apparently. It was expected to know the rules and how to play. I just knew I had to get the ball from one side to the other and into the goal of the other team. I could make sense of that as a basic rule. So in the beginning, I would try to kick the ball to my fellow teammates or try and steal it from my opponents but very often, Mr Moore's whistle interrupted my attempts and called 'offside' or 'foul'. I hardly touched anyone, so how it could ever be a foul, I never understood. So in the end, they decided that the position of goalkeeper was the best option for me. I'd just have to stand in the goal and wait, hoping I would not even have to do anything. But if I did, I just had to try to catch the ball they kicked at me. Seemed like an easy enough task. But I still didn't like sports. If Mr Moore didn't have the intention of explaining the rules, why should I have the intention of caring for sports. I tried, in some ways, but if I was honest to myself, I didn't really, and that was pretty evident. And that probably added to the fact that Mr Moore didn't like me. Well, if he didn't show any effort, why should I? It was just typical that he would only tend to his favourites, which was everyone but me, obviously. And all of his favourites knew and loved any kind of sports, and so Mr Moore had a nice and easy time being the best and most encouraging teacher there has ever been. For them.

The soccer game started and luckily for me, my team played pretty aggressively, so that the action took place mostly in the other half of the field. This gave me a sense of calm and relief... until it didn't, when Zac's team dribbled their way towards me. My eyes tried to stay with the ball as focussed as possible. "Maybe they will lose the ball on their way," I hoped. But the ball came closer and closer until Mike took the shot. It was a straight forward shot not in any of the corners but right down the middle where I was standing. I didn't know if this was intentional or not. I only knew that the ball hit me in my crotch with such force and speed that I immediately fell to my knees, holding my crown jewels. Sweat dropped down my cheeks. For a short moment, I couldn't tell if it was sweat or tears. I was so surprised and shocked by the hit, it left me dazed. It might as well have been tears because I did feel like crying. But I didn't. "Get up," Mr Moore shouted while blowing his whistle, as if to emphasise. I got up slowly, struggling, in pain. Mr Moore rolled his eyes and said, "Go and sit down then and take a rest." The annoyance in his voice was difficult to miss. "Pussy!" I heard Robbie yell. Everyone else was laughing. I didn't say anything. I didn't look at anyone. I just stumbled over to the benches at the wall near the exit and sat down for the rest of the class.

The game continued promptly without any more fuss. Benji took my spot in the goal, and he held the other two shot approaches from the opposite team. Of course, he did. The game ended in a draw. The two team captains came together at the end to shake hands. The high-pitch sound of Mr Moore's whistle arose. "Well done, boys. Off you go and hit the showers. See you on Wednesday."

Ugh, Wednesday.

I always avoided the showers. I was way too uncomfortable to be in the same shower space with the other guys. Even though there were separations, it was still open showers and anyone could see you. I was already so self-conscious, both about myself and about them, what they would say or think, so I naturally decided to only do a quick wash under my arms to wash away the sweat. I didn't bring my deodorant but what could I do. I got changed in a rush, back into my 'holesome' pants... Sonya's puns were clearly rubbing off on me. I grabbed my things and headed to the benches in the school yard.

Sonya was already waiting there.

6. At home.

As I walked the way back from the bus stop to my house, I could pick up some smells. Smells that would lure me directly to my place. I opened the door and could confirm for myself... Mum made her special spinach and tofu pasta. The garlic and onions made the dish exceptional. My mum always jokingly said, "If I want to make sure you come down to see me, all of I have to do is fry up some onions and garlic. It always does the trick." And she was right. There was something about the smell of that. It made my mouth water. I've always liked garlic and onions. But I had to be mindful of the amount I ate, especially if consumed raw. You'd be able to smell it through pores for days to come. So I tried to modify my intake as much as I could. But no matter how much garlic and onions mum used in this dish, I wanted to eat every little bit of it. Not only was this my favourite lunch dish but after the day I have had, I thought I deserved to go nuts with it.

"Hey, my darling!" Mum saw me coming in and hanging up my blue hooded jacket next to her rose-patterned cardigan. "Hi mum." I went into the kitchen and smiled at her. "It smells good." Mum was stirring the pot with a wooden spoon, turned her head over the left shoulder and said, "It's your favourite." She took the wooden spoon out of the pot and let it glide across the room towards me and into my mouth. "Here, have a taste." I took in the mouthful of pasta goodness. My tastebuds were exploding in awe. "Sit down, sweetie."

Mum served up a plate for her and a plate for me. She always put more on my plate even if I said I didn't want more, she did it anyway. I didn't know if this was because I was so skinny. I could eat as much as I wanted, my metabolism seemed to be very fast. So I was always quite skinny, and yet often I would think that I wasn't and would question my body in the mirror when getting dressed in the mornings.

Mum put the plates on the table. Before she sat down, she took off her apron. My mum loved her aprons. She had a whole collection of them with all different kinds of prints on them. This one said 'I'm still hot, it just comes in flushes now'. It always made me a bit uncomfortable because it was weird to look at your mum as a 'hot person'. Yes, of course, she was pretty but it was still strange to think of her as 'my hot mum'. But if it made her happy, I was okay with that.

She sat down opposite me and said with a playful grin, "Let's dig in." Excited and hungry, I devoured the first few bites of the meal. "How was your day today, Spencer?" My excitement for the pasta diminished abruptly. The thoughts went back to school and what had happened. It was reflected on my face. Mum took my right hand and held it with both of hers, gently stroking.

"I just want to be unnoticed sometimes," I said. I ripped my hand out of hers in anger. Not at her, but at the people at school. My mum reached for my hand, pulling it back into the comfort of her touch. She looked deep into my eyes, smiled at me warmly, slightly showing her well-kept teeth, her eyes full of love and care. "My darling, you will never be unnoticed. You are too special to ever be unnoticed. Has it ever occurred to you that that's why Robbie and the others put so much focus on you? It's because you cannot be unnoticed. Your presence is so real and alive and bright. They cannot not notice you even if they wanted to because you, sweetheart, are one special person. You just haven't allowed yourself to notice yourself yet."

"You just haven't allowed yourself to notice yourself yet." This sentence kept repeating in my head, over and over again. I went upstairs to my room and fell on my bed. The same bed I was struggling to get out of in the morning. Every school morning. Now I was back here, back in the peaceful and cosy space I valued so much. But something was different, the voice of my mother rotating in my head.

"You just haven't allowed yourself to notice yourself yet."

"You just haven't allowed yourself to notice yourself yet."

"You just haven't allowed yourself to notice yourself yet."

With that on my mind, I fell asleep.

7. In the morning.

The daylight was shining through my curtains. My eyes slowly but gradually opened. "What time is it?" I rolled over to check the clock. It was 5.35am. I woke up before my alarm today. 10 minutes early. That didn't happen too often. I turned off the alarm setting and rolled over to the other side of the bed for a few more minutes. Breathing deeply. Calmly. Peacefully. With another deep inhale, I moved over to the edge of my bed. I threw the blanket to the side, put my two feet on the ground while sitting there for a moment. Exercising a few more deep breaths. This always helped me to get into a healthy headspace. With every exhale, I tried to breathe out the negative energies that occupied my body. With every exhale, I added a smile to farewell the dark clouds that entered my system.

I got up and stretched my arms and legs. I walked to the window over the creaky floorboards, pushing the curtains to the sides, inviting the sunlight to shine directly on me. I closed my eyes and enjoyed the warmth that the sun was gifting me. A few more deep breaths. A few more smiles. I sighed in contentment and stepped to my bathroom that was attached to my room.

I turned on the tap and waited for the water to warm up a bit. I took a couple of good handfuls and splashed it onto my face. "Ah, that's nice." I took the towel next to the basin and dried my face. I looked into the mirror. I looked closer. "What is that?" I got even closer to the mirror to get a better look. I rubbed the top and sides of my nose. I rubbed the skin under my cheeks. I kept rubbing, again and again. I rubbed my skin so hard that my face turned red. But the redness didn't take away from what I could see. I stared at myself in disbelief. "Wait, am I actually awake?" I was doubting that this was real. Was this all a dream? Maybe all I had to do was wake up. I slapped myself, first gently, then more forcefully. I looked around. I was still there. Still in the bathroom, still staring at myself with the yellow-striped towel in my right hand. I dropped the towel. Not intentionally but in shock. It was settling in. I started to realise what was happening. Well, not what was happening exactly but what I was looking at. I took another look at myself to confirm. I looked at every corner of my face. I stood still. And then, I screamed. "AAAAAHHHHH!!!"

"Darling, are you okay?" I heard my mum as she stomped up the stairs and entered my room in a hurry, knocking over the guitar in the corner behind the door. She stumbled into the bathroom. "Darling, what's wrong? Why are you screaming?" I turned around and looked at her, tears starting to form in my eyes. "This is why," I said and pointed at my face. Mum seemed unsurprised and almost immediately said, "Aww, sweetheart. You have freckles."

"YES, I HAVE FRECKLES!" I repeated loudly. "Freckles, mum! Freckles! Why do I have freckles?" I just couldn't believe it. Nobody in my family had any freckles, not even one tiny spot that would indicate that I or anyone else should have them too. And weren't people usually born with them? Wasn't it genetic? They didn't just appear, or did they? "It's okay, my dear. It's perfectly normal to have freckles," she tried to comfort me. "Yes, but how do they just appear over night? How is that possible? What am I going to do? I can't go to school like this."

A million thoughts were running through my head. What were the kids at school going to say? Didn't they have enough to make fun of me about already? They will tease me so badly with these ugly spots. "Oh honey, they're not ugly." I seemed to have said my thoughts out loud. "They are not ugly," mum repeated. "They are lovely. You know, people also call them angel kisses… or sun kisses." Sun kisses? Hmm, I did just stand by the window, absorbing the sun rays. But surely, those few seconds couldn't have caused that? Could they? Surely not! No, that was ridiculous. "I don't even spend much time in the sun, mum. You know that. I always look for a spot in the shade." I walked to my bed and sat down. Mum came and sat right next to me, putting her arm around me. "Spencer, the freckles are not ugly. *You* are not ugly. I think they are a wonderful feature. A feature that not everyone is lucky enough to have. They are special. They don't call them angel kisses for no reason." I looked at my folded hands, listening to her words but they didn't make me feel better.

"You know," she continued, "we did have members of our family who had freckles, too." We did? That was complete news to me. "Really?!" I looked at her curiously. "Oh yes. Well, *one* member," she clarified. "Then how come I have never met them?" I asked. "Well, they lived a long time ago, long before your time. Long before my time. My great-grandmother told me about an Uncle James. She didn't know him personally either because he lived well even before her in the 1700s, but he's known among us. The reason for that is that he was the first and only person in our family, thus far, to have had freckles. They just appeared over night. Just like yours. Nobody knew why. But there you are, Spence, it can happen, and it's perfectly normal." It still didn't make any sense to me. But the story caught my interest. There hasn't been any other freckled family member for hundreds of years?! Until now? Until me! My mind was blown.

"Now, come down and have breakfast with me, will ya?" she said as she took my hand and gently pulled me off the bed. "Okay," I said and walked downstairs, still in a daze over what just happened and over what my mum just told me, still deep in thoughts. But I got yanked out of this daze very quickly as she started to sing. "Haaaaaaaaaaappy birthday to you, happy birthday to you, happy birthday, my sweet Spencer, happy birthday to you." She was a decent singer actually. She liked to sing along to songs on the radio. And if the opportunity arose, she also shook her hips to those songs. It was really lovely to see how much she enjoyed music. So it was no wonder that she has always been the first one to initiate the "Happy Birthday" song.

Oh my God, what? I forgot my own birthday? It was like I was walking into my own surprise party. The surprise being that it was my birthday. Oh my God, I couldn't believe myself. I was just so preoccupied with the recent school happenings, and the discovery of my freckles really got me out of whack. My head was everywhere and with everything but my birthday.

"Oh my goodness, mum. What is all this?" She decorated the table with lots of candles, 16 of them. She hung up paper pom poms in all colours of the rainbow, with a flower pinned to each of them. And there were fairy lights above the table. Not only were they fairy lights, she also attached pictures in between with colourful wooden pegs Pictures of when I was born, pictures of when I was a toddler and fell asleep in my mum's arms, pictures of Sonya and me in kindergarten at our secret hollow tree, pictures of my first day of school, pictures of me doing an Easter egg hunt with a basket that was almost as big as me. "Oh wow, mum!"

I looked over and beamed at her with undisguised admiration. I stepped closer to the pictures. My mum joined me, took my hand and kissed it. "This is how I see you, Spencer. These are a series of moments of light. And they are light because you are in it. You're the best thing that has ever happened to me, my darling. And I wish you the happiest of birthdays." She paused, she sighed, she tried to collect her thoughts. "You're 16 now, my boy. 16! Where has the time gone…" She ran her hand through my red wavy hair. "I remember like it was yesterday," she went on, "when you were 4 years old and you fell down the basement stairs in our old house. You were so fascinated by the basement because you thought it was inhabited by ghosts - but you were not scared." I remembered that too actually. She was right, I was fascinated by anything supernatural. It made sense that I was later obsessed with "I Dream of Jeannie". It might have always lived in me, this interest, this fascination, this feeling.

"Mum, thank you so much for this. This is everything. I love you so much." I embraced her tightly. "I love you, too. I love you so much." She kissed me on my forehead which was always her way of comforting me. Forehead kisses always made me feel like I was in good hands, that I was safe and understood, that I could just be.

We sat down at the table, the fairy lights dangling above our heads. There were pancakes with mixed berries and coconut yogurt and sprinkles of cinnamon. Another source of comfort. Pancakes. They were so fluffy and light, they melted in my mouth, the berries adding a sour relief to the sweetness of the pancakes. Mum knew how much I liked them, and she made them so well. But today, they tasted differently. Even better. Even tastier. Even more satisfying. Even more magical. Magical in the way that they took my mind off things. The whole birthday surprise did. It made me forget all my worries, even just for a short while. And more than that, it made me see the light all around me. Little did I know that this day would also spark a new light within myself.

8. Within myself.

With a spring in my step from the birthday morning, I got ready for school. I went to the bathroom to brush my teeth. I looked in the mirror, there it was again. That new face. My new face. The freckles. How could I soften the blow that I would undoubtedly get from my so-called classmates. I went to my wardrobe. I skimmed through my clothes until I landed on my oversized, cream-coloured hoodie. I could tug the hood down deep over my face. I felt a bit like Amanda Seyfried in "Red Riding Hood". It was almost humorous. The hood serving as a disguise while trying to manage the way through the forest without getting noticed by the wolf. That seemed very familiar to me.

"Well, the hoodie will do," I thought. At least for the way to get to school. I walked to the bus. Eddie greeted me as usual with his broad smile. "Hey Spence, is that you in there?" he asked, leaning in to catch a glimpse of my face. I pulled the hood over my head even more as I moved past him. There was a whole free row of seats right behind Eddie. "Yes," I thought. "At least that." I didn't have to face Robbie, Zac and the others who sat at the back of the bus as always. I could hear their voices but their words had a veil over them. They were faint echoes in the distance, my thoughts far away from the present moment. I also saw Adrian, sitting by himself with a book in his hands. He glanced at me over the corner of the book. He probably thought I wouldn't notice but I did.

I sat down behind Eddie, staring at the back of his head. His half-long dark brown hair spilling over from under the cap. "So he must have hair then." My thoughts were running away with me to various fields of notion.

The bus stopped abruptly, yet again. Yet again, pulling me out of my day dreams. "Have a good day, folks," Eddie warbled. Tsssss - the sound of the opening doors that released air pressure. Ironically, the pressure that was released by opening the doors caused more pressure to enter my mind, to lay on my shoulders. Because I arrived at school. I exited the bus, the hood still over my face. I could, however, still see Sonya. I didn't necessarily have to see her face to know that she was there. Her well-worn Doc Martens were a giveaway. "Happy rat day." She swept her hand over my head, causing the hood to fall back, revealing my face. She gave me a firm, yet gentle push against my right shoulder. Then, she went in for a hug. "What do you think about my face?" I asked her right away. "What do you mean?" She clearly hadn't seen my new friends yet, or she just ignored them to make me feel less conscious. "Oh, the freckles," she finally said. "They're cute, they suit you."

I was stunned. Why did nobody think it was unusual for me to suddenly develop spots on my face. "You don't find it weird?" I asked the obvious question. "No, many people have them, or get them at a certain phase of their lives," she casually responded. "Do they?" I shrugged my shoulders. "Yes, many people get them in summer through the sun and some people call them…" I interrupted her before she could finish her sentence. "… I know, I know, people call them sun kisses." Sonya looked at me, almost in disgust. "Umm ewww, I wasn't going to say that. That's so cheesy. No. I was going to say people call them sparkles." She looked at me with a slight grin. "Sparkles?" I asked, astounded. "Yes, rat, sparkles. Little face dots, with every one of them having their own little sparkle within," she said with conviction, which I truly didn't expect. "Ok, well, THAT is cheesy," I replied and looked at her in an instant of pretend annoyance, patting her on the head with my maths book - until we both broke out in a belly laugh.

That felt nice.

The rest of the school day went as expected. Sort of. As I had to eventually abandon the hoodie during class, people noticed the freckles. Some people mumbled among each other, some tried to hide their surprise. It was that look that you got when you saw a person who you'd always known to have glasses, and then one day, they showed up without glasses, having switched to contact lenses instead. They went through a transformation, a change, and this change could make others unsure how to deal with it. They had only ever known the person as one thing, and now that one thing had completely changed.

While my freckles indeed symbolised change, it didn't change the fact that I was still the weirdo in the class, maybe even more so now with a sudden change of feature, something so unexpected that it made me appear all the more different, all the more odd. It was an open invitation for Robbie to take a shot at me. "Hey Penny, did someone shit at you through a screen door?" He thought he was so clever, coming up with this comment. He cracked up laughing, his minions joining in to form a cackling storm. "Good one, mate," Mike praised Robbie for his remark before they all high-fived each other.

"You would know best, Robbie," Sonya intervened. "It takes shit to know shit." Sonya was my hero. She knew how to put Robbie in his place. I could never do that. I never knew what to say but choked up inside, my heart racing faster and faster, my blood pumping through my veins intensely. No matter what Robbie said or did to me, it was a stab in the heart, not just emotionally but physically as well. I couldn't move, I couldn't talk. I couldn't react. I wanted to but in those moments, I never could.

Afterwards, once I did have more time to breathe and think again, I always thought of what I could have done or could have said. But in the actual moment, it was a different ball game. I could even try to prepare something in advance, prepare myself for a nasty comment - but when it came to it, I would always forget. I just froze, just stood there motionlessly. I couldn't do anything but let it happen. But in my numbness, in my pain, in my anxiety, I always had Sonya. She knew how to step in and hand it back to Robbie.

Robbie's face collapsed. He inhaled sharply and parted his lips but before he could say anything back, Mrs Anderson entered the classroom. "Hello class," she greeted us jovially as usual. It was clear that Robbie wasn't happy about not being able to retort to Sonya's feistiness. He had to swallow the bitter pill, and that felt like a small victory. Sonya and I looked at each other and chuckled. I reached for her hand under our table where we exchanged a celebratory high-five. This high-five seemed like a direct, unspoken response to Robbie's high-five with the boys earlier. It evened out the battlefield. A battlefield that for the remainder of the school day was unoccupied. Non-existent even. Thanks to Sonya.

When I got home from school, I found Aunt Ruth and Uncle Hector sitting around the still decorated table, chatting with mum. "Hey, it's the birthday boy," Uncle Hector exclaimed. He got up and gave me a firm handshake before he patted me on my shoulder a few times. Aunt Ruth stayed seated. I walked over to her. She turned her head towards me and opened her arms. "Happy birthday, Spencer, my sweet." She gave me a hug, planting wet smooches on my cheeks, leaving marks of her bright red lipstick. "Thanks, guys," I said while attempting to rub off the smudges on my face. "Grandma Rose and Grandpa Doug are on their way," mum said. "So go put your stuff down and let's get the party started." Mum was so awesome, but also a bit cringe sometimes. "Get the party started for Spencer's birthday," she started to mimic P!nk's song before I stopped her. "Alright, alright, mum, we will," I said in a mix of embarrassment and laughter. I liked that she was so excitable, and I knew she just wanted for me to have a nice day.

Soon after, Grandma Rose and Grandpa Doug arrived. They were my mum's parents and the only grandparents I had left. My dad's parents had both already passed. I liked Grandma Rose and Grandpa Doug, they were funny. They had been married since they were 20 years old. Amazing. While they were bickering constantly, you could still feel their affection for each other. It was their love language. It was simply how they were, and I found it quite amusing and sweet. They were just in one of their arguments, when Grandma Rose suddenly stopped and stared at me. "Aw, Spencer. How adorable."

For a moment, I wasn't sure what she meant. Was there still residue from Aunt Ruth's lipstick? I took the sleeve of my shirt and wiped it over my face. But then it clicked... My freckles. I had totally forgotten about them by this point. Everything felt so normal again. Especially with nobody acknowledging them. Everything was as it was before, except that in reality, it wasn't anymore.

"Oh yeah, that." I said, short and plain. What else was I supposed to say. "Come here." Grandma Rose waved me over to sit next to her. "You know, it's a gift to have those freckles. Especially in our family. Many generations ago, there was a kid just like you. His name was James." She gently patted my knee. "Oh yes, mum told me about him this morning. He was the freckles pioneer," I said with a subdued smile. "Yes, you could say that," Grandma continued and smiled. "Legend has it that from the time James had developed those freckles, peculiar things would happen." This story was getting more and more intriguing. "What do you mean, peculiar things?" I asked. "Well, things would disappear into the nothing, or they would appear from seemingly nowhere. Nobody knew for sure what was going on, but James always appeared to be nearby when those things took place," she paused ominously. "And nobody ever asked Uncle James about it?" I wondered. "This is as far as the story goes, this is all that is known about him." She raised her eyebrows and pressed her lips together. "And why are you telling me this? Are those peculiar things connected to his freckles? Is this all connected to *my* freckles?" I asked in anticipation. "We don't know if anyone found out the reason for these occurrences," Grandma answered. "Nobody even really spoke about it much, and it was kind of forgotten about. It was put in the back of our family's memory. But it all seemed to happen when James grew freckles. On his 16th birthday."

I was stunned. His 16th birthday. My 16th birthday. You couldn't deny some similarities there, but I didn't feel like him at all. I didn't feel like I could move things. I didn't feel like I could make things appear or disappear. I didn't feel that I was like Uncle James. I *wasn't* like Uncle James. I just wasn't. I convinced myself of it.

"Well, Sonya says they're like little sparkles." I tried to move the conversation into a different direction while deep down still processing the newly discovered facts about my family. "Aww, that's gorgeous," my mum agreed. "They *are* like little sparkles, aren't they? *You* are a little sparkle. Oh..." Mum hopped up from the table as if she had been stung by a bee. "Sparkles. That reminds me. It's time for cake! Are you all ready for cake?" Mum disappeared into the kitchen. "I made your beloved cherry cake," Grandma said while giving me an endearing look. "Yum, thank you, Grandma." Mum came back into the living room with the cherry cake which was topped with 16 small candles.

"Haaaaaaaaaaappy birthday to you, happy birthday to you, happy birthday, dear Spencer, happy birthday to you." Again, mum initiated the singing but everyone else promptly joined in. Grandpa Doug topped it off with an encouraging "Hip Hip" that the rest matched with a merry "Hooray". Three times. Hip Hip Hooray. Hip Hip Hooray. Hip Hip Hooray.

The afternoon quickly turned into the evening. After an extended dinner, Aunt Ruth and Uncle Hector left, together with Grandma Rose and Grandpa Doug. The front door closed and there was an immediate moment of silence. And reflection. It was a great day. I had a nice time. But I was tired. "I'm going to go to bed now." I dragged myself over to the living room where my mum put away the last few dishes. She came over to me and embraced me while holding one of her treasured porcelain candle holders. "Ah honey, I hope you had a good day. Happy birthday, my sweet." She gave me another of her familiar forehead kisses. "Thanks, mum, thanks for everything."

I went upstairs, expressing a deep sigh. A sigh of contentment. I swung my arms around playfully. I didn't know why. I just felt good about the day, good about myself. There was a certain sparkle that was awakened. Sparkle. A word that kept revolving around in my head. With that and all of today's singing in the back of my mind, I lay down on my bed, my cosy bed, my safe and peaceful sanctuary. I pulled the blanket towards my chin. I looked up. Up to the ceiling where I had glued star stickers that would illuminate in the darkness. Stars. Sparkles. There it was again, the word, only feeding the spinning wheel within myself.

As I tugged the blanket a little higher, wrapping me in a cocoon of comfort, I found myself melodically mumbling, "Sparkle sparkle, high and deep. Sparkle sparkle, let me sleep."

9. Sparkle sparkle.

My alarm aggressively welcomed me to the next day. "What? How did I fall asleep so quickly?" I wondered. Usually, I would stare at the star stickers above my head for ages while exercising a few deep breaths. This felt different. I didn't even remember any of my dreams, also unusual. What has happened? Confused but still very much comfortable in bed, I tried to retrace my steps from last night.

"Okay," I thought. "I came up here after the birthday party. Yup, okay. I still had all that music in my head and was singing to myself. Wasn't I?" I visually strained my brain. "Oh yes, because of the sparkles," I remembered. Then the rhyme I came up with last night, it came back to me again. As I remembered it, I repeated it loudly. "Sparkle sparkle, high and deep. Sparkle sparkle, let me sleep."

Blank. Everything was blank. Blank. No memory. Just blank. "Spencer." I was guided back to consciousness by the voice of my mum. This time, the voice was more forceful than usual, with a sense of urgency. "Spencer," she continued to call up. "Come on down now, you're late for school. What is taking you so long?" My eyes opened, I checked my alarm clock. Another 30 minutes had passed. I fell asleep again! So deeply. "Spencer," mum called up once more. "I'm coming. I'll be down in a minute," I answered, a little spaced out. "Hurry up," she kept pushing. "You'll miss the bus."

Still in a state of confusion over the sudden sleep I fell back into, I moved myself out of bed. What has happened? I was awake and then suddenly I wasn't. What was different? What happened in between? As I tried to carefully think about a resolution, I always came back to one thing. "Sparkle," I kept thinking. "The sparkle rhyme." I started to form a conclusion. I started to make sense of it. Or did I? Did it have to do with my freckles, with my sparkles? All I knew was that I spoke words about sparkle and then I fell asleep? Was it that? Then my thoughts jumped to Uncle James. "Things would disappear into the nothing, or they would appear from seemingly nowhere." Grandma's voice echoed in my mind. "Appear from nowhere," I repeated loudly. Like my sparkles. "Disappear into the nothing," I softly said. Like me disappearing into the land of no dreams.

It couldn't have been a coincidence. It must have been my sparkles. It must have been the words I spoke. "Hmm, should I try again?" I hesitated at first but then I thought, "What the hell, let's do it. It's probably going to do nothing anyway." I sat on the edge of my bed. I wanted to be comfortable and present for this. I closed my eyes, took a deep breath and said, "Sparkle sparkle, up and neath. Sparkle sparkle, brush my teeth."

The next thing I knew was that my bamboo toothbrush was firmly shoved into my mouth with the perfect amount of toothpaste on it. The toothbrush was moving gently from side to side while I still sat there at the edge of my bed, my eyes wide open in disbelief. I lifted my right hand and reached for the toothbrush. I took it out of my mouth. I stared at it. Was this all a dream? Was my recent sleep not blank at all, and this was the dream I am experiencing right now? I shook my head. No, it wasn't. This was real. I was speechless. But it was starting to sink in. My toothbrush was over there, in my bathroom, and I moved it from there right into my mouth. With my words.

I pushed myself up from the bed and waddled into the bathroom. I put the toothbrush back into the ceramic cup where I kept it, together with toothpaste and dental floss. I leaned against the sink, looking at my toothbrush, then looking at myself in the mirror. "Sparkle sparkle…," I murmured deep in thoughts. As I spoke those words, I saw my freckles light up ever so slightly. It was faint but I could see it. I stood there, seemingly for ages. The illuminations fading. I tried again. "Sparkle sparkle…," I whispered, light starting to shine through my face spots. The brightest one was at the very tip of my nose. I touched it. A small drop of light came off it. A light that was now on my fingertip. What did it all mean? I examined it closely before I touched my nose again. The light drop from my fingertip went straight back into my freckle. I marveled at it for another moment before I said, "Sparkle sparkle, here and there. Sparkle sparkle, brush my hair." Immediately, I saw the comb move from the corner of my eye directly into my red tousled hair. The freckles still shining, still sparkling. Sparkling! "They are sparkles after all," I thought. They were sparkles, indeed. Sparkles of light. Sparkles of… magic.

"Hahahaha," I screamed out in short laughter and excitement while dancing around my bathroom, still in my underwear. I was ecstatic. And yet so confused. "Speeeencer!" As I heard my mum calling persistently, I reacted quickly. I really needed to hurry now. "Sparkle sparkle, be refreshed. Sparkle sparkle, get me dressed." My freckles shone, a beautiful play of rays and light confetti all around me. Then, I looked down. I was dressed in my 'holy' pants and a t-shirt I haven't seen or worn in ages. It was a white shirt that had a grey cloud on it, with the sun peeking over the side from behind the cloud. "Huh," I said while I looked myself up and down. "Good choice!" I smiled and winked at myself in the mirror as I made my way downstairs.

10. Radio Ga Ga.

"This is all so surreal," I thought to myself as I walked swiftly to catch the bus to school. My whole world as I knew it was turned upside down - by freckles. I chuckled at that thought. This was never something I could have ever imagined. I mean, who could have?! Not only getting freckles, randomly and suddenly, but also having those freckles turn out to be *magic* freckles. That was just insane, unbelievable. It was a lot to process. What did it all mean? Was I just like Uncle James after all? Should I tell anyone or keep it a secret? Well, for now at least, I decided to zip it and say nothing. I needed to get my head around it myself first.

I rounded the corner into the street where the bus stop was. The bus had just arrived, picking up some other passengers, and it was about to go. But then it stopped again. I ran towards it and entered through the already open door. "Oh hey Spencer," Eddie greeted me. "I was wondering where you were but then I saw you coming around the corner, so I waited for you." He smiled and winked at me. "Thanks for that, Eddie. You're a legend." Eddie was visibly chuffed by what I said as he straightened his posture, wiggling his shoulders from one side to the other. "Let's go," he said as he closed the front door and turned up the radio. Fun FM, of course.

He really did like this radio station. And he really did like to sing. I sat in the first row opposite him where I could closely view his joy. He was tapping on the steering wheel to drum the rhythm of each song, sometimes trumpeting through his plump lips. He was like a one-man band. Just as he got into shaking his groove thing to Queen's "Radio Ga Ga", the radio sputtered, resulting in static noise interfering with his in-seat performance. "Argh, damn it, not now." He slammed against the radio in an attempt to get the reception back to normal, but it didn't work. He seemed to get quite frustrated with it. A colour that didn't suit him well. But maybe I just wasn't used to seeing him anything but positive and cheerful. He kept banging against the radio with no success. Again and again, with growing agitation. So I thought I better help him. And naturally, after the latest events, I knew exactly how. I looked around to see if anyone was going to notice. Sure, the usual people were on the bus. Robbie and his minions in the far back, Adrian somewhere in the middle with his phone. But everyone seemed to be preoccupied with their own things at this moment. "Ok, Spence, go," I encouraged myself.

And so I mumbled, "Sparkle sparkle, music glow. Sparkle sparkle, radio flow." I could feel my face light up, and a slight but steady tingle was going through my body. I picked up on that sensation earlier too but I wasn't sure if this was because of my magic freckles, or because of my excitement and surprise. It was strange but not uncomfortable. It was just something I didn't know or feel before. It was actually quite a warm and fuzzy feeling.

Eddie was about to put his fist against the radio again but just before he even touched it, the reception came back. The same song was still going. His face transformed immediately, joy flooding back in an instant, as he continued to sing along without missing a beat. Seeing him so happy made me happy, too. "Maybe I can do good things with this," I thought. "But maybe I shouldn't use it all the time." I was in two minds about the New Me. It would be too risky to use it in front of others. I had to keep this a secret. Just like Jeannie did. It was going to be challenging but at the same time, I wasn't a stranger to secrets.

Eddie's voice was reaching a high pitch, just as he drove up to the school bus stop. His voice was as clear as a whistle. Ugh! Whistle. That reminded me that I had to go to sports class again today. Ugh.

11. A Hole New Me.

I headed straight to the gym entrance, the other boys all in front of me, going the same way. As I walked along, I looked down and remembered the hole in my pants. Something that was so far removed from my thoughts by then, I almost didn't even care about it anymore. I had so many other things going on. But being at school and walking towards the gym with the others made me remember the impact it had in the past. So I thought I should better take the focus of something that I could control, that I could make better, that I could make… disappear. I looked up and double-checked if anyone was looking in my direction. The coast was clear. I was good to go. "Sparkle sparkle, don't let in ants. Sparkle sparkle, repair my pants." Lights! Lights of my freckles and all around me. Tingles! Tingles all throughout my body. Whoosh! I checked the area underneath my zipper. The hole was gone. I smiled. Satisfied with myself and the outcome of the spell.

I arrived in front of the gym with the others. We were a few minutes early, waiting for Mr Moore. Some people were leaning against the big windows, occupied with their smartphones, while others like Robbie, Zac, Benji and Mike huddled together, talking indistinctly. I sat down near the windows in a cross-legged position. I got my earphones out and put them into my ears. Right when I got comfortable and wanted to play my music, Robbie turned around and threw a look at me, his expression was all question marks. He turned back and consulted his minions. They all glanced at me.

"Hey Penny," Robbie yelled. "Where is the hole in your pants?" Their eyes were pointed at me in anticipation. And I didn't keep them waiting for an answer. "Don't worry about any of my holes, dude. Start worrying about the hole in your head," I blurted, without any hesitation.

Bam! Wait, what was that? What did I just say? Where did that come from? It just came out, like a bullet out of a shotgun. A shotgun that could easily put a hole in someone's body. But in this case, I was just aiming at the hole that was already there. The hole in Robbie's head.

It was always easier to just let it be and not fight back. But his remark sparkled an immediate reaction in me. Sparkled. Hmm, did this have to do with my sparkles? Did it? I felt a new kind of control and power. A shift in me, a transformation. Not just my outer appearance but my inner self.

And I called him 'dude'. Haha. It made me giggle, thinking about that. I never called anyone 'dude'. To me, that expression was associated with being casual and confident, most of which I was not. I was the quiet and shy weirdo that everyone picked on. I wasn't casual, I wasn't confident. But maybe this had changed now.

Robbie was stunned but managed to react. "What did you say, you freak?" He was angered, his face turned red. He looked at me like a fanatic. "What did you just say to me?" he repeated slowly as if he was talking to a 5-year-old. I was confronted and intimidated by the way he looked at me - like I had always been. I felt insecure. What did I do? Should I have kept quiet, like I always had? "No!" I said to myself. "No!" I pulled all my strengths together. I clinched my fist to give me the courage to talk back.

"I said you should worry about the hole in your head." I sat there, still, my body upright, my chest slightly out as I released a satisfactory and calm exhale. "I'm going to smash your face in, you little shitface," Robbie said with such rage as he started to stomp towards me. Benji and Mike held him back, trying to convince him to let it go. "Come on, Robbie. Leave it. He's not worth it." Not worth it - that was exactly what Sonya said about Robbie. "He's not worth it," her voice resounded in my ears. It was ironic that both parties said that about each other. Which made me wonder yet again, why were we even in this situation if I wasn't worth it? Why did Robbie insist on bullying even when his buddies tried to get him to drop it? To be fair to his minions, this showed a certain kind of integrity. Maybe they did know deep down that Robbie's behaviour was off at times. Yet, they went along with it for the majority of the time. But here, they stepped it up. They pulled Robbie away, back into their huddle. Robbie's eyes swiped me viciously, he sniffed in disgust and anger as he surrendered back to the boys circle.

Mr Moore came out of the teachers' room and escorted us into the gym. I got up, the earphones still in my ear. I pressed 'shuffle' to play a random song to accompany me. I walked at the very back of the pack, like I always did. The music started. I listened to the first few words of the lyrics and I smirked. "This is so fitting," I thought as the Sugababes belted out their song "Hole in the head".

12. Dreams.

I managed to get through the sports lesson. It was the usual scenario. Mr Moore and the boys sharing their mojo. Me being on the sidelines of that. But I didn't care so much. My mind and body were still occupied with adrenaline and joy over the confrontation with Robbie. Joy. It was funny that I found a new kind of joy in this now. It had never been joyful before. It was always a dread, it was hurtful and simply annoying to be confronted all the time. But this felt different. I was up for the challenge this time. I felt exhilarated. But because this was so different to what I had known before, I still had so many questions. First and foremost: Who the hell was I?

I needed to know more. I had a free lesson after sports, so I went into the common room where students hung out in their free time to read or study, some even had a nap there. I sat down in the far corner, pulled my phone out and started to google. Magic. Lots of information came up. Anything from Houdini and David Copperfield to learning courses. Witches - lots of information about witches, too. From witches and the Salem trials to modern day witches in fiction. The Halliwell sisters from "Charmed". Samantha from "Bewitched". Jeannie. Harry Potter. This made me think... All those TV witches were genetic witches. It ran in their families. So I googled 'Wise Witches'. Maybe something was going to come up. But no, nothing. Just articles about the wisdom of witches. I tried something more specific as I typed 'James Wise witch'. As I scrolled through the results, I came across an article about one James Wise, born in 1704. The write-up even featured a drawing of him, which was published in a pamphlet. The headline read "Witchcraft! Boy develops mysterious face spots". It was him! I couldn't believe that I found him.

The article confirmed what Grandma had told me. His freckles appeared on his 16th birthday. And strange things happened after that with James seemingly being in the middle of them all. It caused an uproar in his town. People called for action. They were convinced he was a witch, that he was sinister and dangerous. But was that really true? I didn't want to believe it. Just because someone was considered a witch, shouldn't mean that this was a bad thing. But at that time, it was. Witches were seen as beings with power and the ability to destroy and inflict pain. While I knew that I wasn't a baleful person, it caused doubts in me, nevertheless. There was an inner rift, an inner struggle about the New Me. Was I good? Was I bad? Have I always been bad? Was this what the people at school saw? Was that why they behaved the way they behaved? My mind was running around in circles. The questions repeated on a loop.

How was I going to get closure? How was I going to get the answers? I wished I could just ask Uncle James himself. "Wait," I thought. "Could I actually do that?" I looked up. Just a couple of other kids from other classes on the other side of the room, discussing over a movie they watched. I looked around again.

Ensuring I was safe to do what I was about to do. "Sparkle sparkle, mystery and claims. Sparkle sparkle, speak to Uncle James," I whispered ever so carefully to not draw the other kids' attention to me.

Lights. Tingles. Whoosh.

I closed my eyes for a millisecond and when I opened them again, I felt disoriented. Where was I? I was not in the common room at school anymore. I was somewhere else, outside. The buildings were well-maintained but old-fashioned. They surrounded a square. A market took place here with many stalls selling food and other goods. People shouted out to advertise their products. I was about to go closer as I heard horses neigh right into my ear. "Hey young lad," I heard a voice say. I looked to my left and saw a man sitting atop a horse-drawn carriage. "Watch where you go," he said as he held the reins tight to control the horses. "I-I'm sorry!" I was startled, just like the horses were. Horses? A carriage? What was going on? I shook my head in an attempt to reset my sight. Was I seeing correctly?

I scanned the area around the square again. "Wait, I know this place," I thought. There was the church with its tower and bells, and the well-maintained but old-fashioned buildings were, in fact, our old merchant buildings, all of which I could see so well from the school bathroom window. Well, they were not so old here. They were looking new and fresh. How could this be?

"Free paper, free paper," a young boy exclaimed from across the road. Once the carriage drove along, I walked towards the boy and I asked for a copy. I looked at the date at the corner of the front page. It was the year 1720. I squinted my eyes. Yes, 1720. That was what it said. I looked further down the page and saw the exact article about Uncle James that I had just googled. "Witchcraft! Boy develops mysterious face spots," I read. I folded the pamphlet and put it in my hole-free, semi-baggy pants. Okay, my sparkles got me there but Uncle James was nowhere to be seen. "Where are you?" I murmured. I took a closer look around me. Suddenly, I felt a nudge. I pivoted. A young man stood right behind me and stared at me with penetrating eyes. "Good day," he said. "Good… Good day," I replied with hesitation. "It's you, isn't it?" I said as I got the pamphlet back out of my pocket. I held the paper next to his face to compare. "It *is* you!" I confirmed. "Uncle James, it's you." An unexpected laughter exited his mouth. "Uncle?" he said. "Come on. Call me James, Spencer. You're my age. Don't call me uncle. It's weird." He was right, it was weird. Even though I thought it was also weird not to call him uncle because technically he was still older than me. But yes, it was weird. I had to chuckle.

Wait, what did he say? He knew my name? He knew who was I. "You know who I am," I repeated my thoughts out loud. "Yes, of course, I know!" He smiled, leaving me in suspense. "But how?" I asked. As we strolled towards an empty alleyway, he said, "I had a dream that I would get a visitor from far, far away. I knew it was going to be today, and here, and I knew it was going to be you." I was astounded. He had a dream about me? "That's… that's so cool," I stuttered. "So, um, it's true then, you are a witch?" I asked him straight out. "Yes, it's true," he confirmed immediately. "Why are you in the papers though, James?" I was still a bit uncomfortable to call him that. James cleared his throat and said, "Well, here is the thing. People here know me since I was born, they were always friendly to me and eager for a chat. But then I turned 16 and I got those freckles on my face. And with those freckles, the mood changed because freckles are seen as an indication for witchcraft. And most people have a negative connotation when they think of witches. But the truth is that witches can use their powers for both good *and* evil. And I am not an evil witch. But people judge me simply for what I look like and connect it with what they think they know and what they cannot explain." His words resonated with me deeply. "I know what that feels like," I replied, thinking of all the times when people misjudged me without getting to know a single thing about me. He consolidated me with a warm smile. "People are afraid of what they don't know. People are afraid of what is different, of what they cannot control. People are afraid to open up to comprehend, to learn, to see another perspective." James knew that I understood where he was coming from and what impact that could have on someone. He put his arm around me and carried on, "Spencer, don't be afraid to be different. Don't be afraid to be something that people don't know or understand. You are you. Don't be afraid to be who you are." James' words were empowering, hugging my whole soul. While Sonya and my mum have given me pep talks like this in the past, this one hit differently because it came from someone who was in the same situation as me. He really and truly got what I was going through.

I looked at James with watery eyes. "As long as I can remember, people have been mean to me," I sobbed. "And now that I have realised a new side of me, I wonder if that was justified all along. I don't know this New Me. I know it's there but I don't know what to do with it." James nodded knowingly. "Your freckles!" he affirmed. "Yes," I said. "How does that even come to be?" I was still puzzled about that. "Well, it is a mystery in itself really. It certainly doesn't happen to just anyone. There has been witches in my family before me but that was way back." James raised his eyebrows. "Same here," I said. "There hasn't been anyone in my family since you. At least from what my grandma told me. And now, there's me." James appeared to be just as clueless as I was about it. "I don't know how it works," he said eventually. "I don't know who gets to be a witch and why. All I know is that despite what anyone might say, this is a gift, Spencer. And we are supposed to use it for good things, for justice, for peace. We are supposed to enjoy it. But..." he halted. "But what?" I asked, staring at him before he resumed. "But... at the same time, it's also a curse."

He paused and sighed. "I've been trying to do good things but look where it got me. People prefer to look at the cause of the outcome rather than the outcome itself. They don't see me as a saviour or peacemaker but as a weapon and a traitor." He looked down, the disappointment visible in his eyes. "What happened, James?" I squeezed his hand to comfort him. "Well," he started. "Just the other day, I witnessed a thief stealing bread from that woman over there." He pointed at a stall with a white-haired, frail-looking woman. "I was at the stall next to hers. The woman screamed and called for help. When I realised what had happened, the thief had already passed me, so I put a spell on him that made him run backwards, back towards the stall of the woman. You should have seen the look on his face. It was very comedic." James had a joyous smirk on his face. "When he reached the old lady's stall, I asked him to give back the bread. The woman looked stunned. Then happy. She looked at the thief, she looked at the bread, and then she looked at me. When her eyes fell on me, her whole face collapsed. She yelled, 'You witch, get away from me.' Suddenly, it wasn't about the bread anymore. The bread was doomed in her eyes because a freckled person like me brought it back to her. So she refused the bread, the thief ran off with it, and I walked away as quickly as I could while she insistently continued to accuse me of black magic." James shrugged his shoulders. "That's so unfair," I exclaimed. "You tried to help that woman." It made me angry. James wanted to do something good, and he was assaulted over it. "I know," James said. "But people believe what they want to believe."

It was disappointing to learn that not much has changed between James' time and mine. People were still ignorant, people still had it out for each other. It was disheartening. "What are you going to do?" I asked him after a moment of silence. "I am just going to do what I have been doing," he said. "If I feel I want or need to use my magic, I will use it. I am what I am. And while I don't understand how I became to be like this, I am proud of who I am. I just have to be careful where and how I use it to protect myself, too. Nobody has ever had any real evidence of my magic, nobody has ever *really* seen me use my powers. They have only seen me in the midst of things and then connected the dots which led to their conclusion that I was the reason for whatever had happened. So maybe next time someone steals bread, I will use a spell from a distance, and then someone else can get yelled at by her." He glanced over at the lady and laughed. It was nice to see that he could find some humour in it. In spite of all the injustice. "Have you ever thought of putting a spell on her for being so ignorant and mean to you?" I asked. "I don't know if this is necessarily the right way to go about it but…" James didn't say another word but instead smiled suggestively.

"Spencer. Spencer! SPENCER!!" I heard voices above our heads. We both looked up, then James turned to me and said, "Looks like someone is calling for you. You better get back to your timeline." The calling continued. "Spencer. Spencer!" I knew he was right. "Yes," I agreed. "I better go." I gave James a hug and said, "It was so nice to meet you. Thank you for all of this. Will you be ok?" James pulled me back to him playfully and gave me another hug. "I will. Will you?" He looked at me with his big brown eyes. "I will be okay, too," I said with true belief as I closed my eyes and uttered, "Sparkle sparkle, king and peasant. Sparkle sparkle, return to present".

Lights. Tingles. Whoosh.

"Spencer!" I opened my eyes as I found myself back in the corner of the common room. I turned my head and saw Mrs Anderson right in front of me, seemingly concerned. "Spencer, are you alright?" she asked. "Oh, yes, yes." I said a bit flustered. "Yes, I am fine, thank you." I looked around, took my backpack in a haste and got up. "I gotta go to class." I ran out of the room and left Mrs Anderson standing there, glancing at me with confusion. A confusion that I shared. Did I just fall asleep? Was this all a dream? A dream? A dream! I shook my head. Was I in a dream now? I was still confused. I stopped abruptly, forcing my mind to clear. A thought sank in. "No, it was real." The penny dropped. I smiled blissfully and continued walking to my classroom. Every step felt light, filled with a new-found joy.

I didn't tell anyone about the experience I have had. Not my mum, not Sonya. I felt bad about that. I was going through major changes but I didn't share that with anyone. Everything was so profound. Surreal. But it wasn't a dream. I knew that. I actually travelled through time to meet Uncle James. I had trouble to get my head around that. Travelling through time? It was mind-blowing. Not only did I now have freckles, not only did they come with magic powers, but they also gave me the ability to go through time. It was a lot to take in. And because I was still processing it myself, I couldn't tell anyone. I couldn't deal with the looks on their faces, having to explain something that I couldn't explain to myself. Even James didn't have an explanation. So how could I?

There were still so many questions. Endless questions and no answers. Like when James told me he was having a dream that he would meet me at a specific time at a specific place. Did that mean that dreams could predict the future? Was that a part of being a witch? Or was it just for James? Was it different for me? Well, I *was* in a dream-like state during my time travel adventure. It felt like a dream but it was real. Though I didn't physically leave the common room, my mind did. My mind wandered, like a delicate feather, into a different sphere while I could still consciously feel my body, like I could feel it during waking hours. I was there physically with James, back in time, and yet, I was also physically sitting in the common room.

It made me think of some of the dreams I have had in the past. Like this one recurring dream I had when I was younger. I remembered it like it was yesterday. I was hanging from the ceiling of a room. At the bottom was a dog, looking up at me, barking aggressively and baring its teeth. I held on tight as long as I could. I was afraid. Terrified. At the end of every dream, I couldn't hold on any longer. I let go. I fell down, the dog awaiting me with its death bite. When it bit me, I woke up in horror, with pearls of sweat, gasping. For a long time, over countless consecutive nights, I revisited the exact same dream. It took over my sleep, and even though I had this dream many times before, it was just as real and new and terrifying as it was the previous time. Eventually, it stopped when I wilfully reminded myself that it was, in fact, only a dream and nothing more. That was how I made myself wake up from it, and that was how I got rid of it altogether.

That dream in particular seemed like a metaphor for my life at school. The dog represented the bullies. And me on the ceiling… well, that was just me being me. Scared. Defenceless. Powerless. And maybe not just a metaphor for school but in general. Like I felt scared when my parents fought. When my dad was drunk. When he threatened my mum. Scared. Defenceless. Powerless. I was numb and didn't know what to do. And in the end, I let myself be bitten. In my dream as well as in life. But maybe this nightmare was coming to an end now? I had already proved to myself that I could stand my ground against Robbie. Maybe I could not just wake myself up from dreams, maybe I could turn my dreams around. Maybe I could turn my life around. A life that felt like a dream more often than not. Especially now. With my new secrets. My sparkles. My witchcraft. But it was a dream that I was actually living. I stood firmly and truly in it. And I liked it.

Yes, it was strange and confusing and overwhelming, and I had no idea what to do with it, but I liked it. I embraced it. And while anxiety and insecurity continued their frequent visits, excitement shimmered through. Excitement to see where this new reality of a dream was going to take me.

13. Sven.

I arrived at my classroom just in time for the next lesson. English... In hindsight, I didn't even have to hurry so much to get there, considering it was Mrs Anderson who found me in the common room and who I consequently ran away from. Over all the confusion in that moment, I just didn't think straight. I just wanted to get away and not be faced with any more questions. I hoped that Mrs Anderson wasn't going to make a thing of it when she came into class. I didn't need the extra attention, on top of everything else.

Sonya was already sitting on her seat when I got there. "Where have you been, Spence? I was looking for you. Everything ok?" She looked at me with worry. "Yes, all good. I just got carried away in the common room," I said briefly and vaguely. "Okay," Sonya said hesitantly, unsure of my answer. Her examining gaze wandered over me one more time before she attended to her notepad.

Sonya has been such a good friend. Always there for me. Which was why I felt so bad that I didn't tell her yet about any of the recent happenings. Shouldn't she know all about that? And my mum - shouldn't she know this, too? Wouldn't they understand? Maybe. Probably. But I was still trying to figure things out for myself. Sure, maybe this was going to be better with someone by my side, navigating through it together. Maybe. Probably. But I decided to wait a bit. It was all still too new, too fresh.

Mrs Anderson entered the room. Her presence interrupted the chatter of the class. But it wasn't just her presence that attracted attention. She had someone with him. A tall, blonde-haired, sporty-looking guy. Who was that? He wasn't a teacher, that was clear. He wasn't from any of the other classes. Not that I knew. I had never seen him before. "Who is he?" Sonya leaned over to express the question that the whole class was discussing in a quiet mumble. I shrugged. My eyes went back to the boy. He stood next to Mrs Anderson with both hands in his pockets. He had a somewhat nervous smile on his face. But he seemed confident just the same.

"Everyone," Mrs Anderson finally called out. "This is Sven." He took one of his hands out of his pockets and waved casually to the whole class, his smile a bit brighter but still nervous. "He just transferred to our school from Germany," Mrs Anderson continued, "and he will be our new class addition. So please make Sven feel welcome." Some of my classmates waved at him. "Hi Sven," others shouted out. Everybody seemed quite friendly towards him from the get go. There was no sense of hostility from anyone, also not from Robbie and his minions who simultaneously greeted him silently with a peace sign. Everyone seemed rather curious and captivated by him. I knew I was.

"Have a seat, Sven. And let me know if you need anything." Mrs Anderson tried to whisper in his ear but I could still hear it, her voice soft and calming. This would have made a whole lot of difference for Sven, coming into a new class, a pack of wolves who were either going to tear him apart or welcome him as one of their own. At this stage, he seemed lucky to be accepted right away. Sven sat down in the first row, just a couple of seats away from Sonya and me. Nobody wanted to sit in the very first row, but he didn't have any reservations about being right at the front. He put his backpack beside his chair, grabbed the "Harry Potter" book out and rested his arms on the table, a black pen in his right hand. He looked around from the left to the right, scanning the classroom, getting himself acquainted with his new surroundings. Then he reached Sonya with his kind green eyes. A faint smile. Sonya didn't smile back. She just looked at him, then she looked down at her book. She was funny like that. It didn't necessarily mean that she didn't like him. It was just how she was. Blunt. Dry.

Sven's head turned over to me. A smile still on his face. Undeterred by Sonya's reaction - or lack thereof. He appeared to find her quite amusing even. Then, his green eyes locked with mine. They were piercing through mine. Like a sunbeam. Warm and comforting. They stayed fixed, on me. He saw me. He really saw me. He acknowledged me with a friendly nod and a genuinely beautiful smile that exposed some dimples on his face. I always thought dimples were cute. "Hi, I'm Sven." His smirk persisted. I nodded back ever so slightly. "Hi, I'm Spencer." Our eyes still locked. Still warm. Still comforting. The beam travelled from my eyes across my whole body. My chest was tightening up. My heart skipped a beat. And again. And again. Electricity was running through my veins. Into my stomach. A funny feeling. This feeling… this moment seemed to last for ages. Sonya looked up to find Sven and me stare at each other. Sonya looked at Sven, then at me, then back at Sven. Our eyes continued to share the moment. Sonya couldn't help but smile knowingly.

"Alright, everyone. Let's start looking at the homework I gave you for today." Mrs Anderson pulled us back into the world of here and now. As the class got their notes ready, Sven threw me another look. Another smile. "He really did see me," I thought to myself. "He truly did."

14. Helping hand.

Mrs Anderson's lessons always went quickly. Because they were enjoyable and fun. But today, it went even faster than usual. More enjoyable, more fun. And I knew it was because of the excitement of our new classmate. Not just a new classmate but also a foreign one, which I found intriguing. And not just foreign, but also friendly. That in itself was new and foreign, at least for me.

During the lesson, my attention continuously hovered over Sven's broad shoulders and the way his thick, chin-long blonde hair caught the light. But then, the school bell rang. The lesson was over. And so was my inconspicuous day dream. I looked over to Sven one more time to see if our eyes could reconnect like they did before but Robbie, Benji and the others had already come to greet Sven in person. They exchanged handshakes and bro fists, clearly also excited for a new classmate, for a new potential minion to join them.

I sighed. I knew I couldn't interfere in this scenario without being called out by Robbie. And the last thing I wanted was for Sven to see that and realise that I was the outsider, the weirdo. But I also knew that sooner or later, he would find out. It wasn't something I could hide for long. But at least for right now, I wanted it to be unknown to him. So I turned my back to them, crammed my stuff into my backpack, got up and took my jacket from my chair.

As Sonya and I left the classroom together, she nudged me gently and whispered, "Well, he doesn't seem to be a dick." I chuckled. She chuckled. "Yeah, he seems nice," I said. I felt my face heat up and my cheeks turn red. "Yup, *nice*," Sonya repeated as if to say that I was underselling my opinion of him. She knew me well but she also knew I was quite shy and private with my feelings. She knew how far she could push it and when to leave it alone. She was very intuitive like that. We kept walking down the stairs to the main hallway when we parted ways for our gender-separated sports classes. Ugh. "Alright, rat. I'll see you later for lunch." I looked at her with a slight smile. "Ok, Son. See you then." She could tell that my previous excitement had changed to anxiety. She put her hand on my shoulder in a consolidating way without saying anything. "I'm alright. It will be fine," I said to her.

Yes, I felt better about sports now with my new-found personality traits. But that didn't mean that I enjoyed going there, having to spend time with all those boys who had made my life a living hell for such a long time. It was still draining. Yes, there were moments of light. Definitely. Absolutely. But it was still a pain. A pain that I could fell in my stomach. A pain that took over that electrifying, funny feeling that I had during the English lesson. And now that Sven had seemingly been caught in the web of Robbie, how was that going to be for me?

As Sonya walked on to her gym, I threw her a quick wave. In that moment, Robbie and the others stormed past me, confident as ever, loud as ever, obnoxious as ever. In the midst of that boy storm was Sven, tangled up in it all, being bombarded with millions of questions. Questions that were asked in quite an abrupt manner. It was just the way those boys communicated. Abrupt. Almost uninterested. Yet engaged enough to form an alliance. I tried to catch some of their conversation but it was quite impossible to make any sense of it. It was too loud, too chaotic. Mike bumped into me as they passed, pushing me aside. Sven noticed and glanced at me briefly with a concerned look before he turned back to deal with the overwhelming noise of the boys. I waited a few seconds for them to reach the gym door where Mr Moore was already waiting. The boys introduced Sven to Mr Moore. I slowly followed.

The sports lesson was my version of "Groundhog Day". A warm up of light running in circles before we had a discussion of what to do in this lesson, followed by the same unsurprising outcome. Soccer. Robbie was made captain of the first team. "And in honour of our new student... Sven, you can be the team captain for the other team," Mr Moore frivolously said. Clearly, Mr Moore took an instant liking to Sven, just like the boys did. Just like I did. So he gifted him the joyous opportunity of being team captain.

Robbie and Sven stood next to each other while everyone else lined up on the opposite side. The usual. What wasn't so usual was when Sven called out his first team member. "Spencer." I was shocked. Everyone else was too. All eyes were on me. Mr Moore's eyes were especially wide open. Nobody expected this. Less of all, me. I knew the procedure. I would line up with the others and I would enter a sort of daze, knowing I would be called up last. The daze helped me get over the anxiety and humiliation. It didn't erase the feeling of anxiety and humiliation completely, but it took the edge off it a bit. "Spencer?" Sven called my name again. His voice was like a soft touch that reached to hold up my chin, so he could look into my eyes to see if I would accept the request of being on his team. I opened my mouth in an attempt to say something. Anything to break the silence and the shock that was occupying the gym hall. "No!" Mr Moore cut in. "No, Sven. Spencer Wise shouldn't be your first pick. Take someone else. Pick Benji, or Mikey." Sven calmly took in what Mr Moore had to say. "I pick Spencer first," he confirmed his choice. I listened carefully. This was the first time I heard Sven say more than three words. I recognised a slight accent which I thought sounded so charming.

Visibly agitated by Sven's resistance, Mr Moore said, "Don't be stupid, Sven. Spencer Wise is our worst link. Nobody wants him on their team. Why do you willingly want to pick him?" Without any delay, Sven replied, "Well, I am the team captain, aren't I?" Mr Moore tried to argue. "Yes, you are but..." he started until

Sven interrupted him. "So as team captain, I would like to have Spencer on my team," he said, giving me a friendly side look. "I don't care about how you see him, what he can or cannot do. I just want him to be on my team. And in any case, just because he is so unappreciated by everyone, that doesn't mean he shouldn't be entitled to a chance." I felt very moved by his words, his accent more obvious and more present... and even more enchanting. "This is supposed to be fun for all, so if you think I am stupid for giving Spencer a helping hand, for giving him a chance to have some fun like everyone else, then I guess you're right... I am stupid. Very incredibly stupid." Sven said this with the utmost satisfaction and winked at me, accompanied by a smirk. The smirk he gave me when we first locked eyes in Mrs Anderson's class. The same cute dimples appeared. The same electrifying feeling returned to run through my whole body.

"Alright," Mr Moore surrendered. "Your unwise decision to choose Spencer Wise is accepted." Mr Moore tried to stir in some sarcasm paired with authority. As if anyone really needed his approval to decide who to have on which team. But he just wanted to feel in control of the situation, I suspected, and so he needed to have the last word. Eye-roll moment. Big time. "Or maybe it will be the wisest decision anyone has ever made here," Sven said cheekily, glowing with confidence. Where did that come from? He was the new guy and didn't know anyone here, including myself. And he was standing up for what he wanted, what he believed in. And on top of that, he snatched the last word from Mr Moore. This whole situation was nothing I have ever seen before. Nobody has ever given Mr Moore a hard time over anything. Well, except me for being me. But that was unintentional. He just never liked me. But Sven stepping out of the cool boys circle and doing what he was doing, that took some balls.

"Let's move on, guys," Mr Moore eventually said while clapping his hands to get the game on its way. In turns, Robbie and Sven selected their other teammates before everyone got ready to assume their positions. Sven jogged over to me. "Hey Spence." He rested his hand on my shoulder. "Is it ok if I call you Spence?" I was surprised he asked me for permission but I thought that was sweet and mindful. "Yes, of course, that's fine." I looked down, a little shy and embarrassed, not knowing what to do with myself in this moment. "It's a cute name," Sven said while looking at me intensively. "Thanks." I awkwardly giggled. "Anyway, Spence, which position do you feel comfortable in to play? Name it and it's yours." It was practically always a given that I was going to be in the goal. I didn't think I was going to be any good in any other position, so I told him that goalkeeper would be fine. "Goalkeeper it is then!" Sven gave me a quick fist pump to seal the deal before he went to his own position. He was a defender. Given what he just did with Mr Moore, I thought this was a very fitting position for him.

He was right in front of me. It felt strangely comforting, yet nerve-wrecking. My eyes were naturally pointed at the opposite side of the field but now my eyes were massively distracted by the sight of Sven and his broad shoulders. My eyes followed his silhouette. From the shoulders down to his fit arms and pronounced calves. Then my eyes moved up again from the calves to his well-formed derrière. I couldn't believe that I even allowed myself to look but considering my position and Sven's position, where else was I going to look?! And even if I had wanted to, I couldn't stop myself from looking. It was like I was intoxicated. I was hooked. Hypnotised. And I couldn't stir away from that. So I kept looking. As if Sven could feel the intensity of my eyes examining his figure up and down, he suddenly turned around and waved at me. Another wink. Another smirk. "I am doomed," I thought to myself and chuckled quietly.

Mr Moore's whistle marked the start of the game. Robbie's team aggressively moved forward, trying to get a hold of the ball in compelling tackles with Sven's team. I tried very hard to concentrate on the ball and be ready for when I needed to be. I didn't want to let Sven down. He showed me so much kindness in such a short amount of time already, and he didn't even know me. The least I could do was to not let him down. My eyes got bigger with anticipation and anxiety as I saw the ball enter my half of the field. Benji was the striker of the opposing team, and he made his way steadily towards me. But there was still Sven in between us, Benji still had to get past him. Sven offensively approached Benji in a bid to steal the ball from him. They were both in the zone, each pushing hard to gain the upper hand. It was an even match, a balanced contest between the two. Benji attempted to get around Sven, but Sven held his ground and aimed a low kick through Benji's legs to knock the ball loose. Benji, however, fought to keep control, shielding the ball with quick footwork. After a few seconds of tussling, Benji jabbed his foot into Sven's right leg. Intentionally or unintentionally, I didn't know. But the consequence was that Sven fell down on the ground. My jaw dropped. "No! Sven!" I thought. I was internally screaming. I was unsettled, I was outraged, I was shocked. Mr Moore didn't react. He didn't whistle to call it a foul. Of course, he didn't. The game continued. As a result, Benji was finally able to get around Sven. He ran in my direction, my eyes still distracted by Sven lying on the ground. It all went so quickly, yet everything seemed to happen in slow motion. Benji struck the ball cleanly and it flew right past me, into the goal. The sound of the ball colliding with the wall behind the goal made me vaguely aware of my failure. But I didn't bat an eyelid, I didn't pay any attention to the fact that Benji had just scored a goal for the other team. All I could see, all I could think about was Sven being on the ground. Seconds have passed and he was still lying there. Was he okay? While Robbie's team celebrated their first goal of the game, I ran to Sven. "Sven, are you alright?" He looked at me with his sparkly eyes, his dimply smile trying to shine through. "I'm okay, Spence." I reached out my hand to him. "Here," I said as I moved even closer. "Now let me be the one to give *you* a helping hand." His smile bloomed brighter as he grabbed my hand firmly but gently. As he got up, his upper body bumped into mine. "Thanks," he said, a little out of breath.

The electrifying feeling reoccurred. But it was interrupted by the sharp sounds of Mr Moore's whistle. "Keep it in your pants, boys," he yelled out. It seemed like a random thing to say. Why did he say that? Was he annoyed that I helped Sven up? Has he noticed the apparent spark between us? Or was he just making fun of this very moment which, in his mind, proved him right in the confrontation with Sven earlier. Mr Moore's face was full of malicious glee over Sven getting kicked down and me not holding the ball. He felt confirmed and clearly enjoyed what he saw. But this didn't sit well with me. He could make fun of me all he wanted but not of Sven. It infuriated me. So I looked at Mr Moore and whispered unnoticeably, "Sparkle sparkle, smile to frown. Sparkle sparkle, pants go down."

Lights. Tingles. Whoosh.

The elastic band on Mr Moore's jogging suit loosened, his pants fell to the ground and had him stand at the side of the field in his boxers. Mr Moore's face dropped. The whole class was staring at Mr Moore, who was just as shocked as everybody else. Everyone had the same question written all over their faces, but no one actually asked it out loud: "How did this happen?" I could see Robbie and his minions looking at each other, unsure of how to react. Should they laugh or should they honour the bro code that they had with Mr Moore by keeping a straight face? After seconds of silent contemplation between their eyes, unsurprisingly, they didn't. They didn't honour the bro code and instead burst out laughing so hard that they spat out saliva. The rest of the class joined in the laughter. So did I. So did Sven, who turned around to me and said, "Keep it in your pants, Mr Moore."

We cracked up in agreement and amusement as Mr Moore hastily pulled his pants back up and ran into the changing room. It was safe to say that the lesson was over.

15. Giggles.

I was still giggling when I went to meet Sonya at one of the lunch tables outside. "Hey Spence, how was sports?" I sat down with a big sigh of relief. "Ah, it.. it was nice," I stuttered. "Nice? Sports class was nice?" Sonya asked with a raised eyebrow. "Yes! It was nice," I confirmed and tried to suppress a smile that came all the way from the deepest core of myself. "Spencer, come on. You hate those boys and you hate sports. It couldn't have been nice." She looked at me, trying to read my face, trying to figure out what I was hiding. She could read me pretty well and she knew when something was up. She had that look a few times lately actually... And she was right, I was hiding things. I haven't been entirely truthful with her. I haven't been telling her everything. All the things that have been happening. I needed to change that. I really did. Soon. Or in the words of Eddie's cap: Bald.

She could see that I was holding back my excitement. I didn't even know why I was doing that. Why was there any reason to hide my excitement? Why was there any reason to hide anything for that matter? "Yes, it was nice. Is that so hard to believe?" Sonya's eyes were wide open. "Umm, yes. Yes, it is. After all the bullshit you went through, after all they have done to you and all they have said to you, it was never nice for you. What was different today?" She paused for a second and then, the penny seemed to have dropped. "Ohhh, you mean Sv...," she started before I beat her to it to finish the sentence. "Sven, yes." An amused smile appeared on her face. She knew that her intuition was right all along, she knew that something was up. Her smile lingered. "Tell me, rat! Don't just sit there. Tell me everything!" My cheeks felt hot. I couldn't hold back the smile any longer. I grinned from one side to the other. "Well, ummm. He, he was… umm…" I failed to find the right words. "He was what?" Sonya asked impatiently. I opened my mouth to continue. "He was just…" I noticed a shadow in the corner of my eye come closer and closer. "Hi guys," we heard the shadow say. Sonya and I simultaneously looked up. It was Sven, standing next to our table with his broad shoulders, luscious hair and mysterious smile. He waved at us almost awkwardly. "Oh hi Sven," Sonya said, "Spence was just about to tell me about your sports lesson." I gave her an admonishing look and tried to kick her under the table. But she didn't want to take the hint. Instead, she invited Sven to join us. "Come, sit."

Sven climbed over the long bench with poise and ease. His luscious hair flipped through the air like it was auditioning for a shampoo commercial - and nailing it. He sat next to me and clipped his hair behind his ears. He rummaged through his backpack before he pulled out a metal container. With a quick flick, he opened it, revealing a small folk attached underneath the lid. He grabbed the folk and took a bite of what looked like fried rice. It smelled delicious. "So, what about the sports lesson?" He asked and turned to me. "Well," I told myself to keep it together and be as cool, calm and collected as possible. "I was just saying to Sonya that this sports lesson was kind of nice." Sven enthusiastically chewed away when he almost spat out some of the food. "Oh, you mean Mr Moore's underwear. That was hilarious." He managed to swallow his food before starting to giggle. Sonya was visibly confused and asked for clarification. "Mr Moore's underwear? Why is that even something we are talking about? What about his underwear?" Sven and I looked at each other and smiled. "It was the weirdest thing. We were playing soccer like we always do." I rolled my eyes dramatically. "And then the next thing we see is Mr Moore standing in his boxers. His pants just fell down and there he was." Sonya put her hands in front of her mouth in disbelief. "Oh my God," she said. "That's so strange, and…" She paused for a moment. "…and so awesome. He would have felt so embarrassed." She chuckled. "Oh yes, for sure, he would have," Sven said. "He blushed pretty bad and then ran into the locker room." All of us giggled.

"Alright," Sonya uttered. "I can see now why you said it was nice. Haha. And a welcome change for you, Spence." She turned to me with her caring look. I could tell she was happy for me to have had a positive experience like that. She knew it had been tough for me in the past, so she realised how much uplifting value this moment held. It wasn't much of a secret that I was being picked on all the time. And while the full extent of it was still unbeknown to Sven, he could get a fairly good idea of it during the sports lesson. And I didn't like that. I looked down, a bit embarrassed. I didn't want Sven to think less of me, I just wanted him to like me. Sonya recognised my worried face. She quickly changed the direction of the conversation, stirring it away from my past and bringing it back to the present, wanting to preserve the lightness of the moment. "What were his boxers like?" We all grinned and Sven said, "Oh my gosh, they were so unexpected. White with a banana pattern." Sonya slammed her hands on the table and said, "No way, what?! Ewww!" We all looked at each other and continued to giggle so hard that our cheeks hurt.

16. Rosemary and thyme.

The giggles were carrying me through the day. When I entered the bus after school to go back home, Eddie greeted me with bjs laid-back smile as per usual and said, "Hey Spence, what's up, man? What's funny? You're beaming today." It was obvious that this didn't happen often. So obvious that Eddie had to point it out. "It was a good day today." I wanted to play my cards close to my chest. What else was I going to say to him anyway? He was a nice guy and I was sure I could have spilled my guts out to him at any given time, but I didn't want that. I just wanted to bask in this very moment with the feeling of relief, mischief, mystery and fun. I just wanted to sit on the bus, reflecting. And reflecting I could, because Robbie and the others hardly even noticed that I was on the bus. There was not even an attempt to throw one of their smart ass comments at me. They were distracted, still talking about Mr Moore's banana boxers.

"So," I thought to myself. "My freckles *are*, in fact, a gift." Just like Uncle James said. They helped me to have a pretty good day. A nice day! Satisfied and content, I leaned back in my seat, put my arms behind my head, closed my eyes and just listened to the sounds of Eddie singing to Snap's "I've got the power".

As soon as I opened the door to my house, the smell of rosemary hit me in the face. I knew immediately that mum was making baked veggies. She always added a lot of herbs to them, which I loved. She was especially a fan of rosemary. The aroma filled the house for hours. It was an added bonus. I walked into the kitchen and found my mum bending over the open oven door, about to conduct a taste test. She knew exactly how long the veggies needed to be in the oven, she just liked to have a little nibble while waiting for me. "Hi my darling," she said with an excited smile and turned around, revealing another banging apron of hers: 'Kiss the cook… especially if you want seconds.'

After the initial cringe moment I always felt when seeing my mum in one of her aprons, I confidently went over to her and gave her a gentle hug and a kiss on the cheek. "Oh thanks honey," she said visibly surprised but equally delighted. "What did I do to deserve that?" I thought this was a good moment to point out the obvious. "Well, for starters, you're a great mum…" She stopped and put both her hands on my cheeks. "Aww, thanks darling." I could see tears forming in her eyes. It didn't take much for my mum to cry, she was a highly emotional person. So a sentiment of appreciation was all she required to turn on the waterworks. "Also," I continued, "your apron says to kiss the cook." She looked down on her apron and touched it, seeming to have forgotten she even had it on. "Oh yes, you're right… and do you want seconds?" she chuckled. "Always," I said loudly. She pulled me to her and gave me another hug. "You're a sweet boy." She kissed me softly on the forehead. The kiss of safety, understanding and acceptance.

"Now, sit down and let's eat. Can you guess what I made today?" she asked as if it was a novelty. "Umm, let me think," I went along with it. "Is it something with basil?" I knew she liked when I was playing. "No, guess again," she said and smiled. "Thyme?" I continued to pretend. "It's almost 2pm, why are you asking, Spencer?" she answered and chuckled at her own hilarity. "Let me give you a hint," she said once she got a hold of herself from laughing. "It's the name of your favourite grandmother, and it also rhymes with hosefairy." She liked to make up funny words. It's one of the things I loved about her. She wasn't afraid to be silly. "Hosefairy? Hmmm." I paused, tapping my lower lip in a theatrical display of thinking. "Hosefairy. Closedairy. Rosemary. Rosemary!" I finally concluded. "Yeah! Yes, well done, darling. Grandma Rose would be so proud and happy," mum said with a satisfied smile.

"So you had a nice day at school then?" she asked, recognising my brighter disposition, as she scooped a few veggies onto my plate. "You seem to be in a good mood altogether lately actually," she observed, and added, "That makes me happy." This felt like the right time to let her in on recent events in my life. "Yes, it's been good," I started. "Umm… Well, you know how I freaked out when I first noticed my freckles?" She grabbed my hand. "Yes, your gorgeous little sparkles," she said and touched the tip of my nose. "Yes, my sparkles. Well, actually, since then, I feel different." I cleared my throat in slight discomfort. "Different how?" she asked. "Well, remember how you said that Uncle James had developed freckles out of nowhere, too?" She nodded. "Well, I did a bit of digging and found out a few things about him." I cleared my throat again. "You did? Like what?" she asked curiously. "Like... his freckles were not just freckles." I hesitated to go on as I was afraid it would sound too crazy to her and that she wouldn't believe me. She sensed my uncertainty. "Not just freckles? What were they then?" she asked warmly, encouraging me to continue. I gulped a bit before I spat it out. "They were magic freckles." There it was, I said it. "Magic?" she repeated. "Magic?" she repeated again. "Magic like 'I Dream of Jeannie' magic?" I couldn't tell if she was mocking me or being serious. "Yes, kind of like that." Mum was thinking for a moment. "Umm, well, okay. I guess I shouldn't be surprised," she said eventually. "What do you mean?" I asked. "Well, my great-grandmother did tell me about some magic powers," she continued, "powers that came with freckles but I didn't think anything of it. She told it so well. To me, it was just a fairy tale. A story she made up with characters from our family. I never gave it another thought." She shrugged. "Well, it turns out it was not a fairy tale, mum. It was real." I looked at mum closely. "I mean, not much was known about him - other than his freckles and supposedly strange things that happened when he was around - but how could anyone know for sure what was real and what was made up," she said. "Yes... Well, I know for sure." I pulled out the pamphlet that I got when I visited Uncle James. I've been carrying it with me since that day. To have some kind of proof of my journey back in time. A souvenir even. Something to show for. Something to encourage myself... to tell Sonya, to tell mum. And something that I thought could make things easier to explain when the time came. So here I was, finally, encouraged, handing mum the paper which she looked at eagerly.

Her eyes wandered over the article of Uncle James. Focused. Concentrated. Taking in every last word. Sometimes going back to a word or a sentence. Reading it again. She checked everything carefully. Her eyes moved to the date. 1720. Her eyes grew bigger. She glanced over at me with a questioning look. Her eyes went back to the date. Then back to me. "1720? What is this, Spencer? How did you get this? Is this a joke?" Even though she said she shouldn't be surprised, she did seem quite surprised to me in this very moment. But you couldn't hold that against her. It must have been weird for her to be presented with all of this, even if she had heard stories about Uncle James. "It's not a joke, mum. This is real. Well, you could actually find this article online if you googled James Wise but I didn't get it from the internet," I said as mum's face came up fast from behind the pamphlet. "How did you get it then?" she asked. "I went back in time." I didn't waver - I blurted it right out. No hesitation whatsoever. There was no way I could have cushioned it for her now. It was all out in the open. The bubble was popped. There was no going back from it. And I wouldn't have wanted that anyway. I wanted her to know what was happening, who I became, who I was.

"Okay," mum took a deep breath. "Let me get this straight, you went back in time to the year 1720 where you got this paper?" I nodded. She closed her eyes. "Okay," she sighed and took another deep breath. "Okay. So you went back in time. How exactly did you do that?" She looked at me with assuming eyes. I was pretty sure she knew the answer before she asked the question but she wanted to hear it from my mouth. She wanted to be sure. "With magic." I kept it short in order not to overwhelm her. "You mean your sparkles?!" she clarified. "Yes, that's right." I stopped to give her a moment, but mum signalled me with her eyebrows that she wanted more details. "Well, I came across it kind of by chance on my birthday. The word 'sparkle' kept rotating in my head. One thing let to another, and here I am. Your son with new freckles. Your son with sparkles. Your son with magic powers." My mum's mouth was halfway open as she followed my wishy-washy explanation. "My son, the witch," she said with a hint of pride.

"Okay, Spencer, my darling, my love. This is a lot for me to take in." I took her hand and said, "I know, mum. I'm sorry." She interrupted me. "No, no, no, honey. Don't be sorry. I am glad you're telling me this. I am glad. I really am. I will just need a second to get my head around all of this magic stuff." She was gasping for air. "Yes, of course. I know. It's a lot," I confirmed understandingly. She got up from the table and walked from one end of the kitchen to the other, her arms crossed. Back and forth, and back and forth. Then, she stroked her chin, pondering. "Show me," she suddenly said. "What?" I gasped, blinking like I hadn't heard right. "Show me, Spencer. Show me how you witch." She smiled and stood with her hands on her hips, waiting, wondering. "Okay…" I got up. I didn't know why exactly, but it felt like I needed to stand up for this. "Okay… I will show you." I gave myself a good shake, from head to shoulders to arms and legs, to loosen up my body, and my mind. It felt like a big performance that I had to get ready for, which made me a little nervous, but what was there to be nervous about? I tried to centre myself, to ground myself. "It's fine, Spence," I told myself. "It's just a spell for mum."

I closed my eyes to find the concentration that I felt I needed. I couldn't think of any big spells in this moment. So I decided to do something more simple. But even that proved to be difficult. With the smell of rosemary present in the air, my focus drifted, the thoughts of food, of herbs taking over. Which wasn't much of a surprise since I hadn't had a chance to actually eat that much. I was pretty hungry still. Maybe I should have eaten first, maybe I should have waited until after lunch - but anyway, this was how it was. I pulled myself together, concentrating hard, as I managed to come up with a spell. We stood opposite each other. I took a deep breath and said, "Sparkle sparkle, go and shine. Sparkle sparkle, show the time."

Lights. Tingles. Whoosh.

As I opened my eyes to see mum's reaction, I found her watching me closely. She saw the lights of my freckles. Her mouth was wide open, she was stunned, in awe. Her stare clung to me for a while but then her eyes flickered. She looked around to see if anything had happened. I looked, too. We were both curious. As our eyes travelled around the kitchen, they eventually stopped at one point on the wall. This was where we saw a big round clock, its margins made of rosemary. The numbers made of vegetables. The minute and hour hand made of thyme shakers. 2.07pm. It showed the time precisely.

Mum and I moved forward to get a better look, to examine the clock. We exchanged glances, and then, we laughed. "Oh my G-God, Spen...Spencer. W-What is this?" Mum struggled to articulate as she could hardly control her laughter. This was the funniest and most unexpected spell so far. We both held our bellies as we continued laughing. Clearly, my head was so consumed by food that even with all my concentration, I didn't make it clear enough what I wanted the spell to do. Did I want to know what time it was or did I want to have some thyme added to my lunch? It was clearly unclear. Indeed. However, I loved that the outcome was a fusion of both. I could see the time, and I could see the thyme. It was ambiguous, it was hilarious, it was perfect. "This is the best, darling," mum said. "I didn't expect this." Her laughter died down to a soft chuckle. "Well, I did better in my previous spells. This one was a fluke." I chuckled with her in amusement, but it also made me think.

Before my 16th birthday, before my freckles came along, I had never cast any spells. Even when I playfully pretended to be a witch as a child, it was always without any words, it was just with thoughts. The wishes that I had, and the thoughts that I wanted to make a reality. It was more a focus on that, rather than a spell. Just like Jeannie in "I Dream of Jeannie". This was new territory for me. I wasn't pretending to be a witch anymore. I *was* a witch. An actual witch! An actual witch that could exercise actual magic spells.

The spells. Well, the spells were a funny thing. Obviously, nobody told me or showed me how to cast them, and there didn't really seem to be a need for it either. They didn't feel like an effort to me. I was merely following my instinct in what I was saying, in what I was wishing. I didn't think much about it, the words came to me quite naturally. Even when I unknowingly mumbled my first spell that put me to sleep, the words just came out of my mouth as a result of a subconscious feeling. A fire inside of me. A light that wanted to shine. A sensation that was difficult to describe. It was just... there.

But now that I had used my sparkles a few times, I realised that my magic was a combination of spells and thoughts. Both mattered, both had to be brought together in the exact same moment. Your words. Your focus on your wish. Your commitment to it. And clearly I didn't do that on this occasion. Sure, the thyme time spell was funny. Was it accurate though? Was it what I intended? Well, if I considered what I put into the spell, and what I didn't... Sure, it was accurate to a certain extent. But I knew I had to be careful, more mindful, more precise.

In any case, I was happy that I could share my sparkles with mum, that she could see for herself how they worked, and that we could have a laugh over it as an added bonus. But it became evident that I still had a lot to learn on this new path of magic, and I was pumped to see where it was going to lead me next.

"Thyme will tell," I snickered to myself as mum and I sat back down to continue eating her delicious baked veggies.

17. Inside and Out.

Days passed. But the thyme time hasn't been forgotten. In fact, mum and I have been laughing about the clock, every time we were in the kitchen. Considering she had no idea what was about to happen, what my freckles were all about, I thought she took it pretty well. That was my mum, so open-minded, so easy-going.

It was quite a similar story with my sexuality. I have never had an actual sit down conversation about it with her or anyone else. It was never a big coming out, like I have seen so many times in movies and on social media. I have always loved seeing those stories that people shared, and I have always felt genuinely happy that they have found their way, the way they wanted to walk it, the way they wanted to come out. Though of course, not every coming out story was a good one. Not every coming out ended in big celebrations or accepting embraces. I was well aware that I was lucky. Lucky to have the kind of mother I had.

In spite of this, I had never felt the need to say to my mum, "Oh hey, by the way, I'm gay." She never made me feel like I had to do that. She has always been that open-minded, easy-going woman. She gave me the freedom to do the things I wanted to do - or not do - and how I wanted to do them. There was never any pressure or urgency. She was just there. There if I needed her. There if I wanted to share something with her, and also there just to be *there*. And I loved her for that.

I knew I was different in that way, always have been. It was always there, always a part of me. It didn't just come out of nowhere, I was born that way. I couldn't necessarily put my finger on it at the time, but in hindsight, it all made sense. There were definitely signs along the way that I liked boys. Quite a few even. At least for myself. For example, when I watched one of my favourite movies during my childhood years. This movie was about a love story between a beautiful young woman and a handsome young man. Back then, I thought I was having the hots for the woman, feeling for her as she went through the ups and downs of a romantic relationship. But looking back, I have realised that I was actually more fixated on the man, and that I wanted to be in the place of the beautiful woman, so that I could experience what she did with that handsome young man. An experience of love with a man. This fantasy, that started to come to the surface, was an added drawing point to this particular movie. It made me want to watch it over and over again.

Another childhood memory was when I had my cousins over to play, Oliver and Sam. Oliver was the older one, a year older than I. Again, looking back, I knew I was drawn to him, though nobody ever noticed that in this way. Sure, we were playing, sometimes roughly on the ground, but that didn't count for anything other than normal child play. Interestingly, despite the fact that I didn't consciously know that I was drawn to him, there was a distinctive moment when Oliver, Sam and I were hanging out in my room, just playing and talking. But then, suddenly, randomly, I got up and went into my bed, under the blanket, and… I got naked. I removed my pants, I removed my shirt, my socks, my underwear. I didn't know if it was obvious to them what I was doing in that moment, but I also didn't really care. My head was still peeking out over the blanket, the rest of my body was covered. I removed every item bit by bit, carefully and slowly but determined. Until I was nude. Completely naked. I remembered thinking what could have happened if anyone had just pulled up the blanket and exposed my birthday suit. It would have been utterly humiliating, but I did it anyway. I got naked. I didn't know exactly what drove me to this, especially when Sam was in the room, too. Regardless, somehow I felt this was the time and the place. I remembered that my fantasy was for Oliver to join me in bed. I wanted to feel him near me, not even necessarily naked, but near. Of course, this was just a fantasy, it never happened. My mum called us for dinner, and I told Sam and Oliver, from under the blanket, that they should go ahead and that I would be right behind them. This gave me time to get dressed again. Quickly and inconspicuously. And that was that. This never happened again. The audacity I had, though - it still made me smile. I was 7, maybe 8, so I wasn't even sexually developed yet. But I did remember this feeling of arousal, lust even. It was strange to me then. Exhilarating nonetheless. So there I was, my 7-year-old self, naked under a blanket, hoping my cousin was going to join. I often shook my head at my own boldness. The audacity indeed. The impertinence of hope and longing.

I had never told anyone about my crush for the handsome movie star, or for Oliver. It was always my little secret. But there was one moment that started as a secret but came to light quite suddenly. One day, I returned home from school and my mum was still at work. She was working as a hotel maid at the time. I remembered she kept telling me how boring their aprons were that she had to wear. Occasionally, she came home later because a guest checked out late, or she had to get more cleaning supplies. It wasn't a novelty for me to be home alone for a bit and make my own lunch, since she had taught me so well to do it myself. She sometimes left a small note with basic instructions or things she wanted me to do when she already knew that she would be home late. I looked for a note but there wasn't one. "Okay," I thought, "She's probably coming soon then."

In any case, something possessed me and made me walk into the bathroom. I washed my hands. I looked in the mirror. It was a mirror cabinet actually. I opened one of the little compartments and found my mum's makeup in there. I had always admired mum's makeup. It looked so good on her. I especially liked when she used the light blue eye shadow. Often, I would ask her to put it on when we went somewhere, just so I could look at her and swoon over the beauty of her face. I really liked that eye shadow. This exact eye shadow was the first thing I had spotted in the compartment. I took it out, then looked at my face in the mirror. I looked back and forth between my face and the eye shadow in my hand. Something must have clicked as I took the little brush and started painted my eyelids blue. Hesitant at first, then more assertive, more certain. I painted my left eyelid, then my right one. It was a different face I was seeing now but I liked it. The eyelids were done. "What next?" I thought as my excitement grew. I went through the makeup drawer and found a lipstick. Also one that I had seen many times on mum. One minute later, the lipstick had transformed my lips into a dark purple curtain that revealed my teeth when I smiled. A smile to check out my lips and the effect of the lipstick. The effect it had on my face, and the effect it had on me. A huge effect. So huge that I didn't stop there.

The lipstick reminded me of something... I went to the hallway where mum kept all of her shoes, including my favourite high heels. They were also dark purple, and they had a rose attached to their pointy front. I thought there were so pretty. I put them on. They were way too big for me. I struggled to walk but I loved every single step I took in them. They made me feel something. I came back to the sink, to the mirror cabinet. I checked myself in the mirror again. Something was missing. "Rouge!" I thought. So I grabbed a pink rouge that I saw my mum put on many times. I noticed she was doing it rather sparingly, so I tried to do the same. Just a touch of rouge. But the first dab was a lot more than I anticipated. I tried to rub some off but it only smeared further across my left cheek. So I just went along with it and did the same with my right cheek, to make it look even at least. This made me look a little clownish. Appropriate and ironic, considering that later at school, I would be called Penny Wise.

As I admired my new look in the mirror, I heard a key turn in the door. It was mum. I had completely lost track of time. I was so infatuated by my own doings, by my new look, that I didn't even think that mum could come home from work at any minute. The front door open. I rushed to the bathroom door and closed it, then locked it. She yelled out, "Spencer, I'm home." I responded, "Hi mum, I'm just in the bathroom." I tried to sound as normal and calm as possible but inside, I was shocked, flustered, terrified. Terrified to have my mum see me this way. Terrified to get punished or screamed at. Even though my mum wasn't the type to scream or punish. But in this moment, I thought this was a valid possibility. "Okay," she said. "Hurry up, lunch will be quick and ready soon." I remembered there was some leftover food in the fridge that she was obviously going to warm up in the microwave. So I knew I didn't have much time. I looked at myself in the mirror, panicking. I took a bar of soap, trying to wash away my colourful face. I dried it with the white hand towel that was hanging next to the sink. After that, it wasn't white anymore. I looked up again in the mirror. To my surprise, the makeup hadn't fully come off. After seeing shades of blue, purple and pink on the hand towel, I would have expected it to be off completely.

"Spencer, what are you doing in there? Open the door." I panicked even more. I didn't want her to see me like that. What had I done? The time was ticking. I tried to rub off the makeup residue with the half-wet hand towel but it only made it worse. I was shattered, I was lost. As mum was knocking on the door continuously, I knew I had no other option. I had to open the door. I had to let her see me. I took off the high heels and hid them in the bathtub behind the bath curtain. I tentatively unlocked the door. Still terrified. Mortified.

The door opened and I found mum standing there. She looked at me. A few seconds of confusion defined her face. It was unclear during those seconds what her reaction could be like. I was expecting the worst. I was as prepared as I could be. "Spencer," she said with a stern look. "Spencer!" she repeated. Her face started to light up. Was I seeing this correctly? Yes, I was. She kneeled down and looked right into my face. My colourful, smudged face. "Spencer," she said for a third time. Her lit up face produced a smile. A smile that I was so relieved to see. That smile turned into laughter. First very subtle, then more and more from the belly, more and more from the heart. She clearly found it very amusing. The relief! The weight fell off my shoulders. Relief! "Spencer, you look so fun!" mum said. "I couldn't get it off properly," I told her. She took my hand and led me to the sink. She saw the hand towel and laughed again. She took a new towel out of the bathroom drawers. "Come here, honey," she said as she gently cleaned my face. It took a few minutes to get my old face back but we got there in the end. "Let's have some lunch now, shall we?" she said to me as she lovingly stroked my face. "Yes, let's!" I said, still relieved. And happy.

My mum took my right hand and we walked out of the bathroom together. As she passed the bathtub, I realised that I hadn't closed the curtain enough to hide her dark purple high heels. She clearly caught a glimpse of them, but she didn't confront me, she didn't say anything. Instead, she casually adjusted the curtain which made it close properly. Not a word from her lips. Not a word, *maybe*. But an obvious, knowing smile on her lips, *definitely*. Mum never asked me about it. She never asked why. She never questioned it in any way. She just let it be. She let me experiment. She let me experience. She let me be me.

So yeah, there were definitely signs of my sexual tendencies along the way. Some obvious, some not so much. But I was certain that mum was aware one way or another, and that she connected all the dots, inside and out.

18. Literally and emotionally.

It was the evening. I was lying in my bed, staring at the star stickers on my ceiling, thinking about all the things that happened recently. All the weird things, all the funny things, all the amazing things. All of which I couldn't have anticipated in a million years. The freckles, the time travel, my growing confidence in standing up to Robbie and his minions, the valuable moments with Sven, and my mum.

I still felt a sense of euphoria, having finally told mum about my magic sparkles, but this euphoria also made me feel worse about keeping Sonya, my best friend, in the dark about it. There were many opportunities to tell her, though the timing never seemed quite right, either. But I was certain! I was determined! I had to come clean. I had to create another opportunity, I had to tell her. Now.

A final, conscious gaze towards my star stickers, collecting my thoughts, gathering all my energy and courage. How will Sonya react? Will she be mad? Will she be happy? Or, will she be her dry and cool self and just take it as if I had just told her that I bought a new t-shirt? Which, by the way, didn't happen often. Regardless, now was the time. "So let's go," I told myself. "But how will I get to her place now?" I wondered. It was too late to take the bus and I couldn't be bothered to cycle there. It wasn't that far away but still, bus and bike were no options. I went up to my window and opened it wide. I leaned over and looked outside. A slight breeze greeted my face. It was nice. Then, another breeze, more apparent, moving my red wavy hair to the back. It was like the breeze made me inhale the idea that it gave me... Flying. "Yes," I thought. "Yes. Flying!"

I got excited about the sheer thought of it. I've always wanted to be able to fly, but obviously that was never an actual possibility. Sure, I had all those dreams about flying before. But never in my wildest dreams did I think that I could actually do it. Yet here I was, a different person now. Someone who could make those kind of dreams a reality. Or so I hoped. I still didn't know what limitations there were with my powers, if any at all. While I had tried a few spells here and there, I was still new to all of this. Was I actually able to fly? I could only find out if I tried. It was dark outside, so it was a good opportunity to do it as the probability of being seen was obviously lower than during the daytime. "So let's do it," I affirmed.

I moved away from the window, making sure it stayed open wide. I put on my oversized, cream-coloured hoodie. "It might get cold," I thought. I was ready. I stood firmly, with both feet planted on the ground. I closed my eyes, summoning my imagination - the image of flying. "Sparkle sparkle, low and high. Sparkle sparkle, let me fly."

Lights. Tingles. Whoosh.

My arms spread out into the air, like wings. Then, my right foot left the ground. My left foot still on the floor. My body was shaking, I was trying to hold my balance. I was wobbling around. It must have looked like a beginner's ballet performance. Until my left foot joined my right foot. My body was now fully in the air. I looked around. I looked down. I looked up. Yes, I was floating in the middle of my room, between the star stickers and the creaky floor. I was scared. I was exhilarated. I was... not knowing what I was doing. At all! I floated like a balloon against each corner of my room. I was trying to move forward. Instinctively, my arms cut through the air, as if I was swimming. Unsuccessfully. I was still only floating from one side to the other, carried by the breeze coming through the window. "Okay," I thought, "not as easy as I thought it would be."

I gave myself a moment to regroup. "Alright, Spence," I said to myself. "You *are* in the air right now. You *are* flying. So the spell did what you wanted it to do. But what am I missing here? Hmmm." I kept thinking what else I could do. I still felt a bit wobbly. A bit unsafe even. It was too strange a feeling to be up in the air like this. I felt unsure… "That's it." I had a lightbulb moment. Unsure! I realised I was too *unsure*. Of this situation. Of myself. I had to try to get myself to a better place. Literally and emotionally. I had to be focused. Committed. Didn't I learn anything from the thyme time spell? I knew I needed a better focus on my wish in order to receive exactly what I was using my magic for. Instead, I was still floating. "Come on, Spencer," I encouraged myself. "You are halfway there. You can do this." I closed my eyes, took a deep breath and said loudly and firmly, truly believing what I was saying, "I can do this! Let's fly!"

My eyes were wide open and fixated on the window. I quickly recognised that they seemed to be the steering wheel of my flying body. As I focused on the open window, I moved towards it, no swimming motions necessary. Wherever I hooked my eyes, that's where my body followed. I touched the window frame as I flew out of my room. OMG! It was actually happening. I smiled. A big smile. Being up in the air, floating in my room was one thing, but moving around outside through the fresh air was another. It was everything I had ever imagined, and more. I was on top of the world. Literally and emotionally.

I flew up, higher and higher. My arms and legs stretched out. It felt so good, so free. The wind in my red wavy hair. I flew so high that I could see all the rooftops of my town. All the lights. The cars on the roads. The people on the streets, some of which were so far away that they looked like tiny insects. I flew over the town square with its merchant houses. I flew over the park with the lake. I flew over my school. Seeing my school from above gave me another perspective. Literally and emotionally. It made me feel so far removed from all the bad things I experienced down there. It gave me the feeling of freedom, of breaking away from it all. Finally. It gave me a feeling of strength and confidence. At least in this very moment. I urged myself to embrace it, this moment, this feeling - because I knew that I had to go back there eventually. Back to the ground. Back to reality. I was going to have to face the dark clouds again that followed my path, but that was okay. I was ready to face it all. But for now, I wanted to just be in the present, enjoying the high I was on. Literally and emotionally.

19. Bully.

As I flew over my town, I noticed that I was about to pass Robbie's house. It was easy to spot from just about anywhere. His house was a stand-alone building on a small hill at the fringe of town. It was a mansion with a manicured garden, with statues and gargoyles. A historic yet well-maintained place that many generations of his family had likely occupied. It was no secret that they were well-off. I wondered if they had butlers and other staff working for them. Even though, it was only Robbie and his parents living there now. His brother Toby moved away years ago but he visited occasionally, I sometimes saw him cruising around town on his Harley Davidson.

Consumed by my curiosity, my eyes led my flying body to Robbie's home on the hill. I swooshed over the front gate and along the long driveway to the entrance of their house. A large front door with Roman columns. The windows on the ground floor were bigger than the ones above. As I looked up, I heard voices coming from inside. First, I couldn't quite grasp where they were coming from, but eventually, I could spot movements through the window next to the front door. Still floating in the air, my eyes moved me closer to the rim of that window. It felt strange. Not only that I was spying on Robbie but also that I did that while flying. It was so mind-blowing and... surreal. But I have gotten to know this feeling quite well as I have discovered all the new *surreal* aspects of my life. This was just another one, and I was sure there would be more to come. It didn't mean that it was going to make it seem less surreal in the future, but it was going to feel familiar at the very least. And familiar could mean safe.

The window was covered by long white curtains but I could see through them enough. It was the window to their dining room. The room was filled with bright lights, so bright that it attracted moths which, like me, were catching a glimpse of the scene inside. One moth flapped around so close to me that it got tangled in my hair. Thankfully, I managed to free it, calmly and gently, without drawing any attention, before I shifted my focus back to the view through the window.

A long table was standing in the centre, set beautifully with a colourful tablecloth and three candles placed carefully in the middle between the arrangement of food. It looked nice and yummy, opulent and fancy, but in a way, also cold and sterile. The father was sitting at the left end of the table, the mother at the right, Robbie in the middle. There was a lot of space between them. I continued to hear the muffled sounds of their voices, it was difficult to make out what they were talking about. The father gave Robbie a grim stare, while Robbie studied his plate, moving food with his fork, clearly avoiding his father's firm look. His mother had her elbows on the table, encasing her plate full of food. Her hands were folded, with her chin resting on her fingers. She was silent and watched with concerned eyes. I strained my ears but still couldn't catch the dialogue. And I wanted to know. I was curious, so I helped myself and put my freckles to use. "Sparkle sparkle, I can't hear. Sparkle sparkle, make it clear."

Lights. Tingles. Whoosh.

Immediately, the volume went up. "I asked you a question," the father addressed Robbie, the stern look still defining his face. "I don't know," Robbie answered while keeping his eyes on his plate. "You don't know," the father repeated mockingly. "You don't know why you wrote this average paper." I noticed that the father had a piece of paper in his left hand. He held it up to emphasise what he was talking about. I could see red markings on it, a lot of them. Some sort of corrections apparently. It must have been the essay we had to write in Mrs Anderson's class. The assignment was to choose a character of the "Harry Potter" book and write what we liked about the character, what we disliked, what felt relatable and what didn't.

For my essay, I picked Harry Potter. Clearly, I could relate to him the most. He had a scar, I had freckles. He was bullied by Malfoy, I was bullied by Robbie. Harry had good friends and support in Hermione and Ron while I had Sonya. Both Harry and I had magic powers, unbeknownst to us at first. Of course, I didn't write about my magic specifically. I kept it general and wrote about awareness and the ability to learn and adjust to new situations.

I did wonder though which character Robbie picked. And what he wrote. And how it made the paper an average essay in the eyes of his father. Granted, Robbie never seemed to receive the best grades but somehow he still managed to advance to the next school year. Surely, his parents would have been used to an average essay. The father stood up, suddenly, while slamming his fist on the table, so sudden that Robbie and his mother got a fright. They both looked at Robbie's father. "It's not just average. It's pathetic. You made so many mistakes in this paper. It is pathetic. You…" The father pointed right at Robbie's face, so close it almost poked his eye. "You…" the father repeated. "You are pathetic." He moved away from the dining table. "You're pathetic," he said louder and more forceful. He walked towards the door. "Pathetic." He smiled ironically as he kept repeating it. "Pa-the-tic!" He then turned around and walked back to the table. He sat down. Calmly. He got settled in his chair. He laid the paper beside him, put his index finger on it and said, "You're a disappointment to this family." He picked up his fork and took a bite of the green beans. "Why can't you be like your brother? He graduated top of his class, and now… now, he's going through university with flying colours. Why can't you be like that? Huh? Tell me, Robert. Why are you not like Toby?"

It's the first time I had ever heard anyone call Robbie by his full name, Robert. It sounded strange. The father looked at Robbie while continuing to eat his dinner. Robbie still avoided his father's look as he mumbled, "Because I am not him." He leaned over to Robbie with his hand on his ear. "Sorry, what was that, son? I didn't hear you. What did you say?" Visibly agitated, Robbie finally growled. "BECAUSE I AM NOT HIM, okay? I am not Toby, dad. And I will never be. I am not him because I am *me*, and I'm sorry that I'm such a disappointment to you. I am who I am, dad. I'm sorry that this is not enough for you." Robbie abruptly got up from his chair, threw his napkin on the table and stormed out. "And, my name is Robbie," he screamed from the top of his lungs. "Don't you walk away from me. Come back. Come back this instance," the father yelled as his son slammed the door shut behind him. It was clear that Robbie wasn't going to come back to the table.

His father sighed and looked over to his wife. She was silent throughout all of this. She didn't even try to intervene. She didn't say one word. She just sat there. "What am I doing wrong, Marge?" he asked her. "Nothing. Nothing, honey." That was all she said. Until she took a deep breath. It seemed she was trying to collect every bit of courage. "But Carl, did you even read Robbie's paper?" she finally said. Unlike her husband, she called her son Robbie, and not Robert. He grabbed Robbie's essay. "Pfft! This? You mean this?" He laughed and shook his head. "I don't need to read it to know that it's bad. Look at all the red comments from his teacher. That's all I need to know. It was never like that with Toby." He exhaled sharply before he put the paper down, wiped his mouth with his napkin and stood up. The look of anger and disappointment still apparent. "I'm going to do some more work. Don't wait up for me," he passingly said as he left the room. His footsteps moved further and further away from the dining room into the back of the house. Robbie's mother still sat there for a moment, looking at the table, looking at all the food that hadn't been eaten, until her eyes met the paper laying next to her husband's plate. She got up and moved to the other side of the table. For a moment, she hovered over the essay, scanning the page. Then, without warning, she turned and walked to the cabinet near the window. The window where I was watching all of this unfold. She was coming closer. I was freaking out. "No, no, no! She cannot see me," I said to myself, panic rising in my chest. What would I even say if she did? No, that couldn't happen. She stepped closer. Her eyes wandered across the curtains. She squinted. Could she see me? She came closer, and closer, her eyes still squinted. My heart started to race. I needed to do something, and I had to do to quickly. "Now, Spence! Now!" I urged myself. "Sparkle sparkle, day and night," I started as she arrived at the edge of the window. I could feel my heart beat faster and faster. "Sparkle sparkle," I continued as she reached for the curtains. Forcefully and determined, she pulled them aside, as I finished, "Need to hide."

Lights. Tingles. Whoosh.

In the same moment that the curtains revealed the night sky to Robbie's mum, I felt my body change. I could still see through the window but I could feel something was different about myself. I looked Robbie's mother right in her eyes. I screamed. "Oh no, it's over," I thought. She looked at me with no further emotion. She didn't scream back, she wasn't shocked, she wasn't surprised that she saw me flying - and spying. How could this be? I looked right at her, and she looked right at me. Why didn't she react the way I thought she would react? Instead, she walked away unimpressed, almost annoyed as I heard her say, "Ugh, bloody moths." Wait, what? Did I hear that correctly? Moth? As in the werewolf version of a butterfly? What? I looked at my arms. But they were not arms anymore, they were wings. Four black wings. I looked at my legs. But they were not my legs anymore, they were hairy legs. Six hairy legs. I looked at my body. I was not skinny anymore. I was quite stocky and my body was covered in hair also. A moth. There was no doubt about it. I was, indeed, a moth.

Initially, I was puzzled about this, and I didn't know how the spell came to turn me into a moth. But the pieces of the puzzle came together. Yet again, I didn't specify what I wanted to happen, other than that I needed to hide. Yet again, my focus wasn't 100% clear. My panic took reign of the situation, but in the end, I was happy that it worked out this way. Sure, it was unexpected and I kind of felt like my freckles were having a bit of uncontrolled fun with me. I certainly didn't anticipate to end up as a light-fixated insect but whatever the case, Robbie's mother didn't see me, and that was my main concern right now. That was a very close call. Phew.

As I crawled up the window with my newly gained legs, I saw Robbie's mum walk to the cabinet. She pulled out the top drawer and reached for an oval case. She opened it and took out a pair of golden-framed glasses. She put them on and walked back to the table. She picked up Robbie's essay again and started to read, silently, her lips quivering. What did Robbie write? His mother's face displayed an array of expressions which made me even more eager to know what the essay said. I was too curious to let it go. I focused my thoughts on Robbie's mum. After the last spell, I wanted to get in the habit of being more precise with my magic, so I didn't have to face constant surprises. "Sparkle sparkle, with no doubt. Sparkle sparkle, read out loud."

Lights. Tingles. Whoosh.

"… safe to say," were the first words that left Robbie's mother's lips. She didn't seem to notice that she was reading out loud now. She continued naturally without pausing. "But no matter how cruel Voldemort is to Harry, I'd like to think of Voldemort as a person. A hurt person. Someone who grew up good but then things happened to him that made him into the cruel creature we know today. A creature that got hurt. A creature that turned bitter and angry. But maybe, just maybe, Voldemort will remember the core of his being. Maybe he still harbours a small enough grain of good in him. Maybe this grain will eventually grow to make him into a person that Harry deserved to have had in the first place. A friend. A supporter. A father figure even, rather than an enemy. Voldemort is evil and he did unspeakable things. But even a monster like Voldemort has love and deserves love. Love to show that there are other fulfilling ways of existing. A kind of love that I hope will prevail in the end."

I was shocked. That was Robbie's essay? That was what he wrote? That was who he chose to write about? Voldemort. He picked Voldemort. Well, his choice as such didn't take me by surprise, actually. It was more the different perspective from which he saw Voldemort, as a person rather than a creature. I never thought of Voldemort in this way. While for me, it was debatable whether Voldemort had any good in him to begin with, I appreciated the sentiment. Robbie was seeing Voldemort through the eyes of hope. The hope that a person could change. The hope that a person could be better. The hope that the good will win. Just as much as this was shining a new light on Voldemort, it was shining a new light on Robbie. This whole evening did. His mother held the paper tight to her chest as she wiped tears from her face. She clearly knew what was going on in that house - between Robbie and his dad. And now she knew more clearly what her son was feeling. What her son was hoping for. A friend. A supporter. A father figure.

She took the paper with her as she left the room and turned the lights off.

20. Like father like son.

When the lights turned off, I felt an immediate relief. I was no longer drawn to the light. For a moment, I had forgotten that I was still a moth. Still with six legs, and still with four wings. I scanned my body. Yes, still a moth. I needed to undo that and get moving asap. Without a second thought, I said, "Sparkle sparkle, young and free. Sparkle sparkle, back to me."

Lights. Tingles. Whoosh.

Yay. I was back. I was back to my normal self. I smiled briefly, pleased that the spell went exactly how I wanted it to go. I felt I was starting to get the hang of it, learning from my previous mistakes. "Okay, Spence," I mumbled to myself. "Let's get out of here." I had seen enough. More than I had anticipated. Even though I didn't even know what I had anticipated to see. What did I expect to witness? Possibly a bunch of butlers to confirm my assumption that Robbie's family had their own staff. But I didn't even see them, so I still didn't know the concrete answer to that. As I flew away from Robbie's house, back over the front gate, I decided to head back home, abandoning the plan to visit Sonya. I didn't have the strength to face her now. I had to do it some other time, but not now. I needed to go home and be by myself.

Because what I just saw was a handful. It was a lot. It caught me off guard. It made me feel a little down, a little melancholic. Hearing the words that Robbie had written were words I never thought he would even think, let alone write down in a school essay. He always presented himself as this tough, 'can't touch this' kind of person. Loud, seemingly confident, joking around and making fun of people. Including me. He was always mean to me, so I never considered him to be any other way. In my mind, that was just who he was. Through the assignment Mrs Anderson gave us, Robbie found a way to show a different side, to express his inner self, all the while masking it as his view of Voldemort. Nobody would have ever known that his essay had an underlying meaning, that it was not just about Voldemort, but about himself. Nobody would have ever entertained that idea. Neither would I.

It never occurred to me that this could all be show, an act, a facade. That underneath it all, he was just a boy who was hurting. A boy who was lacking attention from his parents, mostly his father. A boy whose father had a clear admiration for Robbie's older brother Toby but who was treating Robbie like garbage. A father who was not a father to Robbie - but a bully. I just never saw this coming. But I have also never really thought about Robbie and the reasons for his behaviour. Yes, I have thought about why he had a problem with me, but I was trying to find the reasons, the cause of it in myself. I thought it was something about *me* that rubbed him the wrong way. I never invested even one minute of my time to look at the other side properly. Instead, I was always too focussed on ignoring him and his minions. Too focused on staying out of their way - anything to just get through the day.

It was safe to say that Robbie had a challenging time at home with his parents, trying to manage their expectations and trying to deal with the disappointment they projected on him. A disappointment that they expressed in a damaging way. Unfiltered. It all became clear to me after that night. Robbie tried to find an escape, an outlet away from his father. Away from the hurtful things he said to him. Away from the emotional pain. And somehow apparently, this outlet was me. He took all of his anger and frustration and directed it at me. He was a hurt person, out to hurt another, to hurt me. And why? I could only imagine that this could have given him a feeling of control - quite possibly. A feeling of power - clearly. A feeling of self-worth - most likely. He actively tried to feel something other than the home-inflicted pain. And in order to do that, he decided to inflict pain on others, on me.

It didn't diminish all that I went through. It didn't excuse any of his actions towards me. Just because he was being bullied most certainly didn't mean that he had the right to do the exact same thing to me. Making me feel like I was a failure, making me feel like I was nothing, making me feel like I deserved this kind of treatment, making me feel like I was worthless. It did not excuse any of it by any means, because after all, he could have chosen the opposite direction. He could have chosen compassion, kindness and understanding. But he didn't. No, it was not an excuse, but it was an explanation.

Hurt people hurt people.

21. Rose and shine.

Beep. Beep. Beep. My alarm rang. Beep. Beep. Beep. "Ugh. Already?!" I thought. It took me a while to fall asleep after the eventful evening at Robbie's place. I didn't quite get the sleep I wanted. Lethargically and reluctantly, I got out of bed and went straight to the bathroom to splash some cold water on my face. Maybe that was going to help me feel better and ready to take on another day of school. "Ugh!" I sent another handful of water crashing against my face, then gave my cheeks a sharp slap. "Wake up, Spencer," I told myself.

I really wasn't in the mood for school today. I was never really in the mood, honestly, given the steady pattern of remarks and actions from Robbie and his minions. But I was even less in a mood for school after learning what I knew now about Robbie. I was unsure how to handle that. He obviously didn't know that I was at his house, and he most definitely didn't know that I learnt of his family situation. And how was that going to affect me? What was I going to do the next time he made a nasty comment? Was I going to strike back at him, or was I going to let it slide? Did Robbie's situation mean that he got a free pass for all of his past bullying, and for the bullying to come? Did Robbie's situation mean I had to try to ignore it even harder than before? I didn't know what to do. And I couldn't even tell Sonya and ask for her advice. I could hardly go to her and tell her that I knew Robbie's secret. "How?" she would ask, and I would answer, "I flew to his house and spied on him." Yeah, that wasn't going to be a good idea. I truly wanted to tell Sonya everything but not like this. It was too much. "Ugh," I thought, "If only I had told Sonya when everything started to change." But I didn't, and now I was on my own to deal with it.

I had no energy for that at all. I felt drained. So drained that I couldn't even get myself to put some clothes on. I looked at myself in the mirror, water dripping from my face into the sink. I figured that my lack of energy was a good excuse to use my magic to get dressed. At least that. At least something to make the day a little easier. I knew I probably shouldn't constantly use my sparkles. I had to attempt to maintain a fairly normal lifestyle - whatever that meant. But at the same time, I *did* have freckles, I *did* have sparkles, I *did* have magic abilities now... So shouldn't I also make use of them? Otherwise, what was the point? Having those kind of powers didn't represent a normal lifestyle anyway. So why would I want to fight it? I just had to make sure to pick the right moments. And this was definitely a good moment. I was in the safety of my home, and I was lethargic as hell. I didn't have to convince myself much more, that thought sealed the deal... "Sparkle sparkle, I'm a mess. Sparkle sparkle, get me dressed."

Lights. Tingles. Whoosh.

I gazed back in the mirror. The water drops had dried. My face still looked tired but my attire looked fresh. My newly fixed 'holesome' pants, my blue-dotted pink socks, and the recently rediscovered white shirt that had the sun shining from behind a grey cloud. "Yes!" I exclaimed. I sucked in a motivational breath, fist clenched and pumping to gather a little energy. "Yes!" I exclaimed again, "Let's do this."

Taking the bus to school felt almost strange, after having flown all over the town. But hey, I couldn't just fly everywhere at any given time without being seen. And I couldn't beam myself to school either - like I beamed myself to Uncle James. That would have been way too risky. No, I had to be careful. For the sake of not getting found out. It was in my best interest. So I took the bus. Besides, it was also quite nice to be around Eddie. He was always fun with his radio obsession. He made me smile and gave me a sense of calm. It took my mind off things. It took my mind off Robbie. And I needed that right now. I needed a distraction. And the music really helped. I leaned over to Eddie. "Hey Eddie, can you turn up the radio, please?" I asked him. "Your wish is my command, good sir," Eddie replied, visibly delighted, as he increased the volume to grant my wish. "Your wish is my command" - it echoed in my head. It was funny that he used that phrase. It had such a different meaning to me now. "Thank you," I said as I giggled silently.

Just as the bus turned into the street of the school, I saw Sonya enter the street with her bike in the same moment. She looked over to the bus and spotted me. She gave me the middle finger and grinned. Before I could even react, she raced the bus to get to school first. She was so awesome. She was the best. I sighed. I got a little sad and nervous and anxious. "I will tell you, Sonya," I whispered. "I will tell you." I looked down on my knees when Eddie asked, "Spencer, my man, you good?" I glanced up and caught his face, bright and cheerful, the 'bald' cap sitting crooked on his head. "Yes, of course," I quickly replied, "All good." I smiled stiffly, trying to sell my answer. "Great," he said with a genuine smile which made my smile look even more forced and fake. "Enjoy your day at school, Spence." I nodded at him as I exited the bus.

Sonya was waiting for me at the school entrance. "Morning, rat. Ready for another day in the palace of education?" she asked with exaggerated excitement. I smirked at her randomness and said, "Oh yes, I am stoked." Enthusiastically, she grabbed my arm and hooked herself in. We walked towards the main entrance when she suddenly did a single slouchy skip. I looked over at her with an affirming smile before I replicated that single slouchy skip. She smirked and launched into another hop. Once again, I mirrored her with a bounce of my own. We would have looked like two silly bobbleheads, but we didn't care. We continued to skip in turns until our movements evolved into a less slouchy, more synchronised rhythm. We had fun. We started laughing out loud. Yes, Sonya really was the best!

We walked to our classroom, our arms still hooked in together. We could hear that most people were already there. The noise said it all. As we got closer, Sonya looked over to me and pointed her index finger at me. An understanding twinkle flew over my face. And over hers. I stretched out my finger and touched hers. "FTT!"

We entered the classroom and approached our seats when I noticed something on my table. I couldn't quite make out what it was. I squinted my eyes and raised my left eyebrow in confusion. When Sonya and I arrived at our places, it was clear what it was. I sat down quickly, picked it up and hid it under the table, so nobody else could see it. Or maybe everyone had already seen it? I looked around at the class. Everyone seemed to be occupied with their own thing. Robbie and his minions were joking around about something, being their usual selves. They didn't pay any attention to me, and no one else was looking at me either. "Great," I thought. Nobody saw this. It was a relief as I really didn't have the strength for any mocking today.

I whipped around, away from the class, facing the wall behind me, hunched over. I took it between my index finger and thumb and spun it around gently while glancing at it from all angles. Mesmerised. Confused. Wondering. "Look what I got, Sonya," I finally said with a heightened sense of playfulness. I figured that Sonya must have put it on my table and that must have been why she was racing the bus to get to school earlier. She turned around and looked genuinely surprised to see this in my hand. "Oh! A rose. How... lovely," she said with one of her best traits... Sarcasm. "Come on. You don't have to pretend," I said, poking her gently. She looked puzzled. "Pretend what, Spence?" she asked so convincingly that I was doubting my suspicion. "You didn't put this on my table?" I asked while still trying to shield the rose from the rest of the class. "How could I have put that on your table, rat? How was I going to do that? I arrived here pretty much at the same time you did." She raised her eyebrow. "Yes," I said, "But you were going so fast on your bike, and I thought maybe that's why. It would have given you enough time to do it." I shrugged and waited for her response. But she just half-rolled her eyes and pursed her lips. "Spencer, come on. I raced the bus because I am a BBB," she eventually said. "A what?" I had no idea what she was talking about. "A BBB. A Badass Bike Bitch." I stared at her and couldn't help but burst out laughing. And so did she. Her dry humour came out of nowhere sometimes - often. Badass Bike Bitch. That was hilarious, yet accurate. She always took her bike to school. For as long as I could remember, she loved cycling. And she did get a bit competitive at times with other vehicles, or joggers. I have seen it. She just had a competitive nature, at least when it came to her bike. So 'Badass Bike Bitch' was spot on.

Our laughter continued before it slowly died off to a dim chuckle. "Besides rat, you know I hate plants." There it was again. Her dry humour. She was joking, I knew that wasn't true. She had cacti in her room. They were plants. Sure, they were not colourful flowers like this red rose, but cacti were still plants. Plants which she arranged thoughtfully on an otherwise empty bookshelf. It was obvious that she loved having them there, able to look at them from her bed on the other side of her room. But instead of arguing with her, I played along. "Sure, how could I forget?" I said, seasoned with my own sarcasm to match hers.

"Alright, alright," I moved on, "So if it wasn't you... Who else could it be then? I mean, who would leave me a present? And not just a present but a rose, of all things." I couldn't make sense of it. I got a present at school before, but that was a while ago, and it wasn't from any of my classmates who wouldn't waste a thought on anything like that, not for me anyway. I knew it couldn't have been them. But for the sake of it, I scanned every classmate individually to tick off the possibility and to confirm my theory that it wasn't them. "It was probably Robbie, playing a joke on you, Spence," Sonya said. Sure, that was something he would do but I really didn't believe that this was him. Especially knowing how last night went for him... Would he have had time, energy and motivation to plan this? Would he? I didn't think so. He seemed pretty fed up with his dad. I really didn't think that there was any room for planning a mischievous gag. "Nah, I don't think so, Sonya. Look at him." We both looked over at him. He was still messing around with Benji, Mike and Zac. "If it was him, they would watch my every move. They would have commented on it already. No, I don't think it was them." Sonya tilted her head to the right in silent agreement.

Before we could make any other assumptions, Mrs Anderson entered the room. "Good morning, everyone," she said while closing the door behind her. "Let's pick up with..." She couldn't finish her sentence because the door she just closed opened again. It was Sven. "Oh, hi Sven," Mrs Anderson greeted him. "Good morning, Mrs Anderson. Sorry I'm late. I —." She interrupted him by raising her hand. "Not at all, Sven. We are only just about to start. Are you settling in well?" she asked with a caring smile while Sven went past her towards his seat. "Yes, very well, thank you, Mrs Anderson." Her smile remained. "Good. That's great, Sven. I am glad."

Sven dropped into his chair while Mrs Anderson proceeded swiftly. "Now, let's pick up where we left off in our last lesson." As everybody opened their "Harry Potter" book, Sven looked over at me with his kind green eyes and cute dimples. The same look he gave me when we first met. "Hi," he said. "Hey," I replied, almost in a whisper. His green eyes were sucking me in, back into being intoxicated. Hooked. Hypnotised. The more I stared into his eyes, the more this funny feeling in my stomach arose to life again. This funny feeling. That electricity in my body. It was unsettling. It was intense. It was *everything*. Lost in his piercing eyes, I barely noticed his lips starting to move. "Did you get my present?"

The intensity of the look melted away beneath his tender words. I found myself back in sobering reality. A thousand thoughts were running though my mind, but the main one resounded in my head over and over again... It was Sven? It was Sven. It was Sven! Sven gave me that rose. What on earth?! I was beside myself. I couldn't believe it. It was so unexpected. I almost couldn't handle it. I most definitely couldn't handle my excitement of his thoughtful gesture. Sven gave me a red rose. It was Sven? It was Sven. It was Sven!

I tried to play it as cool as I could to make sure he didn't get a grasp of the quiet hysteria bubbling inside me. "Umm, yes," I said, my composure hanging by a thread, "Yes, I did. Thank you." I smiled while feeling the blood running into my cheeks, undoubtedly painting them as red as my hair. As red as the rose. That, I couldn't control. "You're welcome," he replied with a fresh smirk on his lips. The smirk lingered as he browsed through his book to find the chapter we were about to talk about in class.

Still stunned about Sven's present, I tried to sort my thoughts and emotions. I felt my red cheeks persisting, obvious to anyone who would look at me. But I wasn't embarrassed about it. I was happy. They were happy red cheeks, burning bright. Though it wasn't really a burning. It was a shine. A shine given to me through a single red rose.

22. Sooo.

I could hardly concentrate throughout the English lesson. All I could think about was that red rose. All I wanted to look at was that red rose. All I wanted to do was chat with Sven - about that red rose. Sonya noticed my restlessness. It was difficult to ignore. I was drumming my fingers continuously on the table. She was trying to calm me down by putting her hand on my tapping fingers, but it didn't really work. It didn't calm me down. I still was very fidgety.

Moreover, I was constantly checking the time on the clock above our classroom door. "Should I use my magic and make the time go faster?" I kept asking myself. I was very tempted. It would have been so easy. I could have used a more appropriate spell this time. A better one than the one I used with my mum. One 'whoosh' and the lesson would have been over and I could have finally addressed the elephant in the room. Or in my case, the red rose. I toyed with the idea but in the end, I opted to wait it out. I realised that I wouldn't have been entirely focused to do a spell. I was way too amped up, so who knew what could have happened instead. Anything really, judging by my previous mistakes. And I really didn't want to deal with that right now on top of this funny feeling in my stomach, on top of the burning - the shine - on my face, on top of the excitement running through my body and my soul. I didn't want to spoil any of that. So I just had to wait patiently, somewhat, for the lesson to be over.

"And now we will..." Mrs Anderson said, until she got interrupted by the bell. It finally rang and offered an instant ease from the physical and emotional tension. "We will follow up on that next week," Mrs Anderson carried on after waiting for the sound of the bell to stop. "Have a nice weekend, everyone," she said in her usual enthusiastic voice as she gathered all her things and put them in her tote bag. I thought it was quite funny that she didn't have a briefcase or any other sort of bag that you would usually see a teacher with. Instead, she always carried a rainbow-coloured tote bag. That was just another thing that separated her from all the other teachers. She was just somehow more down to earth, she was more relatable, she was almost one of us.

Sonya stood up from her chair and leaned over, winking at me with a cheeky smile. "I'll see you after the break." She knew I was excited. And I knew she was excited for me. I smiled, almost uncomfortably. "I'll tell you everything later," I whispered back. In the moment I said that, it was setting off another trigger in my brain. Another kick in the gut. Another bout of guilty conscience. I hadn't told Sonya 'everything' yet at all. I had told her nothing. But maybe this could be the entry point of that 'everything' conversation that I desperately had to have with her.

"Later, Sven." Sonya gave him the same cheeky smile as she left the room. "Yeah, later," he replied, seemingly confused about Sonya's gesture, but I was convinced that he knew exactly what that was all about. He looked down at his black Chucks, a little flustered, and smiled. Then he looked up again. At me. "Sooo," he said, his eyes awkwardly moved back and forth. "Sooo," I retorted while looking around bashfully. "Sooo," Sven said again, followed by a second of silence before he went on, "Umm… Did you like the rose?" Of course, I liked the rose. I *loved* the rose. And I loved that he was making the first move to open the conversation. "Stay cool, Spence," I told myself, "Stay cool." I nervously ran my hand through my hair while trying to avoid his gorgeous green eyes. "Yep. Umm. Yes, I did. Thank you," I said. "Wh-why… did you give me a rose exactly?" I stammered. I almost couldn't bring myself to ask him that but I wanted to know. I *needed* to know.

"Well," Sven started, "I kept thinking about the time when you helped me up at the soccer match. I thought that you were incredibly kind and thoughtful." My eyebrows lifted in evident surprise. "What? What is it?" he asked as he studied my face. "Well, *I* thought that *you* were the kind and thoughtful one?" I said to him, this time not trying to avoid his eyes but looking straight into them. "Me?" he asked. "Yes, *you*!" I replied rapidly. "You were the one who picked me first as your teammate when nobody else ever did that before. And you didn't even care that I was bad at it," I added and laughed.

Yes, I laughed. If anyone had told me that I would be in the mindset to laugh about the sports lessons, I would have told them to get lost. But the once so traumatic ordeal in sports was suddenly transformed into a dream-like experience. One that I would have never thought was going to be real. But it was. That dream-like experience was real. And Sven made that happen. He picked me first. He showed me kindness and understanding when nobody else in that class did. "Well, I thought you did well," Sven said. "You were able to get me up from the ground after all, and that's not easy," he said and chortled softly. "I was down," he continued while pushing his right hand towards the floor to underline his statement, "and then I rose," he concluded while pointing his right hand at the rose which I was holding safely in the palms of my hand. "Get it? I 'rose'?!" he said and looked at me. I felt a prompt push in my stomach. That feeling was back. No, it wasn't *back*. It was there all this time. It wasn't back. It was more pronounced, more present now. That funny feeling became more accentuated when he made that comment, that silly pun. It was so silly. So cringe. It was perfect. *He* was perfect. "Could he be any more perfect?" I thought. "Hehe," I chuckled, "Yeah, got it. That's funny." I played down the actual glee that I was feeling inside.

"And also," he suddenly resumed, "the rose didn't only remind me of our sports lesson. It also reminded me of you." I was perplexed. "How do you mean?" I asked. "Well, you see," Sven elaborated, "the rose is a delicate flower. Fragile perhaps, but powerful at the same time. It just has something special. That's why it makes so many people happy. It gives people a sense of joy to look at it, to marvel at its beauty, to simply be in its presence." I was bound to his lips, devouring every word that came out of his mouth, so carefully that I didn't miss even one syllable, not one thought that he expressed. "And that's what you give me, too," he continued. "I like to be in your presence."

I had to stop my jaw from dropping all the way to the floor. I said nothing, completely tongue-tied. My fingers played with the rose as I looked at Sven nervously. There was a gentle plea in his eyes, asking, hoping for some kind of reaction. And rightfully so. Of course, he wanted to know what I thought about it. Instead, I gave him nothing. The look on his face persevered. "And you look like a rose," he finally said to break the silence. He bit his lip and tensed up immediately. "I mean, sorry," he back-paddled, "I didn't mean... I didn't want to say that you are..." He was struggling for words. "Stop!" I grabbed his hand that he had been waving through the air. "I get it," I tried to calm him down and chuckled, "I'm a delicate red rose." I pointed at my red hair and threw it back exaggeratedly. I humorously shook my head left and right, pretending to be in slow motion until my head came to a complete stop with some of my hair burying my face.

I could see his face lose tension. A smile came to the surface. That smirk. Those dimples. His left hand travelled slowly but steadily towards my face. He carefully brushed the strands of hair in my face to the side whereby touching my forehead and sliding over my temples ever so slightly. His green eyes pierced through mine. They locked, they intertwined, they danced together through the space of time and imagination.

"Sooo," he said softly. "Sooo?" I responded with a shy look on my face. I wondered what he would say next. "Sooo," he went on,

"Do you want to hang out this weekend?" Oh my God, what was happening? He wanted to hang out! I was screaming on the inside. "You mean, like, just the two of us?" I wanted to clarify. "Yeah, just us," he confirmed. I could feel my face muscles form the broadest smile. "That would be cool," I said. Cool? That was such an understatement. It was so much more for me than just 'cool'. I looked up, at his dimply smile and back into his piercing green eyes. "Great," Sven said. "Great!" I nodded, with my lips firmly pressed together as if to - unsuccessfully - hold that broad smile on my face at bay. "Great," Sven said once again, "Sooo, I'll message you later then." As Sven walked outside the classroom, my eyes followed his every move. His shoulders, his hips, his legs. Wallowing in my own world, Sven suddenly turned his head around, back at me. He caught me staring at him. I was instantly embarrassed and looked down for a second before I took the courage to look up again. He stood there, his head still lingering in my direction. His eyes said it all. He most definitely saw me gawking. He smiled. He winked. And he walked away.

Tingles. Tingles everywhere. Tingles, not from my sparkles, but straight from my heart.

23. Henry Miller.

I leaned against the table for a moment to let it sink in what had just happened. Sven wanted to spend more time with me. I crossed my arms in contentment and snickered. I could have never imagined that the day would turn out like this. From not even wanting to go to school to being given a present. It made me think of the last time I got a present from someone that wasn't my family. That also happened at school. It was from Henry Miller.

Henry was a friend once. We were in the same year but in different classes. His was just across the corridor from mine. We used to spend a lot of time together, not just at school but outside of school, too. We were pretty tight. Often, I would go to his place which I could reach within minutes on my bike. We would do all sorts of things. Watch stupid movies. Play video games. Try to make music. Him on his keyboard, me on my guitar. Our music sessions, much like our friendship, wasn't always harmonious or perfect - but it was still always fun, and always easy.

Mum used to drive us around to amusement parks and gaming halls, sometimes to the cinema. My mum liked Henry, and she liked that I had found a good friend in him. She always had him stay for dinner after a day of hanging out together. That was always a nice finish to the day - for all of us. Mum also invited Henry over when we had family gatherings, so it wouldn't be so boring for me, or maybe just so I had an extra ally around. Someone my age. She just knew that we were good friends, that we liked to be around each other. She wanted him to be involved in my life as much as possible because she could see the positive impact it had on both Henry and me.

One day, at my place, Henry and I watched a movie. Mum had prepared some microwave popcorn for us which she placed in a big glass bowl. As we watched the movie, we freely and carelessly took popcorn out of that bowl. We would often grab at the same time, so our hands would touch frequently. It wasn't anything extraordinary. But there was a specific moment when we both reached into the bowl, and our hands touched longer than they would usually touch. When I looked at Henry, he had a twinkle in his eyes. At least, so I thought. We looked at each other. I looked in his eyes, then his mouth, then the tiny mole on his chin. You could hardly notice it, but I did. And I liked it. I thought it was the cutest feature... then I went in for a kiss. My first ever kiss. Our lips touched. His were soft and smooth, his breath pleasantly minty. No surprise because he always had a chewing gum in his mouth. In that moment, I couldn't believe I even did this. It took me such courage but my feeling was so strong, so I thought, "Just go for it, Spence, just do it." When our lips touched, I felt relieved. Relieved that I did it. I went in for the kiss. YES, I did. YES, our lips were touching. But not for long. Henry pulled back. It wasn't immediate but once he had grasped what was happening, he did. He pulled back.

"What is wrong with you, you perv? Why did you do that?" His face full of disgust as he wiped his lips with his sleeve. I didn't quite expect that kind of outburst. I didn't know what I expected really, but it wasn't that. "I… I don't know." I stared on the ground, utterly ashamed. I couldn't look at him.

Henry stood up abruptly, knocking over the bowl of popcorn in the process. He was stammering. He was trying to squeeze out words, like you would try to squeeze out the rest of a lemon but no more juice would come out. He squeezed and squeezed but nothing came out. He tried hard. Some fractions made it out of his mouth but none of them made any sense. He grunted angrily, his hand in his brown, usually perfectly combed hair. His eyes so wide open, you could see a whole lot of white. It looked scary. It gave me flashbacks to the look that my dad had on his face when he was really pissed off about something.

Henry eventually managed to spit out some words. "Damn, man." He stared at me. "Why," he whispered, the words being carried out of his mouth on a wave of his minty breath. "Why did you do that, Spence?" He turned to the wall, then looked back at me. He stood there for a moment. Completely motionless. A moment suspended in time. Suddenly, he took his jeans jacket from my rocking chair. He grabbed the door knob and wanted to open the door but his hands slipped off. His hands seemed to have gotten sweaty. Sweaty in disbelief of that kiss? Sweaty because he was angry? Or perhaps sweaty because he actually liked it? Despite his outburst, maybe he still liked it? I didn't know. He certainly wouldn't admit it there and then. Instead, he wanted to leave.

Henry tried to open the door again, this time successfully. He stormed down the stairs. "Oh hey Henry, are you not staying for dinner?" I heard my mum ask him as he passed her by. He didn't acknowledge her and ran out of the front door, slamming it shut behind him. I looked out the window and saw him running down the street, hastily and somewhat uncoordinated. He stopped at the corner of the street. He was about to turn left - but he stopped. He stopped to look back at my window. He saw me standing there. He saw me staring. "Ugh, no," I thought as I quickly pushed myself away from the window, behind the side curtains. "He must think I'm such a creep. First the kiss and now staring at him through the window. You're such a creep, Spencer Wise," I scolded myself. I was mad at myself, and I was afraid. "He will tell everyone at school. He will tell them everything, and it will be hell." That thought was hovering over me like a black cloud about to unleash the biggest downpour. So quite fittingly, when I came to school the next day, I expected the biggest shitstorm ever. I expected the roaring thunder of people mocking me, the flashing lightning of harsh comments about to electrocute me. I braced myself. But... None of that happened. No comments, no mocking, no ridiculing. Nothing. Henry never told anyone.

Of course, I was happy about that. I didn't want this to be a public outcry. I didn't want this to become even harder than it already was. When I sighted Henry, I wanted to thank him that he didn't blurt it all out, and I was hoping that we could talk about what happened, and work it out somehow. After all, we had been good friends, inseparable really. So I wanted to make this right, resolve it. But when I tried to approach him, he would ignore me and go the other way. He knew what I wanted but clearly that wasn't something that he wanted. He did all he could to avoid me, but that wasn't entirely possible with our classrooms being opposite each other. He saw me, and I saw him. We saw each other every day. Every time when we left our classrooms for lunch. Every time when we entered it again for lessons. We saw each other every day. Every single day. But we never spoke a single word ever again.

He since switched schools. One on the other side of town. So I hadn't seen him. Out of sight, out of mind - so I told myself. I thought it might be a good thing for me, so that I could finally move on. Finally forget. Forget the kiss. Forget our hangouts, our gaming sessions, our music collaborations. Forget Henry Miller.

It was a nice thought in theory but the reality was very different. Just being in my room brought back memories. Like my guitar. The guitar behind my door. I hadn't played again since it all happened. It would remind me way too much of the pain and embarrassment. Should I have even been embarrassed to begin with? Perhaps not. I was just following my gut, I was following my heart and went for what I thought we both wanted. I was wrong. And that was painful. It hurt. That pain still lingered in a far deep corner of my being. It was still there. I hadn't forgotten about it. But I tried. So I hid away the guitar, gone from my view for most of the time. In the corner behind the door. I could have stashed it in a much better place. A place I'd never have to see it again, not even for a second of any given day. But I put it there. Behind the door. Hidden, yet very much still present.

Why was it there? Why didn't I just get rid of it? Well, I was conflicted. While I wanted to dump it many times, I didn't. I couldn't. I loved music, and I loved that guitar. I loved how it made me feel when I played it. Of course, throwing it away would have meant letting go of Henry Miller, but at the same time, I would have been letting go of what else it stood for, what it did for me, what it represented for me. And I wasn't ready to give up on that. I wasn't ready to give up on new and better experiences that this guitar could give me. I wasn't ready to give up on more fun, on more laughter, on perfectly imperfect moments. I wasn't ready to give up on what I wanted. I wasn't ready to give up on a part of me. I wasn't ready to give up on... me.

24. Scared.

Once I collected my thoughts, I checked the time and realised that the break was almost over. So I quickly got my backpack and rushed out the classroom to join Sonya and tell her what happened. Just as I jogged onto the corridor, I got halted. Sonya was standing right beside the classroom door, seemingly popping up out of nowhere. I jumped so hard I let out a full-on shriek. "Sonya, what the hell?" I held my chest and gasping for air. I hated to be scared like that, and Sonya knew that. She knew that very well, actually. She continuously tried to convince me to watch a horror movie with her. She was a big fan of horror while I was not. So naturally, I always denied. No, thanks. I didn't like the gore, and I most certainly didn't like the scare factor of those movies. Sonya has used that knowledge to her advantage many times over, for her own amusement. She liked to scare people, she thought it was the funniest thing. I never liked it though, I always got annoyed but I always laughed it off in the end.

"What was that all about?" Sonya asked bluntly as if she didn't just give me the biggest fright of my life. She just moved on as if nothing happened. Although her face didn't give much away, I could see a suppressed smile on her lips, secretly pleased with herself. I looked at her in agitation as I walked back into the classroom. Sonya followed. "Come on, rat. Tell me." She jabbed me lightly in the hip with her elbow. "Don't keep me hanging. What did Sven say?"

My face immediately lit up. The scare, the agitation, the annoyance - it all was pushed away. Pushed away by the thought of Sven. Like when the sun pushed aside rain clouds, making way for a beautiful rainbow. "Well, it's nothing really. He... he wants to hang out. That's all," I casually said as I shrugged my shoulders. "That's all?! That's all? Spence, the hottest guy in school just gave you a rose. That is not nothing!" Sonya grabbed my head with both her hands and shook it gently as if to wake me up and make me realise the significance of her words, and the significance of Sven's actions. "Y-Yeah," I stuttered, "He said the rose reminded him of me." Sonya's eyes stretched wide open, she rolled them slightly. An accompanying smile underlined the look on her face. "Okay, that's a pretty weird thing to say if you ask me, but I guess it's also pretty sweet," Sonya said with that smile of amusement turning into a smile of excitement. "Yeah, umm. I didn't expect it, that's for sure. It is pretty cute, I guess, isn't it?" I asked while not actually needing an answer to confirm. It *was* cute. *He* was cute. "Spencer, I know you. You can't fool me. Hello, knock knock, it's me. I know you are smitten with him. I've seen the way you look at him." She was right, I couldn't fool her. She did know me. And it was great to have someone who could read me so well. However, the thought of that gave me a sudden shiver. Did that mean that she also knew that I hadn't told her about my sparkles yet? Ugh. There it was again, my bad conscience. Seemingly disappearing into the background for a while - until it sensationally came back to remind me that it was still there. This wasn't going to go away until I actually did something about it. I was going to. I was determined.

"You are right, Son. You're right," I said, once I pulled myself away from the thoughts of bad conscience, back to the present moment. "I do like him. He's nice, and he just seems different to the other boys here. And I like that. But I am also scared." Sonya leaned on the table right next to me, so close that our arms were touching. "Why are you scared, rat?" She looked into my plaintive eyes for a few seconds, as if she was staring deep into my soul. "Oh, you mean Henry?" She knew. "Yup," I briefly said. "Spence, the whole Henry thing wasn't your fault. You were just being yourself." She was right but it didn't make me feel much better. "Yeah, but that's how I lost a friend." I looked down, my eyes were getting watery. "And I don't want to lose another friend. It's scary." Sonya put her arm around me and squeezed me tight. "I know, rat. It is scary. It's scary to be open, to be vulnerable." I thought it was quite funny but sweet at the same time that this was coming from Sonya, who was not the most vulnerable person herself. "But if we don't show the person that we like who we really are, then what are we doing? We'd just pretend." She squeezed me gently once again as she continued. "Don't pretend, Spencer. Just be you. Trust me. If someone truly wants to be your friend, they will like you for who you are." Our eyes locked, and we shared a connecting smile. "With all those terribly annoying qualities that you have," she added and rubbed my head wildly with the knuckles of her hand. We both chuckled as I playfully pushed her away from me.

I fixed my disheveled hair as the chuckle slowly vanished into the air. I looked back at Sonya before I purposefully stretched out my index finger. And so did she in response. We pressed them together for a while, firmly and tightly. A tender moment of understanding. A moment of comfort that eased the feeling of fear, pain and anxiety.

FTT.

I was still scared but, more than that, I was also excited. The unknown could be scary. Indeed! But it could also be a second chance. A chance that we didn't know we wanted, or needed, or... deserved.

25. Choccies, chokes and cheers.

Ding. I was just standing in front of the mirror in the bathroom of my room, fixing loose strands of my hair when I heard a notification come through on my phone. I walked to my bed and picked it up. It was a message from Sven. "See you soon. :)" The smiley face at the end of his message transformed mine to exactly that, a smiley face. A smile of exhilaration - and relief. Relief that the meeting was still going to happen. I tried to prepare myself for anything, even a message to cancel. But he didn't. I read the message again. "See you soon. :)"

I put the phone into my jeans pocket and went back to the bathroom mirror to make those loose hair strands sit exactly where I wanted them. I checked my face one last time for my own approval before I headed down the stairs. "Mum, I'm going out for a bit," I yelled in her direction as I walked along the entrance hallway. She was in the kitchen, doing some tidying up. She gracefully pushed the kitchen door open with her hip while hand drying a plate. She still wore her apron. This one appropriately said 'Dishing it out daily'. Her apron collection just never failed to deliver.

"Alright, my sweet. Have a good time," she said as she kept polishing the plate. "Thanks, mum." I put on my sneakers and opened the front door. "Where are you going again?" mum asked. "Umm, I, I'm meeting a — friend." I didn't know why I felt so awkward about it. "You mean Sonya?" mum wanted to clarify. "No, anoth-..., a different friend," I replied. Mum looked confused but tried to hide it behind an engaged smile. "Great, well, have fun with your... friend," she said as she went back into the kitchen. She winked at me, threw me an air kiss and used her hip again to shut the door.

Sven and I agreed to meet at the large steel entrance gate of the city park. The park was one my favourite parts of town. Probably my most favourite actually. I went there whenever I could, which was quite often. Sometimes by myself, sometimes with Sonya, sometimes with my mum. It was just a nice place to be. So green and lush in summer, but even in winter, it was stunning. Being there always made me feel calm, it made me able to collect my thoughts. When I was there on my own, I talked loudly among the trees, *to* the trees. Speaking about my wants and needs, my troubles and my worries. When other park-goers passed me, they frequently gave me a side look, most likely thinking I was nuts for presumingly talking to myself. But I ignored them and stayed in my world with the trees which I felt could absorb and understand my words. And they turned them into reassurance. Nature was my saviour. My ally.

When I got to the entrance gate, Sven wasn't there yet. Was I early? I checked the time. 2.09pm. Damn. We agreed to meet at 2. And I would have been on time if the traffic hadn't delayed the bus. I regretted not leaving the house earlier. I was angry at myself. Did I mess it up before it even started? Was Sven here on time? Did he leave when he didn't see me? Did he think I wouldn't come? I should have texted him to say I was running late. I was looking around. In every direction. No sight of Sven. I checked my phone. 2.10pm. No message from him either. I looked around once more. He was nowhere to be seen.

I unlocked my phone and tapped on Sven's name to call him. Toooot... Toooot. I had the phone on my left ear, listening to the unanswered ringing when another ringing sound behind me entered my right ear. Ring, ring. The overlapping sounds kept mingling, seamlessly woven together. Tooot... Tooot... ring, ring. Tooot... Tooot... ring, ring. I turned around, my phone still pressed against my ear, in case Sven would answer. Tooot... Tooot... ring, ring. "Are you trying to call me?" Sven came around the corner with a smile on his face. His phone in one hand, wiggling it slightly to show me that it was ringing. In his other hand, a drink tray with two takeaway cups placed in it. "Mmm, yes," I said, "I'm sorry I'm late. The bus took ages." A bit of a stretch but it made me feel better about being late. "No sweat, all good," Sven said. "I hope you haven't been waiting much," I uttered, knowing exactly that he obviously got there at the agreed time. "Nah, not really. I went down the road quickly to get us hot chocolates. And so technically *I* am late now." He smirked with his dimples making him cuter every time. "That's sweet of you to say. Let's just say we are both late then," I replied with an implicit wink. We gazed at each other in agreement and smiled while holding that look, turning it into a faint stare.

"Soooo, umm..." I awkwardly interrupted the stare. "You got some drinks for us, huh?" Sven almost unnoticeably shook his head as if to force himself out of that staring moment as well. "Umm, yeah. You like hot chocolate, right? I wasn't sure if you drink coffee or not, so I thought I'd be safe with hot choccies." Hot choccies - it's been a while since I had heard someone say that. And Sven pronounced it so accentuated. I found that really infatuating. I didn't even remember the last time that I had a hot chocolate. I did, in fact, have coffee every day. I kinda liked the taste of it. When I was about 8 or 9, I remembered I asked my mum what coffee tasted like as I had seen her drink it every morning, and she seemed to really savour every drop. So she gave me a super weak version of her coffee, and I thought, "Oh yes, that's good." From that day on, I have had coffee. And as I got older, I increased the strength to a normal, single shot per cup. But hot choccies were going to do just fine. "Who doesn't like hot chocolates," I stated enthusiastically, trying to show my appreciation for the literal sweetness of that moment. "Great, I went to that place called 'Dairing'. Do you know it?" Sven asked while handing me one of the takeaway cups. "Yup, I know it." I knew it well actually, because it was notoriously famous for their concept, dairy. Hence the clever - or whatever - name of their cafe. I went in there once to get a coffee and asked for any kind of plant milk, and they were quite rude in telling me that they only served dairy milk and didn't believe in milk alternatives. Great for them, they had a vision and stuck by it. I respected that. But as a customer - and as a human being, for that matter - in an ever-changing world of environmental issues, I felt let down. I never went back there, obviously.

What was I going to do about that hot chocolate though? I didn't want Sven to be offended if I said I didn't drink dairy. It was so lovely of him to get me one of those. A sweet gesture, indeed. But I couldn't not accept it. So I had to do something. "Thank you," I said eventually, "Thanks for getting me one. That's nice." I put my lips on the cup lid and pretended to take a sip. "Hmm." Then, I started to choke, launching into a fake coughing fit - classic stall manoeuvre. "Oh, hey, are you alright?" Sven was visibly concerned. "I'm fine," I said, giving him a thumbs up while still coughing, in a desperate attempt for deflection. I needed to get a moment to myself. I twisted around, away from Sven, hunched over, pretending to get on top of the choking, as I called my freckles for help. "Sparkle sparkle, choccy time. Sparkle sparkle, oat for mine."

Lights. Tingles. Whoosh.

I was sincerely hoping that Sven neither heard me whisper those words, nor that he saw my sparkles light up. I tried to angle myself away and disguise the spell with the choking as much as I could. I felt his hand on my back while I gradually stopped coughing. It felt nice. Comforting. He gently patted to help ease the cough, like when trying to burp a baby. I straightened up from my Hunchback of Notre Dame position and emitted a final cough, drawing my staged choking to a close. "All good. Thanks. I think I just got some chocolate powder in the wrong hole." I didn't realise what it sounded like when I first said it. Until I did. I held my breath, thinking of what next to say. "You're cheeky," Sven said, "I like that." He winked at me with his piercing green eyes. We both chortled. "Shall we go in?" Sven finally asked. "Yes, let's," I replied frivolously. "After you." Gentleman-like, Sven pointed the way with his arms to let me go through the steel gate first.

When he came through the gate after me, he hopped to my right side, bumping into my shoulder, almost knocking my undercover oat hot chocolate. He raised his cup and moved it towards mine. "Cheers," he said, holding his cup high in the air. "Cheers. To sweet things!" The added toast came out of my mouth naturally, I didn't even think about it, it just came out. "Omg, I'm so embarrassing," I thought to myself. I wanted to slap my forehead for being so cheesy. But I couldn't take it back. I already said it. "I'll cheers to that," he said with a mischievous grin on his dimply face. We both took a sip of our choccies and started walking on the wide, long path of sand and gravel with my allies, the trees, left and right, accompanying our every step.

26. Swans.

"Sooo," I broke the silence after a few meters of walking, "you're from Germany?!" I didn't really know anything about Sven, so I was genuinely interested in his story. "What makes you say that?" Sven said. What? What did he mean? Was I wrong? Didn't Mrs Anderson say he came from Germany? My face transformed into one of those wide-eyed emojis, on the verge of short-circuiting from cognitive chaos. "Is it because I have an accent?" He stopped and looked at me with a straight face. I didn't know how to react. Was he offended? But why would he be? He *was* German, wasn't he? I started to doubt myself. "Uh, no. No, I... I mean... yes. I..." I stuttered. I felt uncomfortable. Awkward.

Helpless. I didn't know what to say in that moment. Sven's expression still persisted. No dimples in sight. Until suddenly, his radiating glow beamed through the serious mask. "Spence, I'm just messing with you." He nudged me with his elbow to snap me out of my awkwardness. He chuckled. "Oh," I said and exhaled while swiping the back of my hand over my forehead. The tension washed away, and I was relieved that I didn't ruin this date when it hadn't even really started yet. Was this even a date? "Phew!" I smiled as we continued walking. "For a moment, I thought that you were being serious." Sven abruptly stopped again. "Why? Because I am German, so I have to be serious?" He put his straight face back on for a few seconds until he nudged me again. He was funny. I liked his humour. "Well," Sven said while we kept strolling along the sandy gravel path, "it's true. Germans can be quite serious which is why the stereotype says that we have no humour. But I'm living proof that we are not all like that. We can be funny, you know? And fun." He winked at me. I smirked at him. "Clearly. Haha," I said amused, "you really got me there."

We both took another sip of our choccies. "Do you know any German words?" Sven asked me. "I don't think so, no," I replied immediately. "No?" Sven said in a playfully surprised voice, "I'll have to teach you some then." But then, Eddie and his cap came to mind. "Oh, actually. I do know one word," I said, chuffed with myself for remembering. "Oh yeah, is it a rude word?" Sven grinned. "Often, people know a swear word in another language. Is that what it is?" He looked at me expectantly. "No," I sniffed, laughing through my nose, "but you can teach me?" I grinned back at him. "I think you're way too innocent to be taught rude words," Sven said. "You think I'm innocent?" I asked. I wasn't sure at first if that was a compliment or not. I had never thought of myself as being innocent. Hmm, well, maybe a bit actually - but in a different way. I thought I was innocent in the way that I was a quiet, peace-loving person, someone who didn't lit any fires, who didn't provoke, who didn't push - and yet, those fires, those flames found me and burnt me anyway. I thought I was innocent of the mocking, of the bullying, of the dark clouds above my head. I thought I was innocent in that way. But I knew Sven meant something else. "You seem very sweet and gentle to me." He glanced over at me, then moved his head, so our eyes were perfectly aligned. "You know... innocent," he murmured. His piercing green eyes were difficult to pull away from. They continued to lure me in, into a world that gave me that electrifying feeling. Our eyes still matched each other's stare. The electrifying feeling intensified. It grew. And grew. Stronger. More vivid. It was almost unbearable but I couldn't get enough of it. I didn't want it to end.

"Ahem," I cleared my throat, forcing us back into the present, standing in the middle of the park, some trees hanging over us as if to give us some sort of comfort and safety. "Well, maybe I am, maybe I am not. Maybe you will find out, or maybe not," I said, teasingly batting my lashes. I could be fun too. "Oh, is that a dare?" Sven drawled, "I intend to find out. Don't worry about that." With a glint of amusement, we continued wandering towards the lake in the centre of the park. I could already see it from the distance. "So what's the word then, Spence?" At that point, I had completely forgotten what we were talking about before. "Oh, yeah, umm. It... It's 'bald'." I chuckled. "Bald?" he repeated. "That's a random word to know." The look of surprise on his face at my revelation was unmissable. "Yeah, I know," I replied and told him all about Eddie. "That's funny. And this Eddie sounds like a cool dude," Sven said. "He is. Maybe you'll meet him one day. I noticed you don't take the bus to school though? How do you get to school?" I asked and sipped on my hot choccy. "I walk. We live just off Watson St, so that's pretty handy," Sven said. "Yes, very handy. You'll never be late for school then," I said, not committed to my words, because I knew from my own experience that this wasn't always true. I, too, once lived literally 30 seconds away from my primary school. You'd think that this meant I would be the first one to get there but nah, it was often the complete opposite. "Well, yes, in theory…" Sven smilingly shrugged his shoulders. "But in any case, at least this school is better than my old school," he added.

We reached the edge of the lake where a number of benches were scattered around, each offering a great view facing the water. I had a favourite spot. It was in the same area as all the others benches, but this one was a little different, a little special. It was in a natural nook, small and quaint, but it was a big enough space to fit a bench in that spot. Right behind this bench stood a tree, its enormous trunk hugging - and in fact, forming - that natural nook. It was like sitting under a wiseman who was putting both arms around you while you enjoyed the serenity and beauty of the lake.

"How *was* your old school?" I asked Sven as I took his arm to stir him into the direction of the special nook bench. We sat down and he released a sigh that resembled more of a grunt. "It was alright," he started, "your typical school with typical students who form groups and alliances, with the typical encounter of the odd-one-out." I looked at him in disbelief. "And that was… you?!" I asked, not convinced this could even ever be the case, knowing that he got along so well with Robbie and his minions. "You sound surprised?!" Sven replied. "Well, yes," I said without hesitation. "I mean, look at you." I pointed at him with both of my hands, while still holding my takeaway cup. I then realised how stupid this must have seemed to him. "I mean, um, I mean, look at you how you are so accepted at my school," I back-paddled. "Everyone likes you, everyone gravitates towards you. Literally everyone." Sven moved his head towards me, slowly and smoothly. He raised his right arm to brush his chin-long blonde hair behind his right ear. Like theatre curtains drawing back to expose the stage, his hair, in this moment, revealed his piercing green eyes. Yet again. "Everyone?" he asked with a curious undertone. I looked down, a flush of embarrassment and sudden shyness rising to my cheeks. "Uh, yeah, I… I would say so," I managed to say, internally shaking. Sven smiled.

"Well, I suppose I got lucky here somehow. Maybe people find it interesting to have a new kid in their class. Someone they don't know at all, not even from seeing them in the local supermarket. A complete stranger who could be anyone." Sven stopped for a moment. He exhaled sharply before he downed the rest of his hot chocolate, with his head all the way tilted back to get out every single bit of it. He swallowed contentedly and licked off a drop that tried to escape his mouth. "And that's what I was hoping to be here, to be honest," he threw in. "A stranger?" I asked, my hot chocolate still half full in my hand. "Well, you know. I just wanted to have a fresh start, start new. And hopefully it was going to be better this time around," Sven resumed. "What happened at your old school?" I asked bluntly, trying to get more details of his experience there. Sven stretched out his legs, sliding his bottom over to the side of the bench, dragging his feet with him over the ground, then fanning out his arms before eventually folding them behind his head. He stared at the lake without blinking, deep in thoughts. "The kids at my school were brutal," he said after a while. "They just didn't get me, or they didn't *want* to get me. They called me names all the time." Sven still glared at the lake. "Hmph." He forced out some air through his nostrils in a brief, amused snort. "What is it?" I wasn't sure what he found so funny in that moment. "Look!" He pointed at two beautiful white swans who effortlessly glided through the water. They were in no rush, they were just having a casual waddle, enjoying each other's time. "Oh yeah, the swans. They are so sweet," I exclaimed. "I like swans," I added. "Yeah…" Sven snorted once again. "Me too. They're so graceful, almost fragile but quite magical in their own way." I thought Sven hit the nail on the head with that. "Exactly!" I smiled at him while we watched the swans change course and swim away towards the other side of the lake, frequently touching their counterparts' feathered bodies.

"It's quite ironic," Sven said, his eyes glued to the swans swimming further and further away. "What is?" I asked to clarify. "That I am telling you about my old school, and we are sitting here, watching the swans doing their magical thing." I wasn't following. Sven was talking in riddles. A moment of silence. Then, Sven gestured at the lake. "Swan. That's what they used to call me. Sven the swan," he explained. "Oh… Why though?" I wanted to know. "Isn't that more of a compliment than an insult?" I added. There were far worse things that I got called by Robbie and his minions. Far worse. But at the same time, when the intention was venomous and evil, then any sweet name could slide a dagger into your heart. Wasn't it the same when they called me 'Penny'?

"Well, you're right. It seems like a cute nickname but they certainly didn't mean it as a compliment. They called me swan because for them, it embodied femininity. And they saw me as that. A femboy." I thought that was ridiculous and didn't make any sense at all. "But you're not feminine," I said bewilderedly, "you're tall and strong and..." I paused as Sven looked at me with a raised eyebrow. "And I have long hair," he finished my sentence while pointing at his shiny chin-long hair. "Aaaand…" Sven added, "… and I guess, just like swans, I like the idea of hanging out and sticking with like-minded people who I feel in sync with." The corners of his lips noticeably quivered until they formed a cheeky smile. A smile that persisted for a few moments while my brain was processing the unexpected words coming out of his mouth. They seemed random to me at first. "Oh," I said eventually, somewhat sheepishly. The penny dropped. He was hinting at me. Was he? "Yeah." Sven nodded affirmatively. I felt flattered and awkward all at once and didn't know what to say. My cheeks were blushing.

"People can be so ignorant," Sven deflected as he noticed my speechlessness, and I was quite thankful for that, "I can see it with

Robbie and the others too. I can see how they treat you, how they make you feel. It's not right. That's why I wanted to back you at that soccer game. I don't know if that made any difference to them but I hope that it made a difference to you." He was so sweet. I was internally swooning. "It did," I spoke with a wavering voice, "It absolutely did. Thank you." Sven put his right hand on my left knee. That electrifying feeling. It was back. Ever so present. All that time, I've been wanting to touch him, too. I wanted to take Sven's hand so badly. I wanted to let him know that I understood what he was going through. I wanted to touch his hand, like the swans were touching each other. I wanted to say, "I'm here, I'm next to you, I'm not going anywhere." And now, his hand was on my knee. A comforting touch. A touch of understanding and care. A touch that made me go wild inside. All kinds of sensations and emotions were rushing through my body in ecstasy. Sven kept his hand on my knee. He wanted me to feel him. He wanted me to know exactly what I wanted *him* to know. I looked at Sven, almost uncomfortably. It was a new situation that I found myself in here. I had never felt like this. Never so strongly. Never so aligned. Never so… together.

27. Stains.

As the tender energy with Sven continued, I decided it was a good idea to put down my hot chocolate, still half full, next to me on the bench. I set it down carefully because I knew myself. I could be so clumsy in the worst possible moment. But not now. Now was not the time. I needed to eliminate the clumsy factor. I double checked if the cup was placed securely on the wooden slats. Once I did, I turned my head back to the left towards Sven, his hand still on my knee, seemingly waiting to be joined by mine. My upper body followed my head, shifting to the left before I adjusted my bottom a tiny bit to sit more comfortably, to face Sven. I wobbled my bum from side to side, like a jelly trying to settle into place. Just as my jelly bum eased into its relaxed position, I was about to move my hand onto his. Then… Thud. Splash. Tinkle. I knocked over the cup. Yes, I did. The hot chocolate splattered all over the side of my jeans before it fell to the ground and dripped the rest over my white sneakers. The cup was now empty.

"Oh no, Spence, your choccy," Sven gasped, clearly not realising the extent of the spill on my clothes. My face was filled with shock and horror. Sven picked up on it. "I'll get you another one," he said. If I hadn't been so mortified, I would have actually laughed. I loved that he thought I was upset about the hot chocolate - although, it was actually really good with the oat milk. So it was definitely an additional bummer that I couldn't keep savouring it. But I wasn't in the mood to laugh. I was upset with myself. I just couldn't believe it. I tried to be so careful with it, putting it down to set up a lovely swan-like moment with Sven, and I still messed it up. I stood up, reluctantly, but I didn't want to keep sitting in the puddle of chocolate on the bench. As soon as I got up, the stains on the side of my jeans were displayed. It looked like a chocolate waterfall had taken a detour down my leg and dried there in triumph. I was so embarrassed but I had nowhere to go. And I couldn't use my sparkles this time without Sven noticing. Or could I? My head was scrambling to find a way to get out of this mess. Literally. But my head was empty, leaving me with zero escape plans and 100% awkwardness.

So there I was, standing in front of Sven, my eyes darting away from him, staring at my jeans. "Ah. Uh. I… I…" Words completely escaped me as I looked around confused, not knowing what to do with myself. "Umm, I better go," I breathed out eventually. "What? Why?" Sven said. I could hear the disappointment in his voice. "Because of that? Come on, Spence, it's nothing. You can hardly see it." He came closer to take a better look. He stopped for a moment. His eyes were following the dry stream of chocolate from top to bottom. He stood still. As did I. He then burst out laughing with both his hands covering his dimply smile, as if he was trying to push the laughter back inside his mouth. "Don't laugh, Sven. I'm so embarrassed." I didn't expect him to laugh at me like that but I also didn't blame him. I knew he didn't mean it in a hurtful way. It wasn't the kind of laugh I have received from Robbie and the others in the past. And really, it must have been a funny sight, seeing me standing there, looking like I had just peed myself. Or rather... pooped.

Still, I didn't see the funny side of it yet. Sven saw my uncomfortable face and stopped laughing immediately. He straightened up and pulled his blue sweatshirt over his head. His hair got a little disheveled. He flicked the hair out of his face before he stepped behind me. What was he doing? "Don't move," Sven said with a demanding, yet gentle tone. He stretched out the sleeves of his sweatshirt. "Put your arms up." Ah, he is going to give me his sweatshirt... But how is wearing his sweatshirt going to help me with my chocolate-pooped pants? I didn't know what exactly he was doing but I trusted him. He came closer from behind me and wrapped the sleeves around my waist. He tied together the sleeves just above my belt. "Hold it," he said with a theatrical raise of his voice. I took the tied sleeves while Sven came around from behind to stand right in front of me, brushing against my left shoulder as he passed. I could feel his warm breath hitting my ear. It gave me a shiver. That feeling. That electrifying feeling. It transported me somewhere else.

Sven grabbed the tie and adjusted it, tightening it into a firm knot. He gave it another tug and inspected it with a sharp, thoughtful glance. "Perfection," he said luridly, looking at the knot and then into my eyes. "Perfection," he repeated, more softly, stifled even. "Ahem," I cleared my throat and assessed the sweatshirt around my waist. "See." Sven pointed at the stained area. "The shirt covers it nicely. You don't even know it's there." I was very thankful. "It's great, thank you. I'll give it back to you soon," I said, sweeping my hands across the soft material of the sweatshirt, secretly wondering if I could somehow keep it. "No stress," Sven replied, "whenever." We winked at each other. "I guess we can keep walking then," I said, "if you don't mind having a walk with a person full of stains." I laughed. I was able to now. "You know, stains can be a great thing," Sven said. "How's that?" I was curious to hear where he was going with this. "Well, stains are like temporary scars. They're proof of something. Good or bad. But either way, evidence of a past situation. A memory, if you will. Could be anything. Maybe a delicious meal at a fancy restaurant. Maybe an angry scuffle in the middle of the school yard. Or maybe a lovely stroll at a park with a nice person." Sven smiled at me, his hair slightly invading his face, yet not quite covering the green eyes that were meeting mine in an extensive peer. "Huh," I thought but simultaneously voicing it out loud. "Yeah… huh," I thought about it for another second, "I guess that makes sense." I liked the way Sven was thinking. He had a distinct mindset. A mindset with a different perspective of things. I found that truly refreshing. Inspiring. And challenging in the best of ways. "Do you have any scars?" I asked him. "No, I don't. Do you?" Sven and I continued to stroll around the large sky-blue lake as I told him about the small scar I had above my left eye. I pointed at the scar. "I fell off a pony once," I said and chuckled. While it was a painful experience at the time, I could laugh about it now. Just like I knew I would laugh even harder about my hot choccy pants in the future. Bald.

On my way home, I kept looking at my jeans, at Sven's sweatshirt, at the stain. I could have used my magic to make the stain go away. Nobody would have noticed on the bus. It would have been so easy. But I didn't. I wanted to keep Sven's sweatshirt on, all around my waist. The thought of his neutral breath hitting my ear was still giving me the feels. I didn't want to undo the stain. Not right away. Instead, I wanted to keep the stain, the memory, the thought of a lovely stroll at a park with a nice person.

28. Hangouts.

I had just come through the front door of my house when I got a message on my phone. Was that Sven? Was that him telling me what I wanted to tell him? That I had the best time ever!?! I pulled my phone out of my pants with Sven's sweatshirt still hugging my waist tight. "How did it go, rat?" It was Sonya. My initial slight disappointment that the message didn't come from Sven vanished quickly and turned into increased excitement. I wanted to tell her everything about the date - or whatever that was. I still wasn't sure if it was a date or not. But did it really matter? Did we always have to put a label on everything?

Whatever it was, date or not, it was great fun. So I dialled Sonya's number right away. "Hey Son." I walked up the stairs to my room and fell onto my bed, resting my head on the soft pillow. "Yeah, it was great, more than great. Amazing." Sonya and I talked for ages. From choccies, to swans, to stains and scars - I told her every excruciating detail. Everything she was eager to know about that day in the park. It felt so nice to chat with Sonya like that. The kind of chat we hadn't shared in a long time.

That day at the park was all I could think about in the days that followed. That day at the park was everything and nothing that I had expected and hoped for. I didn't just get to spend some alone time with Sven, I got to know a new side of him. I knew already that he was gorgeous. Obviously. And I knew that he was nice but that day at the park, he showed me that he could also be vulnerable. He wasn't afraid to tell me about his past troubles at school, there was no reluctance to share, and I really appreciated that. As someone who struggled to open up myself at times, I knew it could be difficult. You had to feel comfortable to even want to open up. So this moment really meant a lot to me. I didn't know how much weight Sven put on this, or if he even analysed it like I did, but it was massive for me. Not only did it mean that he felt comfortable with me, it also meant that I wasn't alone anymore. Of course, I was never really *alone*. I had my mum on my side, I had Sonya, and even Eddie. I wasn't alone as such but it was different to have someone who understood first hand what it was like to be bullied, to be the outsider, to be the weird one. There was just a mutual, deeper understanding between those who knew and lived it. Just like Uncle James did. Just like Sven did.

People who were a part of the same journey had an invisible bond. A connection. Like when people took part in a unique experience, such as a reality TV show. Did the audience really know what it was like to be on the show?! The thoughts. The sentiments. The anxieties. Well, sure, they would have gotten an idea of the circumstances and the emotions one would go through. But the ones who truly understood the storm you sailed through were the ones who navigated the exact same waters, on the exact same TV show, in that exact same situation. And that turned out to be Sven. He had a profound awareness of what it involved. This was a huge change for me.

Over the course of the following weeks, Sven and I became two peas in a pod. We spent much time together, after school and on the weekends. We went to the cinema every so often, where we would watch stupid comedies while indulging in soft drinks and popcorn. We only ever got one big bag of popcorn to share instead of two small individual ones. There was never a discussion about it. Sven made the decision and ordered a big bag on our first visit at the cinema together, and ever since then, that was just a given. And I didn't mind. I didn't mind at all. I liked it very much. It made it somewhat more intimate, even though we never really touched. But we didn't need to. The simple act of sharing a big bag of salty popcorn was enough for me to feel close to Sven.

We went to gaming arcades where we would play all kinds of games. Sven liked the pinball machines and the 'Zombie Splash' video game while I preferred the claw machines and virtual reality games. We often combined our gaming outings with a round of bowling. One of the arcades had a bowling alley attached to it, so it kind of made sense to check it out while we were there. I liked bowling, though it wasn't totally my jam. Sven on the other hand thrived on bowling alleys. He was crushing it. In fact, he was crushing me. And he wasn't shy to rub it in my face, showing off his sporty body every time he got a strike. He liked to tease me like that. I pretended to be annoyed. But he was well aware that I was just playing and often started to tickle me to get me out of my fake moaning state. Sometimes, I used my sparkles to temper with his bowling ball, just for my own amusement. While that threw him off a little in the scoreline, he always recovered. I could have given myself the edge in our bowling games. Heck, I could have won them all with my sparkles. But I hadn't actually used my sparkles very often at that point. I didn't *want* to use them, and I certainly didn't want to use them to win. That wasn't important to me. I had more joy in seeing Sven build up his motivation and energy to focus on that one goal: Winning against me, so he could tickle me later.

We went on lengthy walks in the nearby forest. We always took our bikes there and locked them up around a tree, which was full of carvings - names, hearts, dates and memories, before heading into the magical array of nature. We would walk and walk and walk, for ages, but we would often stand completely still to listen to the sounds of the birds and the soft howling of the wind. As the breeze wandered through our hair, I was reminded of the feeling when I was flying that one night. I loved how the wind danced in my hair. It was so comforting, so soothing, so freeing. Even more so when I was up in the air. I needed to do it again soon.

We went to each other's house where we would hang out, often without doing anything in particular, sometimes just sitting on the floor on opposite sides of the rooms, reading our books but always secretly looking up to check on the other person. During our hangouts, we learnt a lot about each other. Our favourite food, our favourite colour and our favourite movie, all of which we had in common. Pasta. Blue. "The Wizard of Oz". I was especially stoked to hear that he liked the same movie as me. A movie, so old but still so popular, still so relevant, still so magical. I loved that we had that in common, and I was excited to discover even more about Sven. While we did talk a lot, we also had moments of silence. Natural silence. Comfortable silence. It was something I had always liked. I didn't have to talk constantly, I also liked the serenity, and to be content in it. I have met many people who were not like that. They always needed to fill the space with words, otherwise, they would feel uneasy. Not me though. For me, filling the space with words that didn't have to be spoken was a waste of an opportunity. The opportunity to appreciate silence. And it was nice to appreciate that silence with Sven.

We spent a lot of time together. Indeed, we did. So much that we turned people's heads at school when we sat in a corner during lunch break with our phones to watch a funny video or to scroll through Instagram posts of our favourite "Drag Race" contestants. Jinkx Monsoon had been my favourite queen from the get go with her hilarious humour and witchy attitude. "No wonder I gravitate towards her," I thought to myself, every time we watched a clip of Jinkx. First, "I Dream of Jeannie", then "The Wizard of Oz" and then Jinkx Monsoon. I realised that this had been a theme in my life, and I had only recently figured that out. Witches were drawn to other witches, even when - like me - they didn't know that they were witches, too. Those interests of mine, those gravitations were signs all along for what I didn't know was going to come.

Yes, Sven and I were becoming good friends, but that didn't mean that we hung out exclusively all the time. Sonya often joined. Her dry sense of humour resonated with Sven, and she got to appreciate his vulnerability and his support. Having someone else in my corner through the continuing bullying attempts by Robbie and his minions made things look a lot brighter - for everyone. We were like a united front against the evil of high school.

Sonya also learnt to like Sven's playfulness. At first, she rolled her eyes ever so slightly at funny comments he made. I found them funny, but she thought they were lame. I often wondered if she had forgotten about the cheesy jokes we made between us, they really were not any better - or worse - than Sven's jokes. But over time, eventually, she came around and realised that they shared more than she would have thought at the beginning. She even ganged up with Sven one time when they attacked me with an impromptu pillow fight, following a heated, yet lighthearted discussion about which actor was the hottest. They both simultaneously said Liam Hemsworth while I vehemently disagreed and pleaded for Chris Hemsworth. One allying eye contact between Sven and Sonya later, and I was the victim of my two soft pillows hitting me left and right.

So yeah, we got on well. We had some fun times. That was for sure. And then, there was that time Sonya, Sven and I had an adventure to the national park...

29. National park.

The national park was located a couple of hours away from our town. I had been there once before but couldn't remember much of it, other than that it was beautiful. Duh! Trees, nature, beauty. Of course. It took a bit of convincing to get Sonya to join us. As she was a self-proclaimed 'plant hater', she didn't have the largest interest in coming along. Sure, I could have gone with Sven alone, and we could have wandered through the park like we did through the nearby forest, but I thought it was a nice way to spend time with both of my friends, together.

Then, there was the discussion on how to get there. Buses were quite convenient, though it took noticeably longer to get there. The other option was to ask any of our parents to drive us. They would have been happy to chauffeur us, knowing the special bond we have all formed. They could have dropped us off at the entrance and gone to a little cafe in the bordering village while we explored the national park. That could have worked nicely. But at the same time, we wanted to be independent, away from hovering parents, strict time limits and numerous questions and conversations we didn't necessarily want to endure from them. So after a tedious back and forth between the pros and cons of both options, we finally decided. We were going to take the bus.

It was one of those fairly comfortable buses. Spacious seats, tray tables, power plugs to charge our phones, and to my surprise, WiFi and an onboard toilet. You could even buy snacks and drinks from the driver. We didn't do that as we had some lunches with us, packed in our backpacks, but it was a nice option to have if we had needed more than what we already had. We felt set to go. We felt happy. We felt ready. We felt excited, even Sonya in her own way. We felt like we were embarking on a journey that we wouldn't forget.

While the bus trip was long, it went pretty quickly actually. We mostly listened to our own music, being in our own zone, with headphones on and gazing at the landscape that passed by our window. We watched YouTube videos, mostly individually but there was a moment when I saw Sven's dimply smile come out over something he clearly found hilarious. I went over to check what he was looking at. It was a cat and dog video. "Animals can be so funny," I said as I joined in the laughter and watched the rest of the video with Sven while Sonya stayed put on her seat, shooting us with her half-amused, half-annoyed eyes. At one point, we even all played a good old-fashioned card game during which the laughter continued, often to the irritation of the other passengers on the bus. Yes, the trip was long but we made the most of it. After all, this was what we wanted. A trip together, without our parents. So no whinging was allowed. That was our only rule.

The bus dropped us just at the edge of the national park, a few metres walk to the entrance point that outlined multiple walking tracks. Some were long and strenuous, others shorter and not so difficult to do. Gorgeous scenery came with every single one of them, so it didn't really matter which one we took. "Let's do the 4-hour return loop," Sven suggested ambitiously. My eyes went over to Sonya, she wasn't ecstatic. It made me smirk. "Too long," she moaned. "Yeah, but we came all this way. Don't you want to see and walk as much as you can?" he tried to argue. And yes, he was right. We came all this way by bus and of course, we wanted to make the most of the time and opportunity we had. But maybe there was a better way to do that. "Why don't we take this trail?" I pointed out a walking path on the map board. "This goes through the forest and comes back alongside the cliffs. Maybe we can find a nice spot for a picnic there and soak it all up?" Sven wasn't fully convinced of my counter-suggestion. "I don't know, we can probably find a spot to sit down on the longer walk, too, somewhere," he said but then looked at Sonya, her displeasure impossible to miss. She raised her left eyebrow, held still and stared at him to make her point. I wanted to burst out laughing, Sonya's expression was hilarious, priceless. I swallowed the laughter as best I could, with only a small remaining flicker of glee painting my face. "Alright, fine, let's do the walk Spence suggested," Sven agreed in the end. "Well… let's go then," Sonya said almost annoyed and wandered ahead energetically as if she had been ready to walk all this time, only waiting for us to get our act together. Sven and I shared a look, and we couldn't help but smile. Sonya was so funny sometimes. "Okay," I quipped, lively and animated, as we followed her to start the track.

As soon as we made our way into the density of the forest, I felt a sense of calm. As I have always felt when visiting my friends, the trees. I tilted my head back, my nose up high, to inhale the fresh air that I was so thankful to breathe in. Not only because it felt nice and invigorating - but in a world of construction and destruction, fresh air was wildly underrated. Underappreciated. As were my friends, the trees… It was them after all who gave us oxygen, and the ability to breathe in that fresh air. They gave us life. And yet, human kind seemed to ignore that fact more and more.

As I enjoyed the slight breeze hitting my face, I heard a thud. And another. And again. Then I realised what was happening. "What are you doing?" I asked Sonya, who forcefully stomped on the ground continuously as she kept walking ahead of Sven and me. "You're going to scare all the animals here!" I said. Sonya stopped and turned around. "Uh yeah, duh, that's the point." She threw her palms up in the air. "What do you mean?" It seemed Sven was as confused about it as I was. "Well, I want to make sure that the snakes know we are coming," Sonya explained. "Aaahh, I see," I voiced my understanding, "Well, that makes sense, Son. Only that there are no snakes here." She looked into the distance of the dense bush. "How can you be so sure?" she asked. "I didn't know that you were afraid of snakes, Sonya?" Sven chimed in. "Neither did I." I literally had no idea. She always seemed so tough with so many things. She had pet rats, for goodness sakes. That was a kind of pet that many people are either afraid of or simply despise. Much like snakes. So it never crossed my mind that there was any animal Sonya could be scared of. I always thought that having a pet rat was badass. And Sonya was definitely a badass. But clearly, you could learn something about your friends, even if you had known them for ages. "I'm not afraid," Sonya insisted and marched on purposefully. She didn't like to show weakness. I got that. But I knew what she was really like. She had a rough emotional armour around her but if you really got to know her, you would find that she was just as human as everyone else.

Sonya was already a few metres in front of Sven and me, so I gestured to him to follow her. Sven mimed an exaggerated stomp and giggled silently. "Don't!" I whispered, snickering briefly. I grabbed his elbow to discourage him from doing it for real. "It would just set her off." Sven nodded with a vanishing smirk as we picked up our pace to catch up to Sonya.

30. Rustle and Bustle.

We continued to walk. Close together in a line of three. Sonya. Me. Sven. We didn't talk much apart from the occasional gasp at either an extraordinary array of fungi or physical exhaustion - even though we hadn't even walked that long. All the enchanting bowling sessions with Sven, and all the stupid soccer games at school seemingly didn't do anything for my condition. Instead... gasps. Occasionally, there was a random sound in the bushes, a rustling. Each time, Sonya flinched. Each time, she gave me a dirty look to say, "No snakes, huh?!" Each time, I smiled and told her that it was probably just the wind, or a rat. I figured the thought of rats would give her more comfort than the thought of snakes. Apart from those interactions, we didn't talk much. We just walked. And marvelled. And walked. And marvelled.

We went further and deeper into the forest. The trees stood tall, and proud, and close. So close that you could hardly make out the sky sometimes. The cooling shade was a welcome relief from the sun that found a way to peek through the clouds more and more. When we got on the bus that morning, and all throughout the bus journey, it looked like it was going to be an overcast day. But the sun wanted to take part in our adventure. The path was winding steadily to the left, signalling that we were getting closer to the gorge with its spectacular cliffs. I was ready for a sit down anyway. And I was sure Sonya was too. Sven on the other hand could probably keep on walking for hours to come. We came to a small intersection with arrows pointing in various directions. One to the right that went straight back to the entrance of the national park. The other merging to the trail that Sven wanted to do. And one arrow stated 'Gorge Cliffs'.

We were all in silent agreement which route to take, even though when I looked at Sven, I could notice a faint sigh and glimpse into the other direction. He still seemed a bit disappointed that we didn't do the extensive return walk. "Man, he must really like walking long distances," I thought. As Sven pulled his eyes away from that track, his full focus was back with Sonya and me. The narrow path wound around tree families with massive trunks. "Woah. Crazy to think how long they have been standing here..." I wondered out loud. "A very long time," Sven immediately reacted. "Yeah, long enough to house some snakes." Sonya couldn't let it go. Just like Sven was still hung up on the 4-hour walk, Sonya was still thinking about snakes. It was hilarious to me.

Then, a thought that I couldn't let go of. Was it mean? Should I? Should I not? Could Sonya and Sven see my face? Was it too risky? No, Sonya was in front of me, and Sven was behind me. They couldn't see anything. Should I though? I played ping pong with that thought for a bit until I came to a conclusion. With a cheeky smirk on my dial, I whispered to myself as quietly as I could, my eyes focused on the left side of the track, just ahead of Sonya. "Sparkle sparkle, rustle sound. Sparkle sparkle, rat be found."

Lights. Tingles. Whoosh.

The leaves on the ground were rustling instantly. Sonya shrieked. "Rat," she yelled. Her body was overcome by an obvious shudder. "Yes, what?" I asked, pretending not to know what was going on. "No, rat. I mean *rat.*" Sonya quickly moved behind Sven's broad shoulders, silently asking for protection. He was completely lost in that moment. "What?" He looked around himself, trying to figure out what was happening. "There was a rat coming out of the bushes." Sonya pointed at the spot where the rustling came from. "I thought it was a snake!" Sonya glanced at both Sven and me, detecting a teasing grin on our faces. "It could have been, okay?!" she insisted, turning back to check the side of the path once again. "Well, the only snake that I see is this long path slithering around all these enormous trees," I tried to take the wind out of her frightened sails and lighten the situation. I chuckled. I felt a little bad to scare her like this. But it was all in good fun. How many times had she scared me to death? So this was my chance for a small payback. I knew she could take it. "Yeah, yeah." Sonya rolled her eyes with a forced smile and trotted on without any further words about it.

It wasn't much longer until we reached an open space, filled with a mixture of earth, gravel, grass and colourful flowers. The wind was more apparent and enjoyed a wild ride through the leaves, through the grass and flowers, through our hair. We stretched our upper bodies while walking aimlessly through the open space, simply enjoying the perfect blend of the sun's warming glow and the cooling breeze of the wind. I opened my arms and spread them as wide as I could, I closed my eyes and started to spin. I felt like Julie Andrews in "The Sound of Music", spinning around and around and around, light and slow. The smells of nature entered my nostrils while the rustling of the tree leaves gave this moment an authentic soundtrack. I kept twirling with my eyes closed, feeling my feet going around each other like two children playing tag. "Watch out, Spence!" Sven suddenly grabbed my arm and knocked me out of my Julie Andrews era. "What?" I blurted, almost rude which I felt immediately bad about. "What is it?" I said more softly to correct my first impulse. "Rat, the cliffs," Sonya cut in before Sven could explain his rushed action. I looked to my side and realised that I had moved from the middle of the open space to the brink of the cliffs. There were no barriers, no fences, no signage, nothing, just the cliffs leading down to the blue and green coloured gorge.

Sven still got a hold of my arm. "Don't do that to me, Spence." He huffed in anxiety, his face in red blotches. I looked into his piercing green eyes, distress clear within them. As I realised the gravity of the situation, I gradually moved away from the cliffs. It was just sinking in how close this was, how serious this was, and how catastrophic this could have been, had it not been for Sven looking out for me. I sat down on a luscious spot of grass. Deflated. But happy and grateful. "Phew," I said, once I steadied myself a bit, "I don't know what to say." Sonya sat down next to me, and Sven followed, sandwiching me between them. I felt both of their hands on my back, trying to comfort me. From the corner of my eye, I could see that they exchanged looks of worry and relief. "I was so lost in that moment, I didn't notice I was moving that far to the edge," I explained. "It's easy to get lost in something that feels so good," Sven said with a faint wink. Was he referring to me? To us? It looked like Sven was going to say something else. But he didn't. He paused, his mind clearly elsewhere. "Is there a 'but' coming?" I asked him. "No, no 'but'…" He paused again for a brief moment before he kept going, "I just wanted to say, always expect the unexpected." He looked at me deeply while Sonya nodded in agreement to Sven's vague, yet profound words.

A sudden rustle appeared in the bushes. This time, that wasn't me. Sonya immediately jumped up from our sandwich position, ready to attack - or rather flee from any possible snake coming out of the forest. Or was it going to be a rat again? Well, it couldn't have been either though. This rustling sound was more pronounced, more insistent, suggesting something far bigger than a rat or a snake. "Are there bears here?" I asked hesitantly. I had no clue if this was a habitat for bears at all. The size of the thing in the bushes was definitely big enough to be a bear. It was getting closer, heading towards us. All of our eyes stared at the point where the sound was coming from. The rustling intensified, until finally, you could see a big stick peaking out of the bushes, trying to create a path through them. With a large swing, the bushes separated and revealed the creature.

"Robbie!?" I exclaimed loudly.

Well, I certainly did not expect *that*!

31. Cliffhanger.

"Ugh, Robbie," I thought. And judging by Sven's and Sonya's faces, I wasn't the only one with that thought. I looked at Robbie, then at Sonya and Sven, then back at Robbie. We were all stunned. Of all the people that we could have bumped into, it had to be Robbie?! Why, universe? Why? What were you trying to tell me? What was the message here? I had no idea. I just stood there, perplexed. Frozen. In shock. But also in annoyance. Couldn't I go anywhere without him around me, either mentally hovering in the back of my head or physically being in front of my face?!

"What the fuck, Robbie! What are you doing here?" Sonya broke the silence, speaking the words that we were all thinking. "I could ask you the same question," Robbie said, seemingly cool and untouched by the encounter. "And why did you go through the bushes when there are proper trails to walk on?" Sven asked Robbie. "Man, it's way more fun to go rogue." He smiled at Sven, trying to get some sort of male bonding reaction back from him. "Yeah, but you're destroying plants in the process," Sven confronted him. I was proud of him for that. "And the snakes and rats you could meet in the process," Sonya whispered into my ears. We both snickered silently while Sven continued. "Don't you find that a bit reckless?" Robbie rolled his eyes and threw his hands in the air. "Dude, don't be so boring and uptight. I thought you were cool, man," Robbie argued. Sonya was quick to react as she stepped in, "You can be cool without being a dick, Robbie." My head was going back and forth between Robbie and Sonya and Sven. They certainly gave Robbie a run for his money. It made one thing crystal clear to me, yet again. Between Sven and Sonya, I felt really safe, taken care of, supported and backed. I knew I could count on them.

"Are you… are you here on your own?" I finally managed to join the conversation, even though I barely got those words out of my mouth. Robbie looked at me, and I was almost certain he would say something nasty. Why would this moment be any different to school anyway?! His face was filled with anger and mischief. An expression I only knew too well. He was going to say something mean but I was ready for it. "Nah, my folks are here somewhere. They wanted to do the 4-hour loop, but I told them I'd meet them here." Robbie looked down, trying to avoid eye contact. Okay, what was going on? He didn't make fun of me? He had the opportunity and he didn't insult me? Instead, he actually just answered my question, like a normal human being. Well, here I was again… I did not expect that.

I also didn't expect that he came to the national park with his parents. Knowing what I knew, I didn't think they would have much quality family time together. Rather, I thought that Robbie would want to spend all his spare time away from them, from his father particularly. Where were his minions? Didn't he spend time with them outside of school? Were they only his schoolmates but not actually his friends? My head was spinning with questions.

Robbie walked past us towards the red-budded flowers which grew comfortably and effortlessly through the layer of gravel. "My family and I used to come here a lot when Toby was still around," Robbie said with a sense of melancholy that I had never seen him show in front of others, let alone us. "Who's Toby?" Sven asked. "It's his brother," Sonya answered jeeringly, standing next to us with her arms crossed. For her, Robbie and Toby were the same, both annoying and loud, both condescending and both taunting other people. Sven leaned over to me, his pleasant breath travelling into my ear. It gave me goosebumps. It made me tremble. It aroused me. But I knew this was not the time and not the place. I shook my head vehemently to snap out of it. So strongly that Sven saw it. "He's not his brother?" Sven asked me, thinking that I disagreed with what Sonya said. "Oh, uh, no, no, he is," I said awkwardly. "Is he dead?" Sven mumbled. "No, man, he is not dead. He is alive. He is just not at home much. Geez. Be real, man!" Robbie seemed to have really good ears to be able to hear Sven's question.

Robbie moved further away from us, turning his back on us, clearly agitated by that question. Or maybe not even by the question but the actual fact that his brother wasn't around much anymore. Did he face away, so we didn't see that he was upset? Maybe. Quite possibly. After all, I knew that there was a different side to Robbie. A side that he didn't want people to notice. A vulnerability that he was hiding behind a thick wall, creating a facade, an illusion of who he was, of how he was seen. But I knew, ever since the day I flew to his house… I knew he wasn't all that.

"Hey Robbie, watch out over there. The edge is quite slippery," Sven shouted as Robbie continued to walk further away from us, towards the cliffs. "Dude, I have eyes! I know!" Robbie hastily turned around, hitting Sven with an evil look. "I can take care of mys—" As Robbie spoke those words, he tripped over an inconspicuous rock right next to him. The evil look on his face changed immediately. Into fear. A scared look on Robbie's otherwise always so confident face. What happened next was what felt like five seconds compressed into slow motion. Robbie's arms were trying to balance off his tumble. But he kept struggling to steady himself. His right foot slid behind his body, towards the edge. *Over* the edge. The rest of his body followed his right foot, bending backwards, Robbie's arms waving in the air, helplessly. "Robbie," we screamed in eerie simultaneity. Robbie's left foot tried to force a grip on the ground but instead, it pushed him away, away from the edge. *Over* the edge. His body was completely in the air, half-turning away from us, facing the gorge below. His arms still waving like crazy, in a desperate attempt to stop this from happening. But it was obvious. Robbie was in trouble. He was falling. *Over* the edge.

Naturally, we were all struck by horror, overcome by a surge of disbelief at what was playing out before our eyes. I knew I had to do something, and I had to act quickly. My mind immediately went to my sparkles when I saw Robbie losing his balance. Could I do it now without anyone noticing? Yes, that thought ran through my head for a millisecond. I didn't want anybody to see.

Of course, I didn't. I strived to be so careful with when and where I used my magic, but ultimately, I knew that it didn't matter now. What was important was that I had to do something, anything. This was the only way out, the only way to prevent Robbie from falling into the depths of the gorge. It was a matter of life or death. Anxiously, I ran towards the cliffs, screaming on the top of my lungs. "Sparkle sparkle, loudly calling. Sparkle sparkle, stop the falling."

Lights. Tingles. Whoosh.

The wind turned into a strong gust, so strong that it scooped up Robbie's body and pushed him back onto the edge of the cliffs, right next to the rock that he had tripped over. It looked like Robbie was flying upwards and backwards. Away from the gorge and back to the safety of land where Sven and Sonya witnessed what had just unfolded, with their eyes and mouths wide open. "Spencer, wha—" Sonya started as I ran over to Robbie who was crouched down on the ground. "Are you alright?" I asked him with a big sigh of relief. He was. Robbie was safe. Sonya and Sven came running behind me to check on him. "Are you okay, man?" Sven echoed. Robbie was lost for words, collecting his bearings. He looked around, touched his chest, and arms and head, and looked around again. "I... I was there, over the edge, and now I am here." Robbie's voice was quaking. "Wha-...What just happened?" He glanced at me, then shifted his gaze over my shoulder to Sven and Sonya standing behind me. He kept staring at each of our faces, trying to get an answer, an explanation. "You, uh, you tripped and were about to fall, but you managed to get your balance back." I couldn't tell him the truth. And I didn't think I needed to either, since Robbie couldn't have seen or known what really happened. He didn't see my sparkles in action. So I opted to tell a white lie instead, though I wasn't entirely sure if he bought what I said. I knew that Sonya didn't. She had seen everything but she didn't say anything, not a single word about it. Neither did Sven. He was just silent and avoided looking at me.

Robbie staggered to his feet. "Oh right. Yes, that's right." He was still confused but ultimately agreed to my explanation. "Robbie!" We suddenly heard a high-pitch voice coming from behind us. We all pivoted. It was Robbie's mother. His father a few metres behind her. "There you are, Robbie. We were looking for you," she said. I couldn't tell if she was annoyed or worried. If only she knew what they had missed, what they could have found instead of a living and breathing son of theirs. If only they did know. But they had no idea. At least not at that moment, and who knew if Robbie was going to tell them about it. It was very possible that he was going to keep it to himself. "Yeah, mum, I'm right here," he said to her with rolling eyes and a face that suggested he was uncomfortable, embarrassed even. She walked up to him and gently touched his back. "So, Robbie, who are your friends?" she asked as his father joined the gathering. She smiled at us. A friendly smile, defined by fine wrinkles around her eyes and lips. Robbie glared at us, the air thick with an awkward silence. His father looked at us, then at Robbie, awaiting an answer. "Robbie, your mother asked you a question?" he said with a stern tone. Robbie didn't respond, allowing the silence to stretch on.

"Hi, I am Spencer," I remarked to shatter the stillness and shook the hand of Robbie's mother. As I reached for the right hand of Robbie's father, I pointed at Sonya and Sven with my left hand, just about to introduce them. But Robbie stopped me in the process and stepped right through the proposed handshake with his father. "I wanna go," he said and stormed off to the trail that led back to the entrance of the national park. "Uh R-Robbie," his mother yelled, unsure of why he just walked off like that. "Robbie, come back here," his father screamed, his voice terrifyingly intimidating. Robbie ignored him and kept moving ahead. "Ah, uh, it was nice to meet some of my son's friends," his mother said as she galloped after Robbie. His father nodded at us, stone-faced, before he squeezed out a faint smile. If you could call it a smile. With big, almost clumsy steps, he walked behind his wife. Towards the exit.

"Well, they are gone," I said, trying to make a joke to start a conversation with Sven and Sonya. A conversation that I was bound to have with them one way or another. A conversation that I should have had ages ago. Of all times, I didn't think that this conversation had to be on a day that was supposed to be a fun day out. "I'm gone, too," Sonya said, "I wanna go home." She grabbed all of her stuff and stomped away - this time not to scare off any snakes but to emphasise her disappointment. "But we haven't even had our picnic…" I desperately tried to turn around the situation and get us all to sit down and have that conversation. "I'm not hungry anymore," Sonya yelled as I watched her contour disappear behind a hill. I turned my head towards Sven. "Yeah, me too, Spence, sorry." Sven seemed less angry but equally disappointed as he started walking towards the hill that would eventually swallow his silhouette, leaving me feeling empty, standing in the open space, beside the edge of the cliffs of the blue and green coloured gorge.

Even the wind seemed to have stopped its playful romp through the tree leaves, holding its breath as the weight of the moment settled in. Shock. Relief. Disappointment.

Silence.

32. Apart.

The bus trip back was draining as hell. For starters, the bus was delayed, so Sven, Sonya and I were standing at the bus stop, silently, waiting anxiously for the bus to arrive. We mostly looked down or on our phones. Occasionally however, we did exchange uncomfortable glances while hoping the other person wouldn't actually look in that moment. Well, *they* did. *They* hoped for that. I didn't. I caught Sonya's eye a few times, despairingly trying to get her attention, to listen to me, to let me explain. "Sonya!" I attempted a conversation at one point. "Don't, Spence," she immediately shut me down while putting her hand right in front of my face. She didn't want to talk to me, and she didn't want to look at me. She made that abundantly clear. And if that wasn't obvious enough, her face was giving me even more 'resting bitch face' than usual. It was kinda scary and intimidating, so it was an effective chat deterrent.

Sven was equally standoffish, although a little more lenient with his act of avoiding. "Sven, let me explain," I softly said to him while wanting to look into his piercing green eyes. But those piercing green eyes lost the spark they once inhabited. His eyes were full of disappointment, of sadness, of … defeat. I touched him gently on his muscly arm, trying to find a way through to him by affection and intimacy. A moment we have shared in the past. A moment I hoped could help me in this one, too. My gentle touch was quickly rejected. He pulled away and turned his back, facing the entrance of the national park. "Sorry, Spence, I need a bit of space right now." I appreciated his clear voice of instruction, telling me what he needed. It didn't make me feel any less helpless though.

It was ironic. We came here as a content and united trio, we entered the national park as a content and united trio, but we came out completely different. Still a trio but separate, split, demolished. Hurt and confused. Confused! Well, confusion seemed to be a consistent aspect of my life. Or was it just a teenager thing? So many experiences, new and old, that led to utter confusion. A splish splash of the mind. How did anyone navigate through their teenage years unscathed? Was that even an option? Being a teenager seemed to be brutal and unforgiving at times. Just like the behaviour of Sven and Sonya was right there and then.

I could, of course, understand their anger and their general disgruntlement. Of course, I understood. I was well aware that I did wrong. I left my two best friends in the dark about my secret. I should have opened up to them. I knew I should have. I recognised that. But we all knew that it wasn't always that simple. No matter who you confided in, no matter what about. It wasn't always a straightforward process. But that was still no excuse. I messed up. And now, there was this big revelation. For them, it came out of nowhere. Just like my sparkles themselves appeared out of nowhere. Without any warning whatsoever. Of course, they were shocked. "Spencer is a witch," they would have thought. Thinking it, spelling it out. It was a thought so surreal that you didn't even think it was real at all. It was a thought that I had many times. I knew what it was like to think it, to be faced with the impossible. "It can't be real!" The thought would linger in my mind for days, weeks even. And I still pinched myself about it on occasion, thinking that this was all a dream. But just because you thought it, didn't mean it was true. The reality was often different, and reality certainly became *real* for Sven and Sonya. What they had known before going into the national park had changed into something different altogether by the end of it. A new view of things. A new perspective. A familiar scenario that I have encountered so often in the past when I had a walk of solitude in nature, among my friends, the trees. They always encouraged me to see things in a different light, and ultimately, they observed a change in my perception. And that was exactly what the trees had witnessed with Sonya and Sven. A shift in their perception as they were confronted with a new perspective of me.

That new perspective of me continued to divide us. Quite literally. When the bus eventually came, we sat in random seats on the bus, far away from each other. There was no joined video session, no old-fashioned card game together, no laughter, no interaction between us. The bus ride back, just like the bus ride to the national park, was long. This time, however, it felt a whole lot longer. We still didn't break our rule 'No whinging allowed'. But I really wouldn't have minded some whinging. Anything would have been better than this deafening silence. "Come on, somebody say something about something. Anything!" I kept thinking. I knew I could have used my sparkles to manipulate the situation, to make them talk, to make us connect again. But it was wrong. I dismissed the initial temptation. My sparkles were not the means to make us reconnect when they were what made us disconnect to begin with. They were what put us in this situation. I knew they were not the answer to get us out of it. So for now, I had no choice other than to just sit it out, wait for this bus ride to be over, wait for this uncomfortable, unbearable awkwardness to be over.

Once we got back to our town, Sonya was the first to exit the bus. She grabbed her bike which she locked up at a wooden fence across the road from the bus stop. She swung onto it, cool and casual, as she did. A moderate breeze brought her pigtails to life, like two flying kites twirling freely in the wind, as she rode off towards her house. She didn't look back. She just rode away. Sven started walking to his house which was in the opposite direction to Sonya's place. His broad shoulders carried his sunken head as his strong legs wandered on the sidewalk, one firm step at a time, bit by bit carrying him farther and farther away. It felt metaphorical, the distance, the division between the three of us. The way Sonya and Sven left in opposite directions. The way I was left in the middle of a street that - for a weekend - was very quiet, very empty. The way I stood there. Quiet. Empty. Alone. Miserable. Apart.

33. Flashbacks.

I hadn't heard from Sonya or Sven for the rest of the weekend. And I didn't expect any different. But I was anxious. I was anxious to see them again at school the following Monday. I was hoping for a small miracle. The whole weekend, I thought of them, about the trip to the national park, about our friendship, about how we could mend this dent in our relationship. I was hoping that it would, in fact, just be a dent. A brief ripple on the calm sea of our bond. A small hiccup in an otherwise intact connection. But of course, it was more than just a dent, more than just a ripple, more than just a hiccup. It was a lot more than that. Like a giant waterfall of vomit, caused by an upside down stomach, caused by indigestible food, fed by... me. And this waterfall was flooding the connecting roads of our beings.

I held on to that hope, strongly, continuously, desperately, until I got to school on Monday, where I was met with the unsurprising reality that this hope wouldn't be fulfilled. I spotted Sonya and Sven before class, not together, rather in their own worlds, away from each other, and certainly away from me. I wondered why they didn't converse, or band up. It could have easily been a two against one situation. But it wasn't. Everyone was very much to themselves. In class, it was extremely difficult not to harass them to speak to me. They were so close to me, uncomfortably close, awkwardly close. They were right next to me. The words were lining up on my tongue, ready to slide out. The words were ready. But Sven and Sonya were not. They gave me nonverbal signals. And I received and read their signals. They wanted no piece of me, they wanted their space. Undeniably.

I couldn't help but think of Henry Miller. How he ignored me, how he didn't want anything to do with me, how it was impossible to get a hold of him after the 'incident'. How helpless I felt, how hurt, how desperate, how devastated. How much I adored him and how much I wanted to reconcile. Unsuccessfully. Those flashbacks struck me deeply, a harsh reminder of the past, with its evident resemblance to the present. I did something that wasn't liked or understood but rather despised. And while the result of my actions was the same one, it was still different. I was truthful to Henry, I was just being me, showing him my feelings by wanting to kiss him. In this case, with Sven and Sonya, I was not truthful, I was not fully being me, I was not showing or sharing all of my feelings, not sharing all of me, of who I was.

With the relief of the school bell, the class was dismissed for break time. A relief that was so obviously felt by all three of us. A relief from an uneasiness. From dealing with me. From being confronted with the truth about me and my magic sparkles. I thought of them once as a blessing but maybe they were also a curse. Just like Uncle James told me when I met him. "They didn't see me as a saviour but a traitor," he said. It hit home. And it hit hard. I now knew exactly what he meant by that. While I saved Robbie's life, the focus was not on that but on the act of how I saved him. I was not a saviour. I was a traitor. And as such, I was treated by Sonya and Sven. A traitor.

More than a week passed with the repetitive scenario of trying to avoid each other and trying to get through awkwardly uncomfortable interactions in must-do class activities. We were no longer the united front against the evil of high school. We no longer turned heads at school for spending most of our time together. Instead, we caused endless whispers about the apparent end of our togetherness. It became quite obvious to others that we were on our own. Sonya was always comfortable on her own anyway, she didn't have many other friends, she was too dry, too weird for most. Never too weird for me though, I always loved that about her. But weird or not, she always did her thing, and she did it fully at peace with herself. It was admirable.

Sven was a different story. Once Robbie noticed the disconnect between Sven and me, he took Sven under his wing, integrating him into his group of minions. Indeed, he seemingly became part of them, hanging out with them in the school breaks and cheering with them over goals at soccer in sports lessons. What Robbie and his minions saw was another brother, another alpha male, another ally, another of their own in their midst, another cool kid who finally joined the right crowd. But what I saw was a boy who was lost and confused, who let himself go and be with people he never really gave the time of day before. He spent time with people that he fought against, stood up against - for me. He was a boy with a strained smile at their jokes and comments. A boy who, somehow, unwillingly got swept away by the wave of Robbie's minionhood. It was like he wasn't himself anymore. While Robbie only saw Sven as someone who came to his senses, I saw the truth underneath. I saw Sven as the boy who didn't come to his senses but who lost his senses.

And then, there was me. I was pretty used to being on my own, although I did always have Sonya. So this was a definite adjustment. Often, I strolled aimlessly through the school hall. I couldn't decide where to sit. Should I join the science nerds? Should I try to make friends with the clique of musicians? Sure, I could have done that. But I had no genuine interest. Just for the sake of not having lunch alone, it wasn't worth it. Sometimes, I just ate on the go while roaming around. I planned on doing this again after another draining day of playing hide-and-not-seek with Sven and Sonya. That was when I saw Adrian hunched over, sitting under a tree, close to the lunch tables, yet well removed from them to be undisturbed. As per usual, his nose was in one of his books. I decided to go over there. I wandered through the thick grass in my white sneakers that were once covered in magically altered hot choccy.

I reached the tree and stood right in front of it. Adrian was sitting on the other side, facing away from the lunch tables area. A part of me questioned if I should join Adrian at all. How many times had I tried in the past to connect with him? How many times did I try on the bus? Only for him to snub me and just keep focusing on his book or phone or whatever he was hiding behind at the time. What was going to be different now? "Nah, not doing this," I thought and backed up my conclusion by starting to walk away. But I got stopped. "Spencer?!" I turned around and saw Adrian peeking from behind the big tree stem that only revealed his straight black fringe and brown eyes. "Did you want to sit here?" Adrian asked as the rest of his face emerged. "I-I don't want to intrude," I said, maybe more aware than ever of other people's sacred personal space. "No, no. It's fine. Come sit." Adrian waved me over. I hesitated for a second. I was a bit stunned by his sudden and inviting willingness. It took me by surprise, but I accepted his invitation. I slipped behind the tree, facing away from the lunch tables and sat down beside Adrian.

He had his backpack next to him, half open, a few school books sticking out, including "Harry Potter" which we still read in Mrs Anderson's English class. There was also a container filled with sandwiches and fruits that he had been nibbling on. He had himself a nice and cosy picnic time. As I looked around and inspected Adrian's little nook, I had to think of the picnic that Sven, Sonya and I were supposed to have in the national park. A picnic that never took place. A picnic that I denied them. "Grape?" I froze up in the world of my thoughts but Adrian managed to pull me back to the immediate present by holding a thick and juicy purple grape under my nose. The scent was fresh and fragrant. I couldn't resist that. "Um, yeah. Thanks." I took the grape out of his hand and shovelled it into my mouth. The taste was rich and satisfying, invigorating even.

"So, what are you reading?" I asked as I enjoyed the last fibres of that delicious grape gliding down my throat. "Ah, just the 'Harry Potter' book," he said. "Oh yeah? How are you finding it?" I was curious. "Yeah, it's... it's good..." Adrian seemed hesitant. "But?" I asked with eager eyes. "But... umm," Adrian stammered, "well, do you think the friendship between them is pictured realistically?" I didn't quite know what he was getting at. "What do you mean?" Adrian took the book from the top of his backpack, randomly skimming through it. "Doesn't it seem too perfect for you?" Adrian noticed that I still didn't quite understand. "For me, their friendship seems too good to be true," Adrian started to elaborate. "I mean, there are no conflicts between them. That's not real life," he concluded as he looked at me, his eyes seeking a response. I sighed softly. "Well, Harry and especially Ron didn't necessarily like Hermione when they first met. But things developed and changed, and they did become friends, even if Ron and Hermione still bickered. As you do sometimes with friends, right?" I answered, focusing solely on Adrian's criticism of Harry Potter's friendships while realising that there was something else that was on Adrian's mind.

"Yeah, I guess," Adrian muttered, staring on the ground, dejected. He put the book back on top of his backpack. "I noticed that you haven't hung out with your friends as much this week," Adrian pointed out. "You mean, not at all," I corrected him, "we, um, we are going through a bit of a rough patch." I kept it vague. I didn't want to share the whole story, especially not about my sparkles, and especially not with someone who continuously refused to chat with me in the past. And now, all of a sudden that he did, it just didn't feel right or appropriate. While I knew Adrian, I didn't really know him at all.

"Yeah, I get that." Adrian attempted a smile. "I had a good friend once. He was my best friend actually. But things didn't go so well." Adrian continued to surprise me. While he not only invited me to sit with him, he also chatted to me. And not just a casual chat, he did a lot more than that, he shared a personal story with me. With me? Why me? I was utterly perplexed about the turn in his attitude, but I tried to hide my sentiments as I didn't want to ruin the moment. I felt that he *wanted* to share, and that he wanted to continue to share, that he was aching for someone to reflect with, someone to simply talk to. And maybe there was nobody else? I certainly never saw him with anyone else at school, Adrian was always a bit of a loner like that. So, this felt like Adrian needed a listening ear for a story that he may have kept inside himself, until now. "What happened?" I asked gently with a voice that conveyed comfort and understanding.

"Well, we were good friends for quite a long time and then, one day, he told me that I wasn't cool enough to be his friend. After all that time of hanging out, I suddenly wasn't cool enough, apparently." Adrian exaggeratedly shook his head and shrugged his shoulders. "That sounds very sus," I said as more Henry Miller flashbacks got triggered. "Yeah, I knew that was bull. That wasn't the real reason," Adrian said. "And what was?" I eagerly asked. I didn't want to overstep or be too pushy but I really wanted to know. Adrian didn't seem to care but rather welcomed my interest as he continued to talk. "I was at his place, like I was many times, but on this day, his father was going off at him like a wild animal." That sounded oddly familiar to me. "Why?" I asked to gather more information. "It was totally stupid. He poked around in his food because he didn't like the asparagus in the pasta bake that his mother cooked for dinner. Meanwhile, his brother got all the praise for finishing all of his plate. It was super random, and ridiculous and…" Adrian scrambled for words. "… and just uncomfortable." Adrian took a deep breath and exhaled, his upper body deflating like a tired balloon. Yes, deflated was the right word. He was deflated but at the same time full of relief. Relieved that the air, the burden, the story that the balloon inhabited was finally out. "And the next day, Robbie told me I wasn't cool enough," Adrian concluded.

"Wait, what?!" I was flabbergasted. "Robbie?" I stared at Adrian with an open mouth and big eyes. "Your friend was Robbie?" I really didn't know why I was so surprised. I knew that Adrian's story sounded familiar, like a story that I have heard or seen. But yet, I couldn't put two and two together, it didn't click. That was also because I had still been so overwhelmed by the sheer fact of an unexpected lunch break with Adrian, sharing grapes as if we had been friends forever. It was weird, definitely. But it was also something that gave me some form of distraction. Or rather an alleviation of my own struggles with Sven and Sonya. And I was thankful for that. Yes, it was random and weird to sit under that massive tree with Adrian, but I was thankful for it. Truly thankful. So I listened to Adrian and his story closely. I listened to every single word he had to say, I was glued to his mouth. I was so blinded by all of the circumstances that I simply didn't have the capacity to make the connection. Adrian and Robbie were best friends.

That was a bombshell moment. But thinking about it, it kinda made sense. It made a lot of sense actually. The fact was that he didn't ever cop it from Robbie. He never said anything mean to Adrian, or said anything at all to him. Adrian was invisible to Robbie, therefore simultaneously immune to his bullying antics. Adrian was under some sort of secret protection, disguised by Robbie's ignorance, probably so Adrian wouldn't tell anyone about Robbie's home situation. Robbie was obviously so embarrassed to have this happen in front of Adrian that he couldn't bear being friends anymore. So instead of leaning on a friend to get him through this, he decided to push him away and be around his minions, a more superficial kind of friendship where no danger occurred of being exposed. And it also made sense that Adrian just buried himself in his book or phone and didn't seem to interact with anyone, certainly not me when I tried. He must have felt hurt for so long that he didn't want to engage with anyone else, not even with another outsider like me.

"Yes, Robbie," Adrian confirmed. "We were such good friends and then something big happens and he shuts me out. I thought this would bring us closer as friends but it tore us apart." He was visibly upset. I felt a little apprehensive and wasn't sure what to do in that moment. A moment so personal, with someone that I didn't know so well. Not well enough to know how best to react, what best to say. But I let my intuition lead the way. After all, I understood the pain of losing a friend. And there was no doubt that Adrian must have truly cared about Robbie. That was all that I really needed to know. So I put my arm around him. Adrian leaned towards me to welcome the gesture. As he shifted to the side, his backpack fell over, all of his books and pencils fell on the ground, knocking over the container with some leftover grapes in the process. But that wasn't important. As the grapes tumbled out of the container and scattered all around the thick grass, Adrian and I just sat there, under the massive tree, in silence, my arm still comforting him. We sat still. Adrian stared at the ground right below him whereas I blankly looked at the trees in the distance. My friends, the trees.

Bubbles of memories emerged, gently floating in all directions in the space of my mind. Bubbles so fragile, so delicate but filled with strong memories. Bubbles of uncontrolled laughter during bowling sessions, bubbles of ever-bonding FTTs, bubbles of heart-racing intimacy, bubbles of pants with holes and pants with choccy stains, bubbles of rats and swans. Bubbles of memories that touched my core, so deeply that my eyes began to water, too much water for my eyes to hold. A plump tear drop made its way out of the corner of my left eye, down my cheeks, past my sniffly nose and into the corner of my mouth. Another tear closely followed down the same path into my mouth. The salty, almost bitter taste reminded me of what I didn't want. I didn't want the friendship between Sonya, Sven and me to become bitter. I wanted it to be *better*! I didn't want those bubbles to pop. I didn't want them to drift away into the unforgiving darkness of my mind. I wanted them to keep floating, I wanted them to stay strong and present and relevant.

Another tear drop escaped the water tank of my eyes. But this time, it didn't make it past my cheeks. Instead, I wiped it away with the sleeve of my hoodie. "This couldn't happen to me! This couldn't happen to me again! I couldn't lose a friend again. It just couldn't happen to me, to Sonya, to Sven, to us," I thought as I kept staring at my tree friends in the distance. The sun started to come around the tree, gently touching my face with its warm glare. The rays of the sun fortified a sense of uplifting determination and filled me with rays of hope, manifesting one thought.

I couldn't let this happen.

34. Silence.

I knew neither Sven nor Sonya wanted to speak with me. I've tried that many times, and it got me nowhere. Just the cold shoulder, accompanied by an icy gaze that spoke volumes. I didn't need to see the look to know how they were feeling. Obviously. But I did need to somehow communicate with them. To explain and to ultimately change the look on their faces when they saw me. But how was I going to do that?

Back in Mrs Anderson's class the next day, I sat quietly next to Sven and Sonya. No attempt to talk to them. I complied with their wishes of giving them space and time. My eyes roamed over to Sven. Undetected. I didn't move my head. Only my eyes. They wandered. From Sven back to my notebook, then to Sonya. When I glanced over to Sonya, I noticed our elbows. My right elbow and her left elbow formed a perfect triangle shape respectively. The tip of the triangles faced each other in faultless alignment. They were mirrors of each other. They were the same but completely different. They were different but still in sync. They were in sync but totally broken. They were broken but holding close. So close that our elbows almost touched in a subconscious approach to each other. Our elbows. They reminded me of our FTTs. Those FTTs were our conscious approach to each other in the past. A gesture that didn't need any additional words, no explanation. It worked perfectly in silence. We just understood. And that was what I wanted to get back. I smiled faintly. Unnoticed, just like my wandering eyes. I realised I needed to mend things with Sonya and Sven separately. There was no group solution for this problem. I couldn't sit them both down at the same time, just because it was easier. I had to go about in a different way, giving each of them the time - and respect - that they deserved, to explain my sparkles, to explain myself. I owed them that. It only felt right wanting to start with Sonya first… and I had an idea how.

Whether you wanted to call it fate or simply perfect timing, it so happened that Mrs Anderson just gave us a silent task. How fitting, right? Silent! The task was to write a review of the Philosopher's Stone in "Harry Potter", what it could do, what impact it could have, and how it could change a life. Ironic, really. The Philosopher's Stone was like my freckles. Magical. Powerful. A symbol of personal transformation. A transformation that I had to learn to accept, just like every other aspect of myself. It wasn't always easy, no doubt about that. It was a process. But a process that was so worth going through. Just like a friendship, with its ups and downs, its challenges that forced you to reflect and grow. To be better, and stronger.

As I started writing, my elbow stayed in the exact same position, angled, pointed, determined. Sonya's also didn't move. Was she aware of our elbow positions? I had no clue, but if so, she may not have associated anything with it. In any case, my take on the book translated onto the page quickly, the review practically wrote itself. This gave me time to pull out another piece of paper and write down my elbow-affiliated thoughts. My hand steadily formed the words that I wanted this note to say. They were not many words, but they were enough to get my point across, or so I hoped. It all made sense to me, and I hoped that Sonya could find her way through the maze of my thoughts, that our minds could be aligned, just like our elbows had been all this lesson.

Once I finished writing both the essay and the additional note, my eyes travelled to Sonya's side. My head still motionless, only my eyes were enjoying the freedom of movement. I was getting quite good at this. The still position of the head but the information-scanning action of the eyes. I spotted Sonya's little black notebook in her backpack. I didn't exactly know what she had this for, but she always had it with her. I often saw her write something down in it, or read through it, sometimes even ripping pages out. I asked her about it once, but only once. She kinda skimmed over it. "It's just my book," she said back then. Well, I knew that. I knew it was her book. Duh. And if there was ever any doubt about that, you just had to look at the cover. It was a picture of her three rats Alvin, Simon and Theodore with the sentence 'I give a rat's.' written above them. I found it a bit cringe, for Sonya anyway, but I also thought it was cute that she had such a strong affection for pets. So yeah, the book was unmistakably hers. But what was inside was a mystery. I imagined she would put down her thoughts, similar to a diary, or maybe it was something completely different. Heck, I really didn't know. But what I did know was that she opened it every single day, multiple times a day.

The school bell unapologetically cut through the silence. Its three second ring couldn't come soon enough for most of my classmates as a sudden chatter amongst them erupted. But not between Sven, Sonya and I. We were still silent together. Sonya started to pack away her English books. Her black notebook was shovelled towards the bottom of her backpack in the process. "Damn," I thought. Once Sonya got all her things sorted, she got up and left the classroom. Sven still sat on his chair and played on his phone, in his own world, unfazed of anything happening around him. "This is my chance," I thought. I quickly folded my note and wrote 'For Son' on top of it - as if it wasn't obvious who it was for. Then, I ducked under the table to reach Sonya's backpack. I rummaged through her stuff, through books and papers and loose pens, until I finally got to the black notebook at the bottom. I pulled it out, opened the cover and slipped my note inside it. I would be lying if I said I wasn't tempted to have a peek at what this book was holding, what Sonya told the book that she didn't tell me. I was definitely tempted. But despite my curiosity, I respected Sonya's privacy and her property of thoughts. Of course, I did. I certainly wasn't in the position to ask to know everything about her when I kept so many things from her myself. That would have made me a hypocrite. So of course, I respected it.

And I didn't have a lot of time anyway. I knew she would come back shortly. So as soon as my note was inside the cover, I closed the book and slid the black notebook back underneath all of the other junk. I tried to meticulously put everything how she left it. Right when I placed the last English book back inside her backpack, Sonya suddenly entered the classroom again. I watched her white and slim legs come over to our table in seconds. She was back, standing in front of her seat while I was still under the table. "Damn," I thought once again. This was awkward. I slowly moved my head up from underneath the table which led me straight into Sonya's confused face, or maybe she was angry, or annoyed. At that point, I really couldn't tell. "What are you doing?" She shrugged as she demanded an answer. While I loved that she finally spoke to me, the circumstances were far from ideal. "Hi. Ummm, I...," I said haltingly, trying to come up with a good excuse. "I, I was...," I continued stammering, until I realised I was still holding the pen in my hand that I'd used to write the English review and Sonya's note. "I was looking for my pen. I dropped it," I finally said. I waved the pen in her face to show her. "Found it though!" I rolled my eyes at myself and smiled in a fake-embarrassed way. I tapped the pen against my forehead to demonstrate my clumsiness before I sat back up straight on my chair, trying to avoid any more eye contact with Sonya as she would otherwise sense that something was up - again. That I was hiding something from her - again. Well, yes, I was but this time, it was something to get us back to where we once were. The undercover note-slipping was a means to an end. And I wholeheartedly hoped that it was going to work.

Sonya stood in front of her chair for a bit, looking up at the fluorescent ceiling, unsure what to make of my explanation. Instead of saying anything else, she blew out an agitated sigh and semi-violently pulled the chair towards her until she took a seat on it. In that moment, Adrian passed. As he walked to his table, he slightly turned his head to me. "Good luck," he mouthed. Nobody but me seemed to notice though. He had seen what I did under the table with Sonya's notebook. And he understood. He understood only too well. He could relate, watching a friendship slip away, feeling desperate and alone. And he knew what it was like wanting to change that.

Maybe *that* was the reason why he opened up to me. By picking up on my quarrel with Sven and Sonya, maybe he saw an opportunity to connect over the same struggles. But also a chance to turn his fate around, to let out all the feelings, all the thoughts which had finally become too much for him to bare. His emotions had boiled over, and he had to share it with someone. And that happened to be me. Whatever Adrian's motivation behind it was, I appreciated our bonding session under the tree. I appreciated his honesty and the trust that he put in me. I appreciated that we were able to move past the awkward silence between us that had defined our relationship for so long. And I appreciated his good luck wishes with my attempt to patch things up with Sonya... I needed that. "Thank you," I mouthed back with a wink as the classroom chatter died down to commence our next lesson.

35. Seesaw.

The place was empty, everyone was gone. It was deserted. Empty. Almost eerie. I hadn't been here for ages. When was the last time I was standing here? I couldn't remember. I waited anxiously. I stood still in one spot, almost rooted to the ground, with only my feet fidgeting back and forth. I stood on my toes and then on my heels. Toes, heels, toes, heels. It almost looked like I was dancing and hopping to a song in my head. But I was just waiting. Anxiously. I checked my phone. It was 6.58pm. I was early. Good, because I really couldn't afford to be late for this one. I made sure I was on time, but I was early - even better. It gave me a couple of extra minutes to collect my thoughts, to take a few deep breaths, and to brace myself for the storm that might be coming. Well, I had to at least *expect* a storm. I couldn't expect that Sonya just forgave me without any bumps and hurdles. But would she even come? I checked the time again. 7.03pm. I looked around, no sign of her. I got more anxious and rocked backward and forward like a seesaw. I focused on my movements to reduce my anxiety but it didn't help. I was still unsettled, and now I was nauseous, too. I forced myself to stand still completely. I looked down on my white sneakers, then back on my phone. 7.09pm. Was she really not coming? Was I maybe not clear enough in my note? Did she not find the note? Did she not use her black notebook today? Or did she open the notebook, find my note and just threw it away without reading it? Or did she read it but was still too upset to face me? Did I really upset her so badly that she didn't want to see me?

I gazed up into the clear sky. It was on the brink of turning dark as the sun slowly set behind the neighbouring row of gabled roofs. I loved sunsets. And I loved sunrises. The start of a day, full of hope and possibilities. The end of the day, full of gratitude - and hope yet again that the following day would bring more hope, more possibilities, more gratitude. What today's sun would set its light on was still very much in the air, an unwritten passage of the unknown. But whatever this day, this night brought, I knew that I tried. I have tried many times, over and over again. And I wanted to keep on trying. I didn't want to give up, because this friendship was something I couldn't and wouldn't just let go of. I checked my phone again. 7.27pm. My anxiety turned into sadness. It wasn't like Sonya to be late. If she wanted to be somewhere, she was there on the dot. You could always count on that. But here I was, standing on the same single spot for the last half hour, alone. I was convinced... Sonya just didn't want to be there with me.

I looked down on my shoes once again and rocked from side to side to ease my anxiety, my sadness, my desperation. Then I paused. I took another deep breath and put my energy towards accepting my failure in getting Sonya here. I raised my right foot from the spot that was now visually bruised by my seesawing. Just when I was about to take a step away, I heard a car pull up. As soon as the car stopped, the high beam came on and shone directly into my face. Did someone forget something and come back? What would they say if they saw me here, lingering around this property? Or did someone already call the police and that car was them? That would not be ideal. I couldn't see who was in the car but I saw two silhouettes. One of them got out of the car, slamming the door shut. The silhouette walked in front of the car, the high beam still shining bright, following their every move. Why did the car have its annoying lights on? The silhouette extended to a hat, not a cap but a hat. Was that a … police hat? Was this actually the police? Was I trespassing? I panicked. Their steps headed towards me. The figure went from a faraway statue to a person coming closer and closer, getting bigger and bigger, the hat getting more and more pronounced and reassuring that this was going to be a police officer.

The lights were blinding, I raised my hand, trying to shield my eyes from the harsh glare. But not entirely successful. I squinted, hoping to be able to make out who was approaching me, though it didn't help me to draw a definite conclusion. I couldn't be sure. But it was probably the police. So I had to be ready. I closed my eyes, feeling a sudden relief from the relentless beam. I started to whisper, "Sparkle sparkle, invisible me. Sparkle sparkle, set me fr —" I was just about to speak the last syllable of my spell when the person arrived and stood right in front of my face. I could feel their breath. I could smell their scent. Was that…? Wait, I knew this smell. Was it… incense? "Fucking hell," a voice said just as I confirmed my assumption. Yes, it was incense. I opened my eyes. The car was gone, taking its blinding beam with it, and finally giving me an unobstructed view. It was Sonya.

36. Makeover.

Sonya wore her peaked hat that very much resembled a police hat. Of all days, she had to wear it today? It gave me a good fright, that was for sure. She got the hat from a second-hand store a few months ago. I was with her when she bought it. I remembered that day well. I loved that day. We went into the shop just to see what was there but ultimately, we wanted to try on as many things as possible, no matter how silly or outrageous. We had a movie night once, and we were inspired by the makeover montages in those movies. I particularly was a sucker for a good makeover, so it was really only a matter of time until I created my own sequences. It looked so fun, so I was eager to do it myself. Sonya initially snubbed the idea but consequently joined, mostly because I bribed her with dinner afterwards. We had a good time though, including Sonya. She may not have wanted to admit it but she visibly had a blast. Funnily enough, it was not me but Sonya who bought a few things from our montage shenanigans. Including the peaked hat, which she wore occasionally on casual outings, with her pigtails left and right. It suited her badass personality. Was that why she chose to wear it for this meeting? She wanted to look badass, maybe even intimidating, as a way of keeping up her emotional wall? Well, in any case, she certainly made an entrance. I had to give her that.

She stood in front of me and sternly looked at me in a brief face off before she brushed past me and sat down in front of a tree. She reached into her pocket and pulled out a piece of paper. "I got your message," she said concisely as she unfolded the note I had written. "Oh, umm, good." I was still a bit startled by her sudden appearance. "I thought you wouldn't come," I said shakily as I slowly moved towards her. "Well, I am here," she replied while pretending to read the note again. "I... I thought maybe my note was too cryptic, and that's why you wouldn't come. Well, that and..." I sighed. "...and because you hate me." She looked up and as soon as her eyes met mine, she looked down again. "Well, yeah," she said, unclear what she was referring to. I waited for her to elaborate, but she didn't. "Yeah what?" I hesitantly asked, even though I didn't want to hear her confirm that she hated me. But I asked anyway. "Well, yeah," she said again, "your note was cryptic AF but I knew what you meant." She paused for a second. "Well, your note wasn't that cryptic really." Sonya took the piece of paper in both hands. "Meet me at 7pm where it all began," she recited my written words. She glared at me over the top of the paper. "Really, Spence? Could you be any cheesier?" she said -

with a straight face, even though this was the kind of comment we would normally both laugh out loud about. And that was the exact reason why I wrote it like that. A reminder of our bond, our common humour, our friendship. But she said it with a straight face, no smile, no laugh, no emotion. Just a stare over the top of the paper. "Well, it is though. This is where it all began," I said and pointed at the tree that Sonya sat in front of. "It's our tree. The hollow tree. This is where we met." Sonya turned around lethargically and glanced at the tree for a short moment. "I know." That's all she said as she wheeled around again. "And why am I here?" she asked indifferently. "Well, I thought it was a good place to talk, to remember how we met, all the things that we have gone through together, including my current fuck up. Maybe you will let me explain. And maybe we can go back to how we were before I pissed you off?"

There! I didn't hesitate to voice my intentions. I put it all out there in a short and sweet summary. My emotions, my hope, my desires. I just wanted my friend back. I looked at Sonya, awaiting any form of reaction. Anything at all. Suddenly, she crumpled my note and shot to her feet. "Pissed me off? You're damn right, you pissed me off," she raised her voice. "I, I… I know, you're mad," I said defensively while holding both my hands in front of my body in an attempt to calm her down, but also as a shield, in case Sonya was going to hit me in her rage. "YES, I AM MAD," she yelled as she took a confronting step towards me. "You think I don't remember how we met?! Of course, I remember, Spence." She was offended. "But do *you* remember?" Her eyes were wide open. "Do you remember, Spence?" she repeated. I opened my mouth but I was cut off before I could even speak. "We promised we were going to be there for each other, and be honest. FTT, remember? F.T.T.," she echoed intensely. "So stupid. Pfft. FTT. Fingertip touch. It should rather stand for Fuck This Thing. That makes a whole lot more sense to me right now. And that's how you seemed to have seen it lately. Fuck this thing. *This*." Sonya frantically wagged her index finger back and forth between the two us us. Her anger was bubbling out of her like a volcanic eruption. "No, Sonya, it's not like that. It had nothing to do with that." I tried to calm her horses. "Oh, didn't it? It had nothing to do with our friendship? Then why didn't you just tell me? Why didn't you tell me that you were a witch, Spencer? Why, huh? Don't you trust me? Have I ever given you a reason not to trust me? No! No, I haven't. I have always been there for you. Who was there when Robbie mocked you over and over?" She hastily pointed at herself repeatedly. "Who was there when he made fun of your pants and I stupidly burnt a hole into my own?" She kept pointing at herself. The answer was clear, even without the pointing. "Who, Spencer, who?" She clearly wanted to hear it, coming from my lips. "It was you," I mumbled. "What?" She came very close to my face. "What was that? I didn't hear you, Spencer?! Who?!" She was so angry and upset that she almost cried. I could see it in her face. It was written all over it. "It was you, Sonya. It has always been you. And I love you for that." Sonya looked at me like she was going to bite my face off. "You love me? You love me, Spencer? Is this how you treat people you love?"

In her outrage, Sonya unintentionally spat out drops of saliva. "It's raining," I said, trying to make light of the situation. It was one of our inside jokes, something we said when one of us spat at the other person's face during a passionate discussion. Inadvertently. It always made us laugh, no matter how deep or serious that conversation was. "What?" She was visibly puzzled and annoyed. "It's raining," I repeated with a flickering smile, hoping that she would join in, like she used to. But she didn't. This might have been the first time we had a spit rain situation and we didn't laugh out loud about it. If I didn't already know it before, I certainly realised it now. This was different. This was serious. Sonya was furious.

"I know, Sonya. I know…" I finally grabbed the initiative. "You are mad. And you have every right to be. I fucked up and I totally deserve this." Sonya surprisingly stayed quiet. "I… I was confused, okay?" I went on. Her eyes narrowed, as if she wasn't buying it. "I… — one day, I woke up and I was a completely different person. Like different different. Yes, I was already different anyway. I was always the outsider, always the one who didn't fit in. And as you know, this has not been easy for me. And I am so grateful that you have been by my side throughout all of that. I don't know what I would have done without you. You made it all bearable, even in the darkest times. You gave me a feeling of belonging when nobody else wanted to be around me. You were my only friend in a world of bullying idiots. You made me come out of my shell, you made me feel accepted, you made me feel worthy. You made me feel less different. You made me feel *good* different. It was a long journey, you know that, but we got there. Without you though, I don't know if I would have ever gotten there at all." I halted. The weight of the words coming out of my mouth hit me like a punch. Seriously, what would I have done without Sonya? It took me a minute to compose myself before I carried on talking. "And then, I got my sparkles on my 16th birthday. I didn't know what was happening, other than that I felt pushed back into the 'different' corner, the one where I was an outsider yet again, the one where I was left alone, the one where I was the only one."

Sonya had been following every single word closely. "But you didn't have to be alone with this. I could have been there for you again," she objected. She was still annoyed, her face showed me that, but her voice sounded much softer. "I know, but I had to get my head around it first. I had to get to know myself again. I had to understand. And nobody could help me with that. I needed time to process it. Much like you did - and probably still do. It wasn't just dealing with physical changes." I pointed at my freckles. "It was about dealing with physical changes that came with magical powers, for Christ's sake! I mean, how *do* you even process that?" I let out a gentle giggle. It was too ridiculous not to. Sonya looked at me with an understanding smile. She got what I meant, and she knew what I had to deal with. Well, kind of anyway. It was one thing to know of someone's magic, but it was another to actually live it. Be it. Be a witch. Sonya shrugged in solidarity. "I'm still mad at you though, Spence. Surely there was a point in time where you could have told me. A time before you decided to save bloody Robbie's life. I mean, come on, rat. So dramatic." The fact that she made a sarcastic joke and called me 'rat' again gave me confidence that we were on a good path, however not entirely there yet.

"I… yeah, I," I stammered while thinking of all the opportunities I had to tell her. "Yeah, you're right. You are absolutely right. I could have told you earlier, once I became more acquainted with my powers. But the longer I waited, the worse I felt for not telling you sooner. Every time that I wanted to tell you, I hesitated. Because I knew you'd be mad that I didn't tell you the moment I found out. So instead of telling you, I avoided it. I was dreading it. I waited longer, and longer, and longer. Argh, I was so stupid. I know that now, but I feared that I had waited way too long to tell you, and that you would not only kill me but abandon me." I submissively sank my head. I realised that my fears did come true as a result of my secrecy. Sonya did abandon me. And I deserved that. I hated it because I missed my friend, but I deserved it. I wasn't the friend that I could have and should have been. I was selfish.

"Well, you're right. I want to kill you. Sooo bad," she said with a playful undertone. "I want to kill you so hard and so thoroughly that you have no chance of ever coming back from the dead. I would make sure of that." Sonya could get a bit morbid at times. "Buuuut," she proceeded, "if I killed you, you wouldn't be able to tell me everything about your freaking magic now, would you?" I lifted my head in surprise and disbelief. I didn't expect her to say that. "So you'll forgive me?" I asked carefully. "Well, I want to stay mad at you, but the thing is that I am mad at myself more." Sonya paused for a moment and exhaled a faint sigh. "It's not entirely your fault, rat." I was startled. What did she mean by that? "What do you mean?" I verbalised my inner voice. "Well, if you were scared to tell me because you thought I was going to be mad, then I'm to blame too." I still wasn't following. "I'm to blame for making you feel that way, Spencer," she resumed. "For making you feel that you can't come to me, no matter how long you wait to tell me. I shouldn't make you feel like you have to tell me anything at any given time. It's not my call to tell you when you should be ready to share anything. It's your call, and yours alone. You are your own person, and you have to make your own decisions, the ones that feel right for *you*. And not the ones that feel right for me or anyone else. I don't own you, nobody does. You are you, and you are great the way you are, even if you are a little weirdo." Sonya was getting mushy, wrapping her emotions in a blanket of a teasing joke. I could even see some water welling up in her eyes. She wasn't the type to cry really but her emotions did get the better of her sometimes, coming to the surface both physically and verbally.

"I…" I turned my face to Sonya to meet her watery eyes, and I took her hands. "I…" she said and glimpsed at me but then quickly looked down to hide the forming tears. "I'm sorry," we finished our sentence at the same time. We both chuckled, then laughed out loud before we shared a warm embrace. "Haha. Who's the weirdo, huh?" I asked mockingly. We both stopped giggling. Sonya threw me a look of pretend daintiness, until she burst out laughing again. We continued giggling so loud that we heard an echo sound coming from the hollow tree. That made us laugh even more. It was just perfect. We both went up to our tree - we almost *rolled* up, that was how much we were laughing - and stood in front of the hole that once allowed us to hide in it during a game of hide-and-seek, the same hole that now delighted us with the echo of giggles. It was like a mirror of memories that made us realise... we came a long way. From a place of hiding and bonding to a place of laughter and reconciliation. We gazed at the hole, still, letting the moment speak for itself, both internally contemplating about what once was, and simultaneously acknowledging the present moment. Our eyes connected, and we exchanged a smile that said more than a thousand words could say. We stretched out our index fingers and whispered ever so slightly... "FTT!"

37. Spark the dark.

Sonya and I sat at the foot of the hollow tree for what seemed like ages. The sun had completely vanished behind the pediments and took its well deserved nightly leave of absence while the moon stepped in with its bright shine to light up a sky of darkness. We sat there and just chatted. There were a lot of questions to be answered, a lot of gaps to be filled. I told Sonya everything. Every little detail that I could remember. How my first ever spells knocked me out, how I got myself ready for school the day after my birthday, how I fixed my 'holy' pants. "You fixed your pants, Spence? What about the hole I burnt into mine? Can you fix that too?" She pouted with mock irritation. Granted though, she did still have a hole in those pants. "Haha, yes, of course, I will fix it for you," I assured her and patted her on the shoulders to ease her pretend annoyance.

I told her how I stood up to Robbie for the first time - though technically without the help of any magic. "I'm so proud of you," she exclaimed and squeezed my hand. How I traveled back in time to meet my only other known relative with freckles, Uncle James. Sonya's eyes were especially filled with fascination as I spilled the tea about my experience in the year 1720. I told her all about my first flight - well, my first and my only flight thus far. How I planned to fly to Sonya that day and come clean. "You did?" She had a shine of surprise and happiness in her eyes. Surprised but happy to know that at least I had intended to tell her earlier. "Yes, I did but then, I came across Robbie's house and I spied on him through a window." The shine of surprise grew brighter, and so did her smile of excitement. "You did what, rat?" I filled her in on what I saw and heard and that this experience ultimately took the wind out of my sails to continue further to Sonya's house. "That's heavy, Spence. I can see why you just wanted to get home after that. It's a lot to take in," she understood as she put her hand on my back. "And that explains a lot about Robbie actually," she added. "Yeah, it does," I agreed, the shadow of pensiveness flickering above us.

To lighten the mood, I gave Sonya an insight into how I almost got caught spying but saved myself just in time by unwillingly morphing into a moth. She cackled hard. "I can picture you as a moth. You already have the hairy legs," she teased me. It felt good to laugh and share all of those moments with her. It was like a load off my shoulders. "And does your mum know?" Sonya asked. "Oh yes, she does," I answered with a mysterious smile, which led into to the story about the thyme time spell. We continued laughing.

A moment of silence arose as we appreciated the night sky with its many stars dotted all across it. Stars dotted like freckles across a face. Like sparkles. Like *my* sparkles. Magical and unique. Just like this moment of silence. A comfortable silence of reflection, of reminiscing, of reconnecting. My head wandered to view the abundance of stars with the big moon in the centre of it all. The bright moonlight led my eyes back to Sonya who also stared at the sky's infinity. As I looked at her from the side, her hat caught my eye. "Why did you decide to wear this hat?" I asked with high anticipation. "Oh that. Ha. I just wanted to make sure you don't forget that I am a badass bitch." So I was right about that. "Haha," I chuckled, "a BBB without one B." I winked at Sonya. "You got that right," she said as she straightened her posture, wiggling her shoulders from side to side, showing off an exaggerated amount of swagger. "I can be a badass bitch even without a bike." There was no doubting that.

"Oh... Which reminds me... you didn't take your bike here?! How come?" I wanted to know. "Yeah no, I had a problem with my bike chain just as I wanted to go. My dad tried to repair it but you know he is not a handyman-type of dad." She giggled. "He was fiddling around with it forever, so in the end, I convinced him to give it a rest and drive me here. That's why I was late." That made sense. Her dad was a great man but he definitely wasn't great when it came to fixing things. One time, he noticed that my helmet strap was broken, so he replaced it with a red silky grosgrain ribbon tie that was more fitted for a 1950s summer hat than a helmet for a teenage boy. Credit to him for trying to help and fix the problem but seriously, I looked so ridiculous that I begged my mum to buy me a brand new helmet - which, after a lot of nagging, she eventually did.

"Ah, okay. Fair enough. I did see another silhouette in the car but it didn't look like your dad's?!" I didn't think anything of it at first but reflecting on it now, I wondered. Was it her dad, and I just didn't look properly? Given the literal blinding of the moment, it was possible that my initial impression was wrong. "Oh yeah, you probably saw Sven," she casually threw in. "Wai— what? Sven? Sven was in the car?" I pointed at the spot where the car stopped before, baffled. "Yes, I mean, we were all in the car. Me, my dad and Sven. But when we pulled up here," Sonya started to explain, "dad dropped his lighter which fell right at the back behind the pedals. So he ducked down, trying to get it during which he turned on the high beams and of course, didn't manage to turn them off right away. Sven leaned over from the back seat, trying to help my dad. It was comical actually." Her lips curled into a slight smile as she rolled her eyes and shook her head in amusement. "But I was already late to meet you, so I just got out of the car and let the boys deal with all of that. So yeah, you probably didn't and couldn't see my dad because he was literally losing it in the car." She grinned. Her humour always cracked me up. I smiled to acknowledge the hilarity but I needed to focus and go back to what she said before. "Sooo, Sven was in the car?! But... W-Why?" I stammered. "Well, I called him," she said without any further elaboration. "Okaaay, but why did you call him? I thought you didn't even speak?" I learnt more today than I expected. "Oh no, we do speak. We have been speaking quite often." I was gobsmacked. "Oh yeah, about...?" I asked. "You, of course, rat." I raised both of my eyebrows, giving her a questioning look. "Well, what you did with Robbie and how we feel about it." I was actually happy to hear that they went through that silent mode with me together. Or at least not as separate as I thought. Maybe they were better friends than I realised. Or maybe this had made them become closer in an unexpected twist? Maybe something good came out of it after all then?

"And... how does Sven feel about it?" I asked carefully but eager to know. "You have to ask him that yourself, Spence," Sonya said softly. "I know. I just thought..." I sighed as I felt Sonya's hand on my shoulder. "And also, rat, you have to ask him now?" she remarked, encouragingly nodding her head. "Now? Wh... Wha... What?" I felt out of it, bewildered, totally lost. "Yes, now. That's why he was in the car with us. I called him to come with me. I told him that this probably wouldn't take long, and that I would send you to him after our talk," she explained. "But where is he?" I looked around to see if I could see him anywhere. "Not here, my dad dropped him at the park to meet you there." My gaze fixed on Sonya, my eyes stretched open in disbelief of what she just told me. "He's been at the park all his time, waiting for *me*?" I asked and felt immediately bad for Sven. It's been ages since Sonya got here, and it wasn't the warmest of nights either.

"I better get going then!" I got up abruptly and checked my phone. "Ugh," I exclaimed. "What is it?" Sonya asked. "It's going to take me forever to get to the park, and it's already dark, and Sven has already been waiting so long," I said, fidgeting, in a mood of panic and desperation. "Spencer." Sonya came up close, both of her hands on each of my shoulders, she looked me deep in the eyes. "You are a witch, remember?" she said calmingly. And she was right. I smiled at her and gave her a big hug. A hug that lasted longer than she may have wanted, but I wanted to express my gratitude and appreciation for her. I was happy that we had this talk with all of my secrets out in the open, I was grateful that she forgave me for what I did, and I appreciated that she even thought of including Sven in a scenario that I had only anticipated for her. I loved her thoughtfulness. She really was a special person.

Sonya slowly but determinedly pulled herself away from me. As the hug concluded, she briefly lost her balance and took an uncontrolled step backwards. She kicked the shoulder bag behind her, not hard but with enough impact for the bag to fall over. Among the things that fell out was her black notebook. She grabbed it and wiped away some of the dirt that had come onto it. "Do you know what this is?" Sonya held her book up in the air. "Your b-book?" I hesitantly stated the obvious. "Yes, my book. But do you know what it is for?" she asked as if I could have any clue whatsoever. I didn't. I really had no idea. It could have been anything. I shrugged my shoulders. "I have this book to write down every time you got hurt, every time you got bullied, annoyed or ambushed. Every single time." She skimmed through the book to show me full pages of words and drawings. Wow! That was a lot of pages, making me realise just how often I faced those tough moments. Seeing Sonya's book was eye-opening.

And Sonya has been by my side through all of that. She was there for the ride, no matter how bumpy it got. A fresh wave of gratitude entered my soul, I wanted to hug her again. "And not just that, I also wrote down who did it to you. Well, mostly Robbie, let's be honest." She stopped for a moment and browsed through the page towards the end of her book. "Oh, and I wrote how I could hurt them," she concluded as she showed me drawings of axes and hammers. She stood still and stared at me, stone-cold serious - until her expression brightened and she laughed out loud. So loud that the echo of the hollow tree joined in. It almost made it sound evil, which made it even more hilarious. "Hahahaha," I cackled as I looked at her admiringly, and I thought, "Wow, Sonya really did give a rat's."

"But enough now, Spence, you gotta go and meet your Sven," Sonya eventually said. "*My* Sven?" I asked innocently. Sonya blinked at me playfully. "Go, rat, go," she urged me. "Okay, okay, you're right. I'm going." I stood in front of the hollow tree, facing Sonya. I threw her a wink before I took a deep breath, closed my eyes and intently expressed:

"Sparkle sparkle, spark the dark. Sparkle sparkle, in the park."

Lights. Tingles. Whoosh.

As I spoke the words, it dawned on me that this was the first time I had used a spell as an open witch to Sonya. It was the first time I didn't have to hide it from her, thanks to our talk that felt like a big coming out. We came out to each other. We came out about things we didn't know about each other. We pushed aside all secrets, and now, we were back on the same page again. I knew who she was, and she knew who I was. Unveiled and real. And it felt so good and so liberating.

38. Dark.

Still exhilarated and uplifted about my chat with Sonya, I arrived at the park at the exact spot where I intended to land. I had focused hard on my thoughts, my vision. There was no room for error. The spell had to be perfect. Sven had already been waiting. Sure, I hadn't known that until minutes before but still, the fact remained, Sven had been at the park all this time. I found myself at the bench where Sven and I sat on our first outing together. The natural nook bench, formed by the enormous hugging tree trunk. I thought that this was where Sven would wait. But nobody was there. *Sven* wasn't there. I checked the time on my phone. "Shit," I whispered. It was almost 10pm. He left. I was sure of that. I looked around and slowly spun in a circle to scan every corner, to see if I could detect any movement, any sign of Sven. But I couldn't. The dim park lights shone on the lake, giving it a somewhat eerie and melancholic vibe. A vibe, a feeling that transcended into my body. I wasn't a fan of the dark, especially not when I was by myself. I loved being by myself, sure. But alone in the dark, that was creepy to me. Spooky. It made me feel uncomfortable and uneasy. This was what I felt in that moment. Uneasy, uncomfortable, afraid. Not just because it was dark, but also because I had missed Sven. I had missed the opportunity to finally speak to him, to finally explain myself. An opportunity that Sonya arranged for me. And I blew it. Again.

Deflated, I sat down on the nook bench, giving in to the melancholy of the lake that crawled over me like a shroud of sadness. I hunched over and buried my face in my hands. I felt exhausted, defeated. Thoughts whirled around in my head. Thoughts like "I should have been here earlier." Thoughts like "I had my chance and I fucked it up." Thoughts like "How am I going to get to Sven now?" The euphoric high that I came here on wore off as quickly as it came. It didn't last. It didn't continue with Sven. Instead, it came crashing down. I was sad and I wanted to cry but no tears would come. I just whimpered, still hunched over and my face still buried in my hands. I looked through my fingers, staring at the ground, remembering the day I took that first stroll with Sven. Just as I felt my eyes grow heavy with emotion, the park lights introduced a looming presence, a shadow on the sandy gravel. Through the gaps between my fingers, I could see it moving towards me, advancing steadily, slowly growing larger, gradually gaining shape. The shadow eventually blocked the shine of the park lights as it continued to come at me… until it covered my whole body. It stopped right in front of me. My eyes were still pointed down as black Converse filled my sight. And what was that smell? Was that … hot… choccy? I finally looked up and saw Sven standing in front of me, with a takeaway cup in his right hand. "Hey," he said.

"Oh hi." I tried to snap out of my pensive state as quickly as I could. I didn't want Sven to see me upset. This was not the time. The meeting was not about me. Well, of course, technically, it was also about me - but it was more about him and his feelings. Either way, I didn't want to take centre stage or play the victim since Sven was the one who fell victim to my insincerity. "I… I see you got yourself a hot choccy?!" Just like on our first date at the park, Sven went to 'Dairing'. Between Thursday and Saturday, they opened late for dinner service. I only knew that because Mum went there sometimes with Aunt Ruth and Uncle Hector but I never joined. So Sven went there again, but this time, he only got himself a drink. "Yep," he replied and took a big sip. "I was feeling a bit chilly." That made total sense. It must have been quite annoying to wait here this long, not knowing when or if I was even going to come. In that way, we were similar. I didn't know that he was waiting, and he didn't know if I was coming. The communication could have been better, definitely. But considering there was no communication at all for some time, I was happy that we got to that point, one way or another, no matter how. What did matter was that I was here now and Sven was here now. That was a big progress.

Sven raised the cup back towards his lips, going in for another satisfying mouthful. He visibly savoured every sip, making it look irresistible… and making me want one too. But I couldn't expect him to get me one this time. These were very different circumstances. And this moment was an obvious indicator for that. Of course, I would have loved nothing more than the simple gesture of getting a hot choccy. Sure, it would have meant that I had to deal with another undrinkable dairy choccy but hey, I would have taken that any day. It would have made the conversation a lot easier to start with. But… there I was, without a cup in my hand.

"Do… you want to sit?" I asked carefully and pointed next to me. Sven glanced at the spot of the bench where he sat once before. "No, let's walk a bit. It's getting cold." He was right. The chill in the air definitely increased. A bit of movement was going to do us both some good. "Okay, let's… let's walk then." I got up and looked over to Sven who was staring straight ahead. I nervously crossed my arms as we started walking. "Sooo," I tried to break the silence between us with a familiar phrase, an expression that had worked so well for us in the past, one that led to a fruitful back and forth dialogue. Despite the different conditions, my hope was that it could be the same even now, and that we could build on that. "Sooo," Sven retorted, initially evoking a sense of optimism in me… but didn't follow up with anything else. Well, okay, so it didn't quite go as I had hoped and intended. And fair enough. I had to do better than that. I had to make the first move to get the ball rolling, and not just with a lame 'sooo'. "Sooo, umm…" I still felt I wanted to use it though. "Umm, I think… I mean, I… I know," I stuttered my way through a conversation that I had practiced in my head so often but now struggled to even start. "I know that I…" I turned to Sven to face him. "I…" I went blank - not just with what I wanted to say but from seeing his piercing green eyes. I missed them. I missed them so much. I missed Sven.

"Why didn't you just tell me," Sven interrupted my stare fest and jumped right in. "I thought we were the same, Spence. I thought we understood each other. I thought we were…" Sven stopped and looked on the ground. "We were what?" I asked softly. I really wanted to know how that sentence finished. "Argh, never mind," Sven dismissed it. "I just thought we were the same," Sven concluded. "Well, we are, Sven, but we are also not. I have wanted so long to be liked by someone like you, by someone who gets me, who's had the same experience, someone who *is* the same. Just as different and weird as me but the same. And we had that going, we were in sync, you and me." I paused and motioned between him and myself. "Yeah, so what changed?" Sven asked impatiently. "Well, how do you tell someone that I am completely different after all?! Completely different on an unimaginable scale. A scale that wasn't on anyone's radar. Not even my own. How do you tell someone who has just accepted me for who I was, and then you yourself realise that you are not who you thought you were. I was not. I was completely different. And that couldn't be easy to understand for you. *I* know because I myself struggled a lot with the New Me. It was an absolute shock to me, Sven. I mean, I wasn't who I thought I was. That thought in itself was so absurd and frightening to me. I was afraid, Sven." I took a deep breath and secretly hoped for Sven to comfort me. But he didn't. He just looked at me, eager to hear more. "I've been wanting to tell you every day. But when I realised that I was… that I *am* so different to you and anyone else, I just didn't want to risk it." Sven stopped walking. "Risk what, Spence? Risk being honest?" Sven intensely exclaimed. "No, Sven, I didn't want to risk losing you. Because this, my sparkles, my magic… that is a whole different thing to anything you and I have known. Well, I know it better now but still," I said, trying to make a subtle joke but I could see it didn't take with Sven who still maintained a concerned face.

"Have you ever used a spell on me?" Sven eventually asked. "Well," I started. "What?" Sven asked intently. "Well, I didn't use a spell on you per se, but on the hot chocolate you got me" I gestured at his cup that he had been sipping from during our walk. "Huh? What?" Sven didn't understand. Of course, he didn't. How could he know. "I… I turned the hot choccy into an oat milk hot chocolate. That's all. Simple spell, simple magic. No big deal," I tried to brush it off. It really didn't seem like a big thing to me. It was just a white lie. "You could have just told me that you didn't want it. You couldn't even tell me that?" He raised his eyebrows and shrugged. "You could have just been honest, Spence." His voice matched the expression on his face. Both were filled with crushing disappointment. "Well, I… I wanted it and I loved that you got me one but I didn't want to ruin the moment or hurt your feelings by not drinking it, so I decided to do a small spell." Sven didn't say anything. "And we had a good day, didn't we?" I asked, hoping he could shift his focus and remember all the fun we had that day. And all the fun following that day. Sven remained silent with no further reaction. He just stayed quiet, and adrift.

All that time, we had been walking aimlessly without any sense of direction. It was like our bodies and our minds had their own separate lives. While our minds were occupied, reflecting on the intense talk Sven and I had, our feet were in charge of the route through the dim-lit park. We kept walking in silence. I glimpsed over to Sven a few times, quiet, disengaged. I didn't know what else to say, so I said nothing more. We just moved along side by side, with an awkward tension hanging between us. Until our minds ultimately became aware of the route our feet had chosen. Bright lights glowed ahead. Not the soft glow of the park, but the harsh glare of the street. We realised that we had wandered all the way back to the entrance of the park. As we approached the large steel gate, I scraped all my courage together.

"What... what are we going to do, Sven?" I wanted to hold him so badly. I wanted to feel his warmth. I slowly reached out to touch his left hand but before I could even make contact, Sven took a step back. "I don't know, Spence. I... I still need some time," he said. "How much time will you need? When can we be friends again?" I knew I sounded impatient and incredibly desperate. And I was. I was desperate. I missed Sven so much. "I don't know Spence, I just need a bit more time. I'll see you." Sven turned around and started walking away from me. Large steps ensured a steadily increasing distance between us. I watched his body, his silhouette, his shadow slowly grow smaller, gradually dissolving into a hazy shape... until I yelled out to him.

"Bald!?"

Sven suddenly stopped. "Yes, he heard me," I thought as I felt my chest tighten up. I couldn't see his face but he stopped. I breathed heavily, my eyes fixed on Sven's broad shoulders. He still didn't move. I felt anxious. And I felt empty. I felt I had tried everything I could to resurrect our friendship. And this was my final attempt to get a new lifeline with him. Another familiar expression between us - and still the only German word I knew. A word over which our first real conversation thrived, a word that ignited a coquette banter, right here in the park. I remembered that day like it was yesterday. And being in the park like we were then made the word even more significant and meaningful. I would have done anything to be back there, to be back where it all began, to be where we first got to know each other. I would have done things differently. And sure, I knew very well that I could have gone back in time to do just that. Easily. All I had to do was activate my sparkles. But I didn't. I didn't want to do that. I didn't because I made a mistake and I needed to deal with that in the present. I knew that the solution was not to go back in time, I had to fix it in the here and now. Yes, I was a witch but I was also still human. And being human evidently meant to make mistakes. Lots of them. So did I want to go back in time every time I made a mistake? Absolutely not. It just wasn't the way to do it. It felt wrong. Mistakes were a part of life, necessary for development and growth. And I still had a lot of growing to do. Even if I did go back in time to alter events, who knew what the situation would have turned into?! It could have even worsened it. This thing with Sven was too precious to me, it mattered too much to play around with a kind of magic that I didn't even entirely understand yet myself.

So there I was, simply me, raw and without any sparkles magic, yelling out to Sven. My chest was still tight. My eyes were still fixed on Sven in anticipation. He still had his back to me. He just stood there. Those seconds felt like an eternity. He eventually moved his head to the side but the rest of his body stayed motionless. I could see the profile of his face. His perfect nose peeked out from behind his chin-long hair. He held his face in stillness. "Soon," he muttered in a soft voice before he slowly brought his head back forward and continued walking ahead. Hmm, soon? He replied with "soon"? My chest felt like it was going to burst. The fact that he didn't reply in German was daunting. But I decided to look at the positive... at least he did reply. At least, he chose not to be silent altogether. At least, he gave me an answer. An answer that was just as vague as it was ensuring. Soon.

Soon - a word I thought about so often. It was always *soon* that I wanted the school day to be over, to be away from Robbie and his minions. It was always *soon* that I wanted to get back home to my space of comfort and safety. And it was always *soon* that I hoped that everything will be over, all the mocking, all the emotional struggle, all the bullying. Just like then, *soon* couldn't come soon enough now. I wanted *soon* to be now. I wanted to have my friend back. I wanted to have Sven back. Not soon but now! But Sven still needed time, and I had to give it to him. If I knew one thing, it was this: *Soon* was always a beacon of hope. *Soon* was a light in the distance that would eventually cover the darkness with its radiant gleam. *Soon* was always near, and yet so far away. But just like I did then, I needed to hold on to it now. That hope, that light. That *soon*.

"Bald!" I whispered to myself, manifesting, as I watched the distance devour Sven, until only darkness remained.

39. Usual.

The next day, I took the bus to school as usual. Robbie, Zac, Mike and Benji sat at the back of the bus as usual. Eddie with his German cap sang along to Fun FM - without a care in the world - as usual. Adrian hid behind his phone as usual. But what was different was that I often sat next to Adrian now. We didn't chat that much but it was enough to make the ride to school a lot more pleasant. What also changed was that Robbie didn't ridicule me, at least not during the bus trip. It was obvious that Adrian and I formed this new connection, and Robbie saw that. Which meant that Adrian's immunity to Robbie's bullying seemingly extended to me. That was a refreshing change, and it was my new usual.

When we got off the bus, I waved Eddie goodbye as I made my way to the bike stands where Sonya waited for me with a comforting smile. Like she did so often before. As usual. She looked at me with her slightly whitened face and black makeup. I smiled back and walked over to her. Excited to see her. Excited to be with her. I had called Sonya after meeting Sven and told her everything about it. Whilst I was devastated about the outcome with Sven, I was also happy. Happy that I had Sonya back. I was happy that I could talk with her again. About anything and everything. Normally. Openly. Like we did before. As usual.

Sonya put her arm around me and gave me a frisky squeeze before we headed towards the school. With our steps in perfect harmony, we marched, then skipped, then stopped as we arrived at the entrance. Through the glass door, we could see Sven, his head immersed in a book, walking upstairs to our classroom. My eyes glued to Sven. Sonya gently bumped her hips against mine. "Are you okay, rat?" She knew how much I suffered, how much I wanted this to be resolved. I lingered in silence as I watched Sven take the last steps of the stairs until he reached the top. "He will understand, Spence. He will come to you when he is ready," she said consolably. "Will he?" I had doubts. "He said 'soon', didn't he?" Sonya reminded me. "Yeah, I guess so." I sighed. I knew I had to give him the space that he asked for but it was agony for me.

It was agony that on one side of my table in class, I had Sonya, reunited and content, but on the other side of the table, there was Sven. He was so close, yet he was as far away from me as ever. "Hi Sven," Sonya yelled out to him, trying to get a conversation rolling. He glanced her way, and while he clearly saw me sitting next to her, he forced himself to only look at Sonya. "Hiya," he said briefly and turned his attention back to his book. "Uh, hi, did you get home okay last night?" I tried my luck to spark a chat, though immediately after I said it, I wished I had come up with something better. Like "What are you reading?" or even just a simple "How are you?". Instead, I sounded like a concerned parent. "Yes," Sven answered without acknowledging me. "Ah, good... that... that's good," I said awkwardly. I looked over to Sonya who winked at me softly as she encouragingly touched my elbow with hers.

"Good morning, everyone." Mrs Anderson walked inside the classroom. A smile on her face and a spring in her step. As usual. I was always engaged in her lessons, always. But today, I struggled to concentrate. I found myself staring at Sven's broad shoulders, his chin-long blonde hair, his long eyelashes blinking in intervals. I was absorbed in my thoughts. In a world where Sven and I went to the cinema and shared a big bag of popcorn. In a world where we bowled all night because it gave Sven such joy. In a world where we once were together. "Spencer," I heard a voice echoing from the distance. "Spencer," I heard it again, this time more present. I started to focus. I lightly shook my head. Mrs Anderson was looking at me expectantly. And so was the rest of the class. I saw Robbie and his minions whisper to each other, chuckling into their hands. I felt my face turn red. I felt vulnerable, I felt caught off guard, put on the spot, I felt… embarrassed. A usual kind of situation.

"I… I'm sorry, Mrs Anderson, could you… could you please repeat the question?" I cleared my throat in discomfort. "I asked, what do you think of the dynamics of Ron, Hermione and Harry?" Mrs Anderson asked gently and patiently. "Oh, I… umm…" I looked down at my desk, then I glimpsed to Sonya, then to Sven, who still didn't look at me. "I think that…" I looked back to Sven, so badly wanting him to look at me. "I think they… they have a good friendship," I spat out at last but stopped without elaborating, staring on my desk at nothing in particular. "Okaaay," Mrs Anderson sounded underwhelmed and a little disappointed, "does someone else want to share their opinion?" She scanned the room for any volunteers. Nobody raised their hands. Everyone tried to avoid Mrs Anderson's assessing eyes.

"They… they have a good friendship but it's not perfect," I finally blurted out. Mrs Anderson turned back to me. "Why do you say that, Spencer?" she wanted to know. "Well, first of all, I don't even know if there is such a thing as a perfect friendship at all. I don't think there is, because we…" I tapped on my chest with the palms of both my hands. "…we as humans are not perfect. Some people think we are, but we are just not. And just like us, the friendship between Ron, Hermione and Harry isn't perfect," I concluded. "Can you give us an example?" Mrs Anderson continued the conversation, ostensibly interested in what I had to say. "Well, Harry lies to them. He is a liar." I realised this sounded harsh, but it was true. "How does he lie to them, Spencer?" Mrs Anderson asked. "He… he was hiding a part of himself. He was hiding the pain in his scar, and he was hiding the fact that he can speak Parseltongue," I reviewed. "But is hiding something the same as lying to someone?" Mrs Anderson dug deeper. "Well, yeah. If you don't tell your friends who you really are, then you are lying to them." I looked down, feeling uneasy, feeling… guilty. "And why do you think he lied to them, Spencer?" I still stared down as Mrs Anderson asked her question. "He lied because he wanted to protect Ron and Hermione. He didn't know what this new part of him was, he hadn't figured it out for himself yet, and so he kept it quiet. He was confused, he was scared, he didn't know what was happening. So he wanted to make sure he knows himself better first before he could reveal his secrets to his friends. He didn't want to worry them, he didn't want them to think he was strange or even dangerous. He just wanted to belong and be friends with them, so he kept it to himself." I slowly lifted my head and saw Sven, not his back, not his side but his full face. His eyes met mine. For a moment, his piercing green eyes engaged with mine. A sensation arose. That funny feeling. Its electricity ran through my veins and into my stomach. That funny feeling. This feeling… this moment, though just short, wrapped itself around forever.

The bell rang and burst my thought bubble, ripping me out of that moment with Sven who immediately looked back on his book and nervously played with his pen. The class got up and started talking loudly as Mrs Anderson tried to cut through the noise. "In conclusion," she started, clapping her hands to enforce a final moment of focus, "in conclusion, lies are bad but if you have good intentions, maybe... just maybe they can be justified. But remember," she emphasised, "letting people into your world with honesty and vulnerability, no matter how chaotic or turbulent or scary - that's the best basis and as close as it can get to a perfect friendship." She halted, her eyes wandering around the class. As my gaze followed hers, I spotted Robbie, looking serious and contemplative. The pause persisted, almost dramatically, until Mrs Anderson finally spoke, "Now off you go, you lot, enjoy your break." The rumbling chatter noise reignited as Robbie, quickly back to his usual self, was the first to exit the room, together with his minions, in familiar alpha male fashion. Loud and obnoxious. As usual.

40. Nest.

Sonya and I decided to take a stroll around the school grounds while eating our sandwiches. It was a gorgeous day, sunny with a light breeze. So we wanted to soak that up a bit. We walked past the outdoor basketball court and down the almost quaint back path with stone benches and a blooming flower bed before we got to the lunch table area. That was when we saw Robbie and his minions harassing a family of sparrows that had woven a nest within the sturdy branches of the tree. The same tree that Adrian and I sat behind. "Typical," I thought, "just so typical Robbie." Apparently, it didn't matter who or what to torment. As long as he could pick on someone, even animals. Unfortunately, I had noticed that often, way too often. Not just with Robbie but other people as well. They thought it was okay to annoy animals just because they were supposedly more inferior. Just because they were animals, it was okay for people to disturb them, to disrupt and ruin their lives, to bully them. I knew early that bullying had a wide spectrum. And bullies had all sorts of reasons - or excuses.

Well, in Robbie's case, I knew where his behaviour came from. But still, I was gobsmacked that he continued to do it and even extended his prey to animals. I found it unbelievable that he couldn't see anything wrong in his actions when he experienced this himself at home. And if Adrian also witnessed Robbie's strained relationship with his father, then obviously, what I saw that one night wasn't an isolated incident. So how could Robbie not see it? Or maybe he didn't *want* to see? Maybe he believed that if he went through pain, others had to as well? In any case, whatever the motivation, it didn't mean that it was justified.

Robbie had a big stick in his hand and waved it underneath the nest, unable to actually reach it. He stood on his toes but he was too short to even get close to touching the nest. Mike, Zac and Benji stood around Robbie in a half-circle and watched. "Give me a piggyback," Robbie ordered Mike who immediately jumped and offered his back. We walked towards the tree as Robbie climbed on Mike's shoulders. I looked at Sonya, a cheeky glint in my eye. "Should I?" She almost choked on her sandwich as she began to chuckle. "Oh my God, Spence, yes. Please do. I dare you." I smiled mischievously and didn't waste another second... "Sparkle sparkle, stick to score. Sparkle sparkle, in his fore."

Lights. Tingles. Whoosh.

Out of the corner of my eye, I caught Sonya watching me in wonder, captivated by the magic of my freckles, before she saw the outcome of my spell unfold. The stick, which Robbie continued to wave around underneath the sparrow nest, suddenly took charge, swirling through the air, away from the nest, until it mildly but effectively hit Robbie on his forehead. "Ouch," Robbie exclaimed as he tried to regain control over the stick. Sonya and I shared a glee-filled look as we approached Robbie and his minions.

"Hey Robbie, stop being such a dick," Sonya shouted. Robbie pivoted, revealing his agitated face. "Why do you care, weirdo?" He spun the other way, tending to the nest of sparrows again. "I care because these animals didn't do anything to you, so just leave them alone." Sonya paused briefly before she stated, "and by the way, Robbie, if it wasn't for Spencer, you wouldn't even be here right now, looking like an idiot on your buddy's shoulders?" Robbie whipped back around. "What are you on about?" he said with a touch of boredom. "Oh, have you forgotten?" Sonya put her hands in her hips, her eyebrows halfway to orbit. "What?" Robbie's annoyance at Sonya grew. "The national park!?" Sonya said, equally irritated at Robbie and his ignorance. "What about it? Get to the point! I'm busy, can't you see?" Robbie said while Mike appeared to struggle to hold him up. "You fell off the cliff, yeah?" Sonya tried to refresh Robbie's memory. "Yeah, so?" Robbie said less annoyed, almost quiet and uncomfortable. I wondered if he had told his minions about that day. I had a feeling that he didn't. "And how did you not actually fall into the gorge?" Sonya asked. "Well, I managed to get my balance back," he replied with simulated confidence. Sonya looked at me before she said, "Bullshit, do you know what really happened?" She tilted her head with a sly smile, letting the question hang. Robbie craned his neck forward, curious to get Sonya's explanation. "Spencer pulled you back up. He saved your bloody life. Without Spencer, you'd be dead. Plain and simple. You'd be toast, Robbie. Dead toast." Robbie shot Benji and Zac an amused look. "Stop lying, goth girl." Robbie was convinced Sonya was just trying to throw him off, distract him, get him to stop harassing the birds. He laughed, and his minions joined it. But then, some doubt crept in. "Is that true, Penny?" he addressed me casually, pretending not to be interested in my answer. "Um, first of all, my name is Spencer, Robert. And second of all, I did grab you and stop you from falling. Yes, that's true. It was me, not you," I said with conviction while staring at Robbie with serious and confronting eyes. I wasn't going to back away from this. Not again. Not anymore.

"Let me down, Mike." Robbie climbed down from Mike's shoulders as he came to stand right in front of me. Robbie's face became red, quickly filling with intensifying fury. "Don't... call... me... Robert," he said slowly and firmly, with undermined aggression, on the brink of exploding. He noticed the steadiness in my eyes, unimpressed and persevered. Pearls of sweat appeared on his forehead as he started to realise the severity of the situation that he had escaped at the national park. "Just... Just piss off." I wasn't surprised about his reaction. That was just typical Robbie. Yet again. Ignorant, dismissive, rude, unappreciative. He turned to his minions. "Let's go, boys." They strutted away from the tree, leaving the sparrow's nest behind. Though he neither directly acknowledged what happened, nor saw any need to question it, Robbie's retreat was a gesture of defeat, a silent concession. He didn't want to argue, he didn't want to fight this one. Because deep down, he knew... He realised that *I* saved his life. Of all people, it was *me*. The person he called names, the person he made fun of.

As we watched Robbie and his minions go back into the school building, Sonya turned to me. "Well done, rat. You've done so well, standing up to Robbie like that," she said proudly. "No, no, you... you..." I repeatedly pointed at her, so excited that I was actually lost for words. "Well, I told you," Sonya said, "I always imagined ways to punish people for what they did to you." Sonya glanced at her black book that was peeking out from her backpack. "Yes, so?" I scratched my head. "Well, I just did that. I punished Robbie," she gushed and took my hand. "*We* punished Robbie!" she accentuated. "You did? We... did?" I asked hesitantly. "Yes, we did..." She looked at me, my features displaying the bewilderment I felt. "Don't you see, we showed him that he is not the one who's always in control but actually had to rely on someone else to help him. We showed him - and his buddies - that he's not the hot shit he pretends to be. And that's punishment enough for Robbie," she said with a satisfied grin. A joining smile pushed aside the confusion on my face. I had a bad conscience though. Should I be smiling with everything that was going on at Robbie's home? I felt bad for him. So I was a bit torn, unsure how to act, how to feel. Although ultimately, Sonya was right. No matter what his situation was, he still chose to be this way. He still chose to be a bully.

But we stood against him, together. We showed him, and there was no denying - it did feel good. We protected the nest. And not just the nest of the birds, but we also protected and strengthened the nest of our friendship.

41. Fight.

It had been about a week since I met with Sonya at the hollow tree, since we got our friendship back and picked up where we left off. It was a week of reconnecting, happiness and comfort. But of course, it wasn't all rainbow and roses. Has it ever been? While I loved having Sonya back in my corner, I missed the other person by my side. I missed Sven. He was still very much not ready to talk to me. Apart from that moment, that look we shared in Mrs Anderson's class, there was nothing. Radio silence. And that bothered me. Of course, it did. We used to be so close, we used to share openly about everything. We used to be friends. Maybe we were more than that? Whatever we were - I missed it. I missed *him*. A lot. And that was quite apparent. I didn't even have to talk it out with Sonya, she knew what was up. She knew I was full of regret for not telling Sven the truth. She knew that I was sorry and that I was hurting.

"Can't you speak to him for me?" I asked Sonya. "I did, rat. I did. I tried to get him to talk to you, to understand, to forgive but he didn't want to listen. He was just withdrawn and closed off about it." I appreciated that she tried. "Why do you think he needs so much time?" I asked. "I don't know, Spence. But everyone is different. There is no rule about how much time it takes to get your head around something or to forgive someone. Everyone heals in their own time. And you have to respect that. I mean, how long did it take you to accept the new Spencer Wise?" She had a point. It did take me a while. And not just to accept and understand my freckles, but also to come forward and tell Sonya and Sven. Although technically, I never sat them down to *tell* them, rather than spectacularly showing them my sparkle powers in an unplanned and unexpected way. "I guess I won't be going to the prom with Sven then," I sighed. "Just wait and see, rat, you never know," Sonya tried to cheer me up. "Well, it's this Friday. And he doesn't want to talk to me, so… I think the chances are extremely slim." Slow steps carried me forward, my head bowed down and shoulders dropping, weighed down by a mix of regret and despair.

Sonya remained rooted in place as she watched me slump down the main school corridor. The same one that all students were passing one way or another, coming into school, going out of school, walking to the classrooms. So of course, it was no surprise that the same corridor was the one that heavily advertised the school prom. Colourful streamers, unnecessary balloons, banners and posters with cheesy slogans like 'Show your inner dancing queen' and 'Don't you wanna dance?', both supported by a pointing finger at the onlooker. Okay, maybe they were not so much cheesy than they were obnoxious. It felt like they were rubbing it in my face. Of course, I wanted to let out my inner dancing queen. And of course, I wanted to dance with somebody. But that somebody wasn't available, he was unreachable. Untouchable. So walking down that corridor could have been really fun and built up a thrilling anticipation for the event, had the situation been different. But instead, I found myself moping, desperately trying to avoid the sight of the decorations.

I kept on walking until a hand grabbed my right shoulder and turned me around forcefully. I gasped. "Come on, Spence, snap out of it!" Sonya's facial expression was a mixture of frustrated and motivating. I looked at her with a half-open mouth, unable to produce any words to come out of it. "You have survived Robbie, you have survived the challenges of your sparkles, you have survived our tumbles. You have proved that you're resilient and that you are a fighter. Now, go rat, fight for Sven," she encouraged me. "But... you just said I have to respect..." I said as Sonya cut in. "Yes, yes, respect his time and his wishes. Bla bla. Of course. But Sven needs to snap out of it too, and there is no harm in trying to speed it up a little. I mean, the prom is on Friday. How badly do you want this?" she asked, though it was more of a rhetorical question. She knew exactly. And I liked her vivaciousness but... I was confused. "And how do you propose I should do that though?" I was hoping that Sonya had a plan to go with her enthusiasm. "That's up to you." An underwhelming response. She put her hands on my shoulder blades. "Spencer. Hey." She looked deep into my eyes as if she was looking at the barrel of my soul. "You can do this. You are Spencer Wise. You can do anything you put your mind to!" She raised her index finger and I thought that she was going for the FTT but just as I flinched to stretch out my index finger, she playfully tapped on my nose. Sonya had so much belief in me. So much more than I ever had in myself. She was always my biggest cheerleader, trying to get the best out of me, wanting me to be happy. And now, I had to fight for that. I had to fight to be happy. I had to fight to get Sven back.

Sonya was right, I couldn't just take a backseat and wait. I had to be proactive. I felt determination rise up from the centre of my core. Determination like I have never felt. I knew I had a goal, and I knew I wanted to get there. I didn't quite know how but I did know that I didn't want this to be another Henry Miller moment. I didn't want to be pushed away again for who I was. I didn't want to lose Sven. Not now, not ever. I wanted his piercing green eyes back in my life. I wanted that funny feeling back in my stomach. I wanted to glide down that school corridor with Sven like the swans effortlessly glided across the lake at the park.

A bright smile blossomed on my face as an idea entered my head. I directed the smile at Sonya. She smiled back curiously. I put my arm around her shoulder, she put her arm around my waist as we sashayed down the rest of the corridor together, our eyes welcoming, inviting, open for all the colourful streamers, all the unnecessary balloons, and all the banners and posters with the cheesy - or encouraging - slogans.

42. Long-lost.

Once I got home from school, I took off my shoes and jacket and went straight up to my room, past the open kitchen door. "Spencer, lunch is ready," mum called after me when she spotted me passing. She had clearly been waiting for me to come home and have lunch together. It did smell delicious, too, but I couldn't eat now. I was on a mission, and I had no time to waste. "Sorry, mum. I will eat it later," I yelled down from my room. I was about to close the door when I opened it again, sticking my head out slightly, calling out, "Thanks for cooking, mum. I love you." I knew that mum was probably a little disappointed that I didn't join her for lunch like I normally did. So I wanted to at least make sure she knew that I valued her. So much. I was sure she knew anyway, but it couldn't hurt to mention. She did so much for me, always, and I didn't want that to go unappreciated.

I saw mum come to the stairs and look up at me. She wore a pair of red oven mitts which complemented the red apron that said 'Don't be afraid to take whisks'. She kissed the top of the right glove, flattened her hand, palm up, and blew me a kiss. "I love you, too," she uttered tenderly with a warm smile before she turned back into the kitchen. Mum didn't ask why I didn't want to eat, she didn't question it. She knew I would have had a good reason. She gave me the space and freedom that I needed. Mum respected my privacy and my needs, knowing that I wasn't a young child anymore. She didn't have to mother me as much, even though I was certain that she wanted to. "You can always come to me. I'm always here," she often said, letting me decide when I needed more mothering, or simply an open ear for what I wanted to share with her. And I was definitely going to tell her all about my motivation to skip lunch. Later.

I slowly shut the door and pushed against it with my backside to ensure it was closed properly. As I leaned against the door, it revealed the object of my plan. My guitar in the corner. The same guitar I put behind the door after the ordeal with Henry Miller. Though I often forgot that it was even there, in a strange way, it always called for me. It always asked to be let back into my life, because it knew that it was meant to be a part of it. It was a part of *me*. While deep down I knew that this was true, I ignored the calls. I wasn't ready. I often caught a glimpse of my guitar, patiently waiting behind the door, always hoping that I would give it any kind of attention. Anything at all. But I never did. Until now.

Still leaning against the door with my back, I took a large step to the left, grabbing the neck of the guitar in haste. It was like ripping off a bandaid. Once you had done it, you couldn't go back. For me, it was the same with the guitar. Once I engaged with it, I knew I couldn't back out again. The sudden moving of the guitar caused a gust of dust to whirl into my face. I coughed, wrestling for some clean air. "Man, I really did neglect you," I whispered as I carefully wiped off the mount of dust on the strings. I was overcome with a feeling of familiarity, a feeling of longing but also a feeling of disappointment and pain. This guitar meant so much to me, even though it held memories that I would have rather deleted altogether. But this wasn't how it worked. I couldn't delete memories, just because I didn't like them. All my memories, good and bad, were who made me who I was. They made me *me*. They were *my* memories. My... scars.

Just like I decided I wouldn't use my sparkles to go back in time to alter certain events, I didn't want to erase any of those painful recollections. Yes, they were unbearable at times. I wanted to forget all about them, and yet, here I was. Standing in my room, holding my long-lost guitar. The very guitar that reminded me of that pain, of that disappointment. But... Sven brought me back to it. I needed it. More than ever. If I wanted to get Sven back, I had to get myself back, every part of myself, *all* of myself. And my guitar was the last piece of the puzzle. The puzzle called life. My life. And it was up to me to try and outweigh those memories of agony with memories of hope and joy.

43. Ready.

Friday was here. Not just any ordinary Friday. *The* Friday. The Friday of the school prom. It came around so quickly. Yet, it couldn't have come fast enough. The corridor decorations were a daily motivator and reminder of what I was planning for, what I was hoping for. It was exciting and terrifying at the same time. There were so many questions waving around in my head, and a good amount of doubt to go with them. However, I tried to block out the negative thoughts and emotions and look ahead, focus, and just do. I still hadn't spoken to Sven, though I kept trying to catch his attention whenever I saw an opportunity. In class, in Mr

Moore's sports lessons, in the lunch break area. Every time I went up to him, he turned his back and walked the other way. Sonya also approached Sven a few times but without any changes in his demeanour. "So it all comes down to this?" she asked me when we stood by the bike racks in front of the school. "It sure does," I said as I exhaled deeply. "You've got this, rat!" With a reassuring pat on my back, she passed on a silent kind of belief - steady and unwavering. "You've got this," she repeated in a softer voice as she stretched out her index finger. "FTT," she said. "FTT," I replied, filled with increasing comfort and decreasing anxiety.

I didn't even know if Sven was planning on going to the prom. I heard Robbie and Benji ask him one day during sports, but Sven only shrugged his shoulders. It wasn't a definite sign that he was going to go, but it also wasn't a definite sign that he wasn't. I could work with that. But then of course, there was the question if he would go with *me*. Even if we did talk again and were still the friends we were before, would he have wanted to go with me at all? And if so, would we have gone as friends, perhaps together with Sonya, or would we have gone as more than friends? The questions churned inside my head like a cyclone without a pause. But every time my thoughts were about to get the better of me, I stepped on the break, took a deep breath and visualised what I set out to do.

The sun started to set, the scarf of the night fell from the sky and slowly wrapped itself around every corner of the town. It turned out to be a crystal clear evening with the infinite orchestra of the stars high above, glistening as bright as ever. I just came out of the shower and sat on my bed, with a large white towel draped around my shoulders. I rubbed it through my damp hair when a chime on my phone announced an incoming message. I tapped on the screen to view it. "You've got this, rat. I'll see you there." No matter how this was going to go, I knew I always had Sonya by my side. Literally and emotionally. At least I had her.

I put the phone on my bedside table and finished drying my hair. "Now, what to wear?" I was so preoccupied with my guitar that I didn't spare a single thought on my outfit. I went to my wardrobe and skimmed through all my clothes. Long-sleeve shirts, short-sleeve shirts, collared shirts, sweatpants, my two pair of jeans, one dark-blue suit that I wore once to Grandma Rose and Grandpa Doug's 50th wedding anniversary. And it wasn't really my kind of suit. Mum bought it for me and I wore it. It was nice, and I liked the colour, but it wasn't me. The shape was just completely off. I went through all of my clothes one more time, but nothing. Nothing stood out. Nothing screamed 'I have to wear this'. Nothing. I went back to my bed and exhaled, releasing a sound somewhere between a sigh and a raspberry. I rhythmically slapped on my thighs, trying to ease my rising anxiety levels. My eyes wandered aimlessly through my room until they got pinned on a photo on the wall near the door. I got up from the bed and walked up to it. It was a picture that Sven and I took in the park. A selfie by the lake. I stuck it by the door, so that every time I left my room, I would pass it and be reminded of that very first date with Sven. No matter how I felt on any given day, the photo always lifted me, put a smile on my face - without fail. I cherished that photo, and I cherished that day at the park and everything that bloomed after that. Every predictable bowling game. Every hilarious movie night. Every moment of comfortable silence. Every unexpected thing.

I stared at the picture and revelled in reflection. Until something caught my eye. Something that I hadn't noticed before. Something in the background of the photo. What was that? I took it off the wall and held it right up to my nose, squinting my eyes to get a sharper look. "Is that...?!" I softly said. I held my breath for a few seconds. I didn't move, I froze. Only my eyes were operating a continuous gaze at the background of the selfie. As the details of the scene entered my mind, a relieved smirk settled on my face. I turned around with my back to the wall, the picture resting on my chest in both of my hands. "Yes." I exclaimed contently. "Yes!" I put the selfie back on the wall and looked at it again, enjoying the wholeness of the moment that was captured. A wholeness that I only now discovered. I touched the photo placidly with my fingertips as if I was stroking someone's soft cheeks. A brighter smile emerged.

Excited, I jumped into the centre of my room. I rubbed my hands together. I knew what to do. I closed my eyes, took a deep breath and focused on the vision in my head. I concentrated strenuously, my temples were throbbing. I wanted to get it right. No more thyme time, no more moth legs. I submerged in the underground of my mind as I searched - and found - the words for my spell. "Sparkle sparkle, get me dressed. Sparkle sparkle, with finesse." A second passed. I kept my eyes shut, I didn't check what I looked like. I didn't want to, and I didn't have to. I had trust. Trust in myself. Trust in my abilities. Trust in my vision. A vision that took more than one spell to realise, so I filled my lungs with another grounding inhale while staying fixated on the image in my head. Then I continued. "Sparkle sparkle, you and me. Sparkle sparkle, with a tee." My face was warming up. It was the familiar feeling that I always experienced when I used my magic sparkles. But this time, it was more present, more vibrant. Warmer than usual. It was like the gentle kiss of the sun, cautiously caressing my skin. It felt different. It felt nice. It felt safe. It felt... right. As my freckles lit up, the rest of my body followed, the tingling sensation running through me. I stood still, my eyes still closed, my arms slightly stretched out, my fingers moving from the tingles within. A faint breeze flew across my face with a few strains of hair dangling over my forehead.

Lights. Tingles. Whoosh.

I was ready to open my eyes. With the feeling of warmth still occupying my body, I turned to the mirror beside my bed. I looked myself up and down, starting from the bottom. My white sneakers. No dirty spots, but clean and shiny. My blue-dotted pink socks from Aunt Ruth. Not hidden but visible for everyone to see, peeking out from the rolled-up light-blue trousers. They were my semi-baggy pants, but they were not baggy anymore. They turned into skinny jeans that proudly highlighted my figure - and personality - instead of hiding it. The jacket I had on was buttoned up over a simple black t-shirt. It was the dark-blue suit jacket from my grandparents' 50th wedding anniversary, but it was a completely different shape that complemented my waist and shoulders. I was in awe. I spun around in the mirror to see all sides of the outfit. I turned left, then all around to my right until I faced myself again from the front. Approvingly, I nodded at my reflection. My eyes moved back to the buttoned up suit jacket. I opened it with both my hands, button by button to show the shirt underneath, like a treasure chest unveiling its hidden gold. I looked at the t-shirt and it put a smile on my face immediately. I couldn't take my eyes off it. It was exactly what I envisioned. It was exactly what I wanted. It was... perfect. My eyes got misty. I felt so happy.

As I wiped away a single tear drop rolling down, I noticed a black box on my bed, tastefully decorated with glitter and a red bow on top. I sat down next to the box and just looked at it for a second. I slowly ran my hand across the smooth box until I lifted it up. It was light, like a pillow. I put it on my lap and opened the lid carefully. When I saw what was inside, all I could do was grin. The grin persisted as I lifted my chin slightly and closed my eyes in gratitude. I took a lungful of air and opened my eyes again. Another deep breath. I closed the box and walked back to the mirror as I buttoned my jacket up again. I brushed over my chest and shoulders while locking eyes with myself. "I am ready," I uttered.

I took a last look in the mirror before I grabbed the black box with one hand and the guitar with the other.

I was ready.

44. Door.

It's been a long time since I walked this way. I had walked it so many times in the past. So many times, I whirled through the neighbouring streets, passing the kindergarten with the half-hollow tree, through little laneways and across the town square with its church tower and merchant houses, each time sparking fond memories of the encounter with Uncle James. I knew this way well, and I always took the same route. I passed my school which eerily stood there empty and quiet. I rigorously ignored its innocent call to give it attention. I didn't want to look at it. While my school experience had certainly improved, that building still housed a lot of pain for me. So I kept walking, forcing myself not to turn my head towards it. I didn't want that energy, tagging along on my way. The way from my house to Sven's house.

As I turned into Watson St, I was always filled with excitement and joy. Arriving at Sven's house always meant that I reached my destination to a fun time, no matter what we planned on doing. This time, however, trepidation was the dominant emotion flowing through my body. Yes, I was ready, and yes, I was excited to be back at Sven's house, but the feeling of worry and anxiety was something I was never quite able to shake off. It was etched into my being, lingering. The contemplation of 'what ifs' didn't always come to the surface, yet it was always there somewhere. But just like any other time when those feelings arose and threatened to take over, every time I had to get ready for school or had to face Robbie and his minions, I tried to focus on my breath. Deep breaths. In and out. In and out, with a smile accompanying every exhale. This unfailingly helped to evict the shackles of doubt.

I stood in front of Sven's house and looked up to his window that was facing the street. His room was lit. He was home. "Okay," I thought to myself, "Let's do this." I went up to the front door and raised my index finger to the door bell. A moment of hesitation prevented me to push it right away. I took a step back. Backing out crossed my mind. Surrendering before I even started, before I even tried. "Ugh," I groaned, shaking off my demons, as I swiftly approached the door and pressed the bell intently. "I did it," I thought. "You can't escape now, Spencer. You can't escape now." I heard footsteps drawing nearer. The door swung open. "Spencer. Hi!" Sven's mother, tall and slim, with blonde hair just like Sven, answered the door. Her kind green eyes looked at me astounded. "I... I didn't know you were coming over..." She was a very organised person and always liked to have a plan for things. She didn't like to feel unprepared in any way. "No, no," I quickly said, "I am so sorry for showing up like this. I... um,... Is Sven home?" She intuitively tilted her head, looking at the stairs that led up to Sven's room. "Y-Yes, he's upstairs. Do you want to go up?" she asked warmly. She was undoubtedly aware of the changes in the friendship between Sven and me. Evidently, I hadn't been at his house for a while. Clearly, she knew something was up. But how much did she know? How much did Sven tell her, if anything at all? "Umm, I think it's better if he could come down?" I asked apprehensively. I didn't think it was a good idea to go up to his room and be stuck there if this didn't go well. I felt it was best to have a neutral terrain to do this. "Sven!" his mum yelled up, "Come down, please. You have a visitor." Maybe she knew that there was a chance he wouldn't come down if she had specifically told him that *I* was the visitor. She smiled at me encouragingly before she walked back into the living room where the TV was still running.

As she shut the door behind her, footsteps echoed from above. I could see the top of the stairs, though the ground floor ceiling blocked most of the view beyond the landing. A tiny gap, however, revealed Sven's shoes coming out of his room and moving towards the stairs. He took the stairs swiftly, and with every step further down, more of his body was exposed. His legs, his hips, his chest and broad shoulders. His movements slowed down as the details of his face gradually unveiled. A moment of tension, of suspense, of nervous stomach tingles. How was he going to react? What would his facial expression tell me? Not much, as it turned out. His face didn't particularly tell me anything, but... I was happy that he didn't go back upstairs the second he saw me standing at his front door. "Hey," I awkwardly said. "Hi," Sven replied as his fingers tucked away his hair behind his ears. "What are you doing here?" Sven asked in a way that was neither confronting and intimidating nor humbled and surprised but interested nonetheless. "I... umm," I stuttered, "I got something for you." I nodded at the black smooth box with the red ribbon on top. "Here." As I handed it to him, Sven opened his arms, almost unwillingly, and received it with an uncertain look. "What is this, Spence? Why are you giving this to me?" I took a step back and looked at the ground, only noticing now that their doormat was different. It used to be a simple black and white one with 'Welcome Home' written on it, but now it was a colourful mat that said 'Home is where the heart is'. Seeing the new doormat encouraged me in my endeavour.

"I... I thought maybe if you wanted to go to the prom,... I mean... umm,... Well, this is from me." I didn't know how to express what I wanted to say. After a brief pause and another glimpse of that doormat, I proceeded. "Sven, I wanted to tell you one more time how truly sorry I am for lying to you. I should have known better. I was scared you wouldn't like me anymore. I was afraid I would lose you, and I let that fear get the better of me. I know I messed up. Of course, I can trust you. Of course, I can tell you anything. I know that now and I knew that then. But I was just too weak to fight against my fears. But that's done now." I took a deep breath. "Now you are not afraid anymore?" Sven asked, some of his hair escaping the ear tuck and falling into his face. "I am scared as hell. Standing in front of you right now scares the shit out of me," I said. "Why?" Sven asked. "Because it makes me realise how much I want you in my life. Sven, I have missed you so much. I miss you every day that we are not friends. I miss you every day that you are not by my side. And..." I pointed at the black box Sven was holding. "Whether you decide to come to the prom tonight or not, I just hope you can forgive me."

"Spencer, I..." Sven seemed lost for words. "I don't know." He shrugged his shoulders. "I don't know if I..." he stopped and looked at the box, and then at me, and then back at the box. He was visually overwhelmed. "It's okay," I tried to comfort him, "You don't have to say anything or decide anything. I just wanted you to listen to what I had to say, and..." I swung my guitar into my right arm. "...as a matter of fact, there is one more thing that I wanted to tell you." This was the moment I had been waiting for. This was the moment I had been skipping lunch for after school. This was the moment I had been practicing for. This was the moment!

As my fingers gently moved over the strings, an emotional shiver washed over me. I took a calming breath until I was quickly transcended into the game of pluck and release, every string eagerly waiting its turn in a series of endless strums, weaving a melody of familiarity and warmth. I strummed, I hummed and I started to sing. "I was born..." I cleared my throat. My voice sounded creaky like a door that needed to be oiled. I cleared my throat one more time and started again, a gentle and harmonic strum across the strings, leading me into the song.

"I was born by the rainbow,
Shaped by the rainbow.
I was shy by the rainbow,
Lost by the rainbow.
I didn't feel free."

I peeked over at Sven. He listened carefully as he put down the black box on the stairs and sat down next to it while keeping his eyes on me.

"Then you came into my life,
Showing me your light, like
The sight of a rainbow,
The feel of a rainbow.
You made me come home."

Sven didn't move one bit. He stared at me, soaking in every word I sang. As I progressed, my voice became steadier and stronger while I felt more and more exposed, more and more vulnerable. It was just me and my song, out in the open, with nowhere to hide. My cheeks were getting hotter and hotter. A slight breeze surrounded my body for a moment. The same breeze travelled inside the house and greeted Sven on the steps before it came back to gift me another refreshing invigoration. A breeze that appeared to encourage our souls to get closer again, to connect again, stimulatingly wrapping itself around both our bodies. It helped me gather the courage to continue singing.

"Home by the rainbow,
Love by the rainbow
When I am with you.
And I hope, I so truly hope
That you feel it too."

I glanced over very briefly, to check Sven's reaction, to check if he received the message of the verse. His body sat more upright than before. His hands rested steady on his knees. But as my eyes met his, his right hand lost its grip and slid off. He awkwardly adjusted the hand as quickly as he could. He smiled nervously at me. I played another chord to complete the bridge, faintly smiling at Sven's sweet clumsiness.

"I was born by the rainbow,
Shaped by the rainbow.
I was shy by the rainbow,
Lost by the rainbow.
But you set me free."

A final stroke of the strings completed the song. A song that I put my heart into. And I was so happy. I did it. I couldn't believe that I just sang for Sven. I had never sang for anyone like this before. Apart from the jam sessions with Henry Miller, I had never really sung in front of anyone. I never considered myself an overly talented singer, though I did enjoy doing solo karaoke in my room every now and again. I liked how singing made me feel. I liked how music in general made me feel. And, I liked how Sven made me feel. So it was only right to combine all of that and reflect it in these personal lines of struggle and comfort and hope and... love.

Love. I hadn't really consciously thought about it until I sat down and started playing around with my guitar. The lyrics just poured out of me, the pen effortlessly leading my hand over the paper. I didn't have to try, I just had to tune in to myself, to my deepest self, and let the words describe what I saw, what I felt. And then my heart, my mind, my hand spelt out the word. Love. I knew it was right. It was genuine. It was real. This was what I saw. This was what I felt. Deep down, I knew that. I felt it all along. How I always wanted to be with him. How I hated when he wasn't around. I wanted a new start. A fresh start. I wanted to share everything with him, openly and honestly. I wanted to share all of me with him. Everything. The good, the bad, the annoying, the magical. Everything of who I was. And I sincerely hoped that this song would convince him of my true intentions.

When I played the final chord, adrenaline flowed through my veins. Excitement and hope and humble expectations. I put the guitar in front of my legs as Sven got up from the stairs. He came towards me, slowly, tentatively. "Spencer, that was…" He sighed, looked down and slightly shook his head in disbelief. His face was difficult to read. Did he hate it? Did I just make a fool of myself? I was freaking out. A moment of silence. Not the kind of comfortable silence I always cherished. It was that kind of silence that hung heavy in the air with jittery apprehension. It was just a short moment but it felt like forever. And it was killing me. But then, finally, I got released from the prison of excruciating silence. "Spencer, that was beautiful. That was… It was… Uh. Thank you." Sven brushed his fingers through his hair. I felt relieved. I wasn't making a fool of myself after all. He liked it. With that feeling of relief, I listened as Sven carried on. "I… I don't know… I really don't know what to say. I… I appreciate it. It was beautiful. Thank you. Really. Thanks for coming all this way to give me this…" He moved his upper body slightly to the side and pointed at the box behind him. As he turned his body back around, he gestured with both palms at me and my guitar. "… and for this," he said, his eyes expressing a mixture of gratitude and helplessness.

Sven was undeniably perplexed. And I didn't blame him for that. After all, I basically ambushed him not only with my sheer presence but with a song that expressed my affection for him, and with an additional present that he hadn't even opened yet. That was surely a lot to take in for him, combined with the still raw and undigested fact that I was a witch. I was aware of that, but I needed to put myself out there. I needed to just go for it and give it all that I got. I needed to fight. And this was my way of fighting for him. I knew what I wanted to do, I knew how I wanted to fight. And I did that. But now, the ball was in Sven's court. I didn't know what I expected or wanted him to say - just something, anything, that would motivate the adrenaline to keep flowing through my body. Anything at all to reignite our friendship and ... that electrifying feeling.

Sven stood in the frame of the front door, uncertain of how to act. "Well," he eventually said, "I better go back inside." I was disappointed. He wanted to go back inside? I just poured my heart out to him and he wanted to go back inside? I was crushed. "Okay," I replied as Sven started to close the door. I knew I didn't expect much, but I certainly didn't expect this. I thought we could at least talk. Why was he being so dismissive? Was it really all that bad? Was it really unrepairable? Sure, I lied to him, and I was definitely not proud of it. But that all felt like a million years ago, though Sonya's voice echoed in my head, reminding me that healing, understanding and forgiveness didn't follow a timeline. Still, I couldn't help but wonder why it was such a big deal to him when it wasn't to Sonya? Why did she forgive me after coming together and talking about it? Why did she and he did not?

The door was almost fully shut, but I could see Sven gander at me through the gap. He didn't slam the door in my face. Instead, he chose to close it slowly. It was almost like he wanted me to stop it. Did he though? He was pretty quick to say he wanted to go back inside. So what did he want? What more could I do? Didn't I do enough? Didn't I just give him everything? Didn't I just lay all my cards on the table? As the door connected with the frame, I suddenly yelled out, "See you at the prom?" The door opened just enough for Sven's face to come into view. He just looked at me. "I'll be there at 8. I... I can meet you at the front?" I said, flashing my eyebrows. "I'd love to see you there." Sven leaned his head against the door. For a second, it was as if his soul had slipped away, leaving him distant, far away, deep in thought - until it returned to his body. "I'll see you at school, Spence. Bye." He waved abruptly as he closed the door. This time, completely. I stood in front of the closed door, my guitar still leaning against my legs. I couldn't shake the feeling that he didn't just close the door to his house, but that he closed the door to *me*, to our friendship, to us. I was devastated. "Bye," I mumbled, deflated, as I half-heartedly waved at the silent door.

45. Stars.

Before I left Watson St, I turned over my shoulder one more time to take a glimpse at Sven's house, fantasising about Sven running after me, romantically acknowledging that he should have reacted differently and that he wanted to be with me, too. But this wasn't another rom-com movie. This was my life. And in accordance with my life, this kind of stuff just didn't happen. I kept walking, further and further away, in the direction of my school. While I didn't end up taking Sven to the prom with me like I hoped, I still wanted to go. Sonya was going to be there, and she was going to wait for me.

I checked my phone. It was 7.30pm. Too early to go to the school hall already, and too late to go back home. I sighed. What was I going to do now? I felt down. Upset. Exhausted. Heartbroken. I just lost a friend. I lost Sven. What I wanted, what I needed was a few quiet moments to myself. But where could I go? I looked around. There was nowhere to sit. No place where people wouldn't pass, and I needed to be away from people for a bit. I needed to be completely alone. "Ugh," I grunted as I raised my head. The stars were twinkling above me, reassuringly, consolingly. Just like the star stickers above my bed, they gave me comfort and strength. "Yes." I nodded at the stars. I knew where I could go. I closed my eyes as I let the magic words unfold. "Sparkle sparkle, up and high. Sparkle sparkle, wanna fly."

Lights. Tingles. Whoosh.

My feet lifted from the ground. I spread my arms left and right, like wings, with my guitar still dangling from my right hand, before I intently pointed my hands to the sky. I zoomed up high quickly, with the soft sound of the wind whispering as I gained altitude. The freshness of the air rippled through my hair. It felt invigorating. I flew around above the town, but I didn't look down. I didn't watch what was happening underneath. I floated on my back with my guitar resting on my chest. I looked up, seeing nothing but the stars. Countless spots of light, distributed across the sky. I loved seeing them, I loved to be around them. A calming effect of relief entered my body. In the air - that was where I could get a better point of view, a clearer mind, away from people, away from troubles, much like I did when I walked in nature among my friends, the trees. The stars, and the trees, were what I could rely on. They were the guidance on my path. In their presence, I could reflect and think.

But what did I think? What did I think of what had just happened? What did I think of Sven's reaction? "I'll see you at school." Of course, he would see me at school, but did he want to go on ignoring me, giving me the cold shoulder? He was sitting right in front of me in class, for goodness' sake. I didn't think I could bare facing him like this every single day, especially not now that I had confessed my heart to him. No reaction at all. Just a "Thank you, that was beautiful". Ugh, I should have just left him alone. I should have just given him whatever time he needed instead of smacking him over the head with a present and a song. Ugh, I was mad at myself. I was mad for acting so stupid. I was mad that I thought that this was okay when really, it was uncalled for. "I should have known better," I thought to myself. I seemed to think that quite often. I should have known better. I should have known better to trust Sonya with my sparkles. I should have known better to tell Sven all about my thoughts and feelings. I should have known better to… leave him be. I should have known better! But what I was left with was exactly what I was left with all the other times when I should have known better.

As I drifted through the night sky, the scene with Sven replayed in my head on repeat. Him coming down the stairs, him receiving the black box so reluctantly that it made me wonder if he ever opened it after I left. Him sitting down on the steps while I played my guitar and sang my song. Him closing the door on me after he said, "I'll see you at school". "I'll see you at school," I kept murmuring. "I'll see you at school." My mind was in a state of daze. Until a single light stepped out of the hovering group of stars and pulled me out of that trance with its bright shine. So bright a shine that I needed to shield my eyes with my arms. It made me wake up and see things in a different light. My eyes opened wide. I had an awakening. "I'll see you at school!" I exclaimed enthusiastically as I snapped my fingers.

Maybe he didn't mean "See you around at school", like "See you next week". Maybe he meant "See you at the prom"? Or did I make that up? Did I just want to find something in Sven's words? Something more, something that wasn't even there? Was I just trying to keep my hopes up, again, for no reason? Or was this an actual possibility? Was Sven going to come to prom? There was only one way to find out. I lit up my phone screen to check the time. It was almost 8pm. If Sven did show up, I couldn't be late. I flipped around in the air to face the world below, moving my body purposefully towards my school. The campus was buzzing with parents, teachers and school kids, so I decided to land in a small alley, a two-minute walk from the school to avoid an unwanted encounter with a passer-by. That was the very last thing I needed now. I focused my eyes on the alley as I mindfully started to descend. Just before I was about to land, I turned my body around in an elegant twist. I winked at that bright-shining star. "Thank you," I breathed out as my feet reunited with the ground.

46. Prom(ise).

I was just about to get going when my legs hit the guitar. I still had it with me. But I couldn't take it to the prom. I looked around helplessly. I couldn't leave it there. While the alley had little foot traffic, I didn't want to risk losing it. It meant too much to me, especially after what I had just done with it for Sven. It held too many memories. I needed the guitar to be safe. I lifted the guitar with both my hands underneath it as if I was presenting it to someone. But I wasn't presenting it to anyone but myself. I wanted to take a moment of appreciation for what the guitar has done for me, for what it meant to me. With an inner voice delivering my gratitude, I softly whispered my spell. "Sparkle sparkle, we'll resume. Sparkle sparkle, in my room."

Lights. Tingles. Whoosh.

In a blink of an eye, the guitar vanished from the palms of my hands. I reeled my arms back in to my body and took another reassuring look in all directions to make sure that nobody had seen me before I started walking.

I swiftly and inconspicuously slipped out of the alley and onto the school grounds, mixing in with the rest of the school kids in their dresses and tuxedos. Just as I approached the steps leading to the school hall, I felt a zooming movement behind me. I turned around. "Hey rat!" Sonya waved at me with freshly painted fingernails. Black, of course. She moved up a step to level with me before she linked her left arm with my right. "You look nice."

She sidled over a little to get another look of my outfit. "Those pants look familiar. Are they…" she said and looked at me, grinning knowingly. "They are, aren't they?" I nodded to confirm her suspicions. "I knew it. They look so different, and yet I knew they were your hole pants, now being *whole* pants. From hole to whole." She winked at me to acknowledge her pun. We both giggled. "But honestly, rat, they look great on you. They are a lot more you. Don't you think?" I looked down on my new skinny jeans, tightly hugging my legs like a second skin. "Yes, they are. And it feels great to wear and do something I was uncomfortable to do in the past," I expressed with pride swelling in my voice. "Speaking of uncomfortable things," Sonya said, "how did it go with Sven? How did he react? What did he say? Is he coming?" Sonya overwhelmingly gunned her curiosity at me with all those questions. And rightfully so. Of course, she wanted to know. And of course, I wanted to tell her.

"Yeah, umm… he received my gift, I mean the box. Umm." I waved around with my hands excessively. "Well, he *received* it but he didn't actually open it." Sonya tried to maintain an encouraging smile. "Okay, and what about the other gift you had for him?" she asked. "The song," I said, "Yeah, the song…" I scratched my cheeks nervously, "Well, he received that too. He sat down and listened." Sonya's eyes glanced at me in anticipation. "And then, … then he said thank you and goodbye," I concluded the story abruptly. "Wait… That's it?" Sonya was as disappointed about it as I was. "So you're telling me that you put your heart on the line, you put all of you out there and all he said was 'thank you and goodbye'? What a jerk!" Sonya's voice developed an angry undertone. "Well, actually," I added, "he also said 'I'll see you at school', so…." I shrugged my shoulders. "So you're hoping he will still come here now," Sonya finished my thought. I nodded. She looked at me soothingly as we took the last few steps to reach the top of the stairs.

We were there. We turned around. A wall of people ascended, passing us on their way into the hall. We looked around, scanning for a sign of Sven. Anxiety entered my body, a familiar feeling of discomfort and fear, of dread und uncertainty. I started to shiver as this feeling seemed to take over every cell of my existence. Suddenly, I felt Sonya's hand grabbing mine. With determination and warmth. She squeezed my hand tight, again and again, as if to adjust her grip, but I knew it was to signal her presence to me, being by my side, literally and emotionally. She slightly angled her head. Her eyes met mine as she smiled at me. We stood there for a moment. Still. Quiet. Without saying a word to each other. And we didn't need to. Our look, her smile told me what it had told me so often in the past, ever since I met her in the hollow tree in kindergarten. I knew what the look meant, I knew what the smile meant. This knowledge, this awareness pushed away the anxiety and gave me back a sense of peace. As my head started to turn away from her and back towards the crowd that came up the stairs, she squeezed my hand again intently. So intently that I looked back at her. I found her eyes still glued to me. She looked deep into my eyes and whispered the words softly into my face in a way that seemed like a spell. A spell without magic freckles, but nonetheless a spell that brought its own kind of magic. The magic of friendship and belonging. She squeezed my hand once again as the words left her mouth and carried them on a carpet of her fresh breath, "I got you."

I gave Sonya a gentle kiss on her cheek. I had never done that but it felt right in this moment. She was such a trooper, such a rock for me, and I loved her so much for that. I loved her. Full stop. I knew she wasn't the biggest fan of public affection, let alone a kiss on the cheek, but she received the kiss without flinching, without hesitance. She knew the weight of that particular moment. She embraced it. She even seemed to enjoy it as she smiled at me with her caring eyes. We both turned our heads back towards the ascending crowd. Another look. Another scan for

Sven. But he was not in sight. I sighed, almost inaudible over the upbeat music of the prom. "He's not coming, is he?" I asked Sonya without actually needing a conformation. I knew he wasn't. I kept all the hope that I still had left to spare and put it on this. The hope that he forgave me. The hope that he understood me. The hope that he felt the same way about me. The hope to meet atop of those stairs where I waited for him, in my new old outfit with my old new hope. The hope that everything would turn out okay.

"Come on, rat, let's go inside. We are here now, so let's have some fun, yes?" Sonya said eventually. I knew she was right. As difficult and sobering as the realisation was that Sven wasn't going to show, I did want to have some fun. I needed some fun. Hell, I *deserved* some fun. After all I had gone through, I just wanted some light distraction from all of it, and I knew I could find that at the school prom, which was kind of controversial really. An event at school to have some fun? When all I knew of school was pain and agony?! It was strange, to say the least, but it felt good to finally feel something else.

Sonya and I shifted our bodies and faced the wide open doors, appropriately decorated with cutouts of musical notes, instruments and dancing shoes. The thumping bass summoned us inside. Sonya softly elbowed me in my hip as she stretched out her index finger. "FTT!" We smiled as we strode along with all the other attendees of the prom until we reached the monstrous space of the school hall. The committee did a great job in creating an inviting vibe. Glitter boas and streamers hanging from the ceiling wherever you looked. A stereotypical disco ball in the very centre to mark the dance floor. The stage, that often served for speakers at assemblies or for the yearly school play, was turned into a wonderland of lights and colour. The usually so ugly and repulsive curtains enjoyed a resurgence of life, provided by the projector that unleashed a kaleidoscope of shapes onto it. It truly was a different room, and it really made me want to be there. I was drawn to it. It felt just... well, magical.

"Wow," Sonya said with a hint of sarcasm as we exchanged looks to acknowledge the makeover of the once so dull school hall. "Yeah." I chortled and opened my eyes wide to take in all of the details that had been thoughtfully arranged to make sure the evening was at least a visual success. I was amazed. The speakers, which were arranged at every possible angle of the hall, kept belting out pleasant pop music that made people bobble, but the dance floor was still very much empty. It was still early, though. I was sure with time, that space was going to be packed with people swinging and swaying. The thought of that made me both happy and sad. Happy because I was there to enjoy it with Sonya. Sad because I couldn't share this with Sven. How amazing it would have been to have my two best friends back, at an event that turned out so beautifully put together. Truly, I was happy that Sonya was there with me, though as much as I tried, I couldn't help but feel sad. Having to adjust to a life without Sven was going to be a whole new challenge. A challenge that I didn't know how to tackle. My thoughts went further into the gloomy passage of 'would have, could have, should haves'. "Let's get some punch, Spence." Sonya pulled me away from my thoughts, literally and emotionally. She led the way to the bar area that was set up to the left of the stage.

The bar was manned by a handful of volunteers made up of teachers and dedicated parents. My mum was one of them. She always liked to help with stuff like that. She even put her hand up once to knit clothing accessories for school plays. Yes, my mum was dedicated. She liked to contribute, and to be involved like this, but I always thought that she secretly did it to keep an eye on me. She would have never admitted it. I asked her a couple of times but she insisted that she just wanted to be of help. And even if she had fessed up to it, I wouldn't have told her not to do it.

Yes, maybe she did this to keep tabs on me, but she also did this for herself. To get out of the house, to feel needed and useful. Who didn't want to feel needed and useful. I would have never taken that from her. So no matter her intentions, I was happy she was there.

She stood behind the counter with a ladle in her hand, ready to dunk it into one of the giant bowls of fruit punch. Mrs Anderson, who was also part of the punch bunch, and my mum were engaged in a conversation, smiling at each other as both of them gestured at the apron that my mum was wearing. Of course, it was one from her unique collection. This one was perfect for the occasion. It read 'CAUTION. May spontaneously start dancing'. When I saw the apron, I shook my head, half cringing, half grinning, internally applauding my mum for being the awesome woman that she was. I could totally see her break out in dance without any warning. That was so her. She did this often at home, with any given song on the radio. For the time being though, her feet stood still as she chatted with Mrs Anderson. They always got along. And I was so happy about that. In a way, they both felt like my mums. Mrs Anderson was the caring person at school, one that you could go to if you had any questions, concerns or problems. And my mum - well, she was my mum. She raised me to be who I was, she encouraged me to be who I wanted to be, she was always there for me. So seeing this union between my mum and Mrs Anderson warmed my heart.

As Sonya and I approached the bar, my mum and Mrs Anderson almost simultaneously moved their heads towards us. "Hi, you guys," Mrs Anderson said enthusiastically as she came closer to the counter, my mum lining beside her. "Spencer. Sonya." Mum reached out both her hands. Her face was filled with motherly pride. She lovingly squinted her eyes and smiled. "So?" She let go of us and rubbed her hands. "You're thirsty then? Want some punch?" Sonya and I looked at each other and nodded in agreement. "Yes, please," we said. Both Mrs Anderson and mum took a glass and filled each with the punch. They made sure we got a good amount of fruit. "Here you are. Enjoy," Mrs Anderson said as they handed us the drinks. "Now go and have some fun," mum added while she gently shooed us away. "Thank you. We will." Sonya and I waved before we made our way to the edge of the dance floor. I took a sip of the punch. The unexpected acidity of the drink travelled down my throat, and I started to cough. "Wow," I said just before Sonya started coughing, too. "Uh... yeah. Wow," she said as she cleared her throat. "It certainly packs a punch, doesn't it?" I snorted. "It certainly does," she agreed and chuckled along. I took another sip and sucked my teeth at the confronting acidic pinch of the punch.

It let my eyes roam around the hall before they stopped at the sight of Robbie and his minions. I was mildly surprised that they came to the prom. An event which they undoubtedly considered lame. At least officially. And yet, they were there, huddled in the corner with bottles of soft drinks in their hands which they frivolously cheered with. They had no dates, just each other. The minion brotherhood. And maybe that was enough for them, but I was curious to see how the evening was going to go for them. Were they going to ask anyone to dance with them, or were they just going to stand in the same spot all night? Were they going to bag the hell out of everyone and everything, or did they actually come to have a good time, leaving any bullying aside, at least for one night? My eyes wandered further and eventually met Adrian who was on the opposite side of the room. He spotted me just as I spotted him. He held up his glass, and I held up mine. We cheered to each other and had a sip of our drinks. I could see that Adrian struggled to swallow the punch just as much as Sonya and I did. "Wow," he mouthed as he wiped his lips with the back of his hand. I smiled and winked at him. I promised myself that I would join him later for a proper catch up. But for now, I stayed standing at the edge of the dance floor with Sonya who was hugging her punch with both hands, but she wasn't drinking it. She just held it and looked at the centre of the room.

The music continued to blare out of the speakers as more and more people tiptoed onto the floor. Many familiar faces that I knew from my class or from seeing around the school grounds, and others who I had never seen or spoken to before. Among the students who wholeheartedly embraced the music were Angie and Angelica. Two girly girls, both extremely pretty, both extremely popular. They were known for being inseparable besties. Two girls who held hands at school or wherever else they went. Two girls who kissed each other frequently without thinking twice about it. On the neck, on the cheeks, on the mouth. Nobody seemed to care or question their relationship. They could just be who they wanted to be and do what they wanted to do without being interrupted or interrogated about it. I was happy for them, but I envied them. The freedom they had. The admiration they had from the whole school. The adoration they had for each other. It seemed so real, so uncomplicated, so beautiful.

Why it was different with them was a mystery to me though!? Was it because it was socially more accepted for two girls to be a couple? It definitely seemed to more accepted among straight males. I remembered watching a show with Grandma Rose and Grandpa Doug once, and there was a gay couple making out. Grandpa Doug immediately reacted to it. "Two women would be fine, but two men together - that's disgusting," he said, visibly repulsed. I remembered this moment well because I felt both excited and uncomfortable. Excited to see people like me on television, doing the things that I dreamt of doing openly. But uncomfortable because I watched it with my grandparents, and Grandpa Doug had such a strong response to it, making me want to dig an ever bigger hole for myself to hide in. I knew that even though the winds of time had shifted and things were generally more chill, more tolerated, there were always going to be morons.

There were always going to be ignorant people who you couldn't argue with or who were not interested in changing their views.

It was certainly evident with Angie and Angelica that times had changed, and they were on the lucky end of it. As I watched them have the best time of their lives on the dance floor, the memories of Sven came back to the surface. All the memories we made together from the day he entered that classroom and sat in front of me and looked at me with his piercing green eyes. While Angie and Angelica continued twirling and laughing, I realised that I might never have that. I thought I could have that with Sven. I thought we could walk the same path together. But our paths hit a fork in the road. And I was the reason for that fork. I didn't embrace who I was. I embraced part of who I was but not all of me. I wasn't there yet, and I should have been if I wanted Sven and I to have any kind of chance to succeed, as friends or as more than friends. I knew I made mistakes but I also knew that I had done everything as best as I could to mend them. The reality, however, was that it wasn't enough. *I* wasn't enough. The upbeat music served as a contradictory soundtrack of my emotions. I was heartbroken, as much as I didn't want to admit it to myself, but I was. I was heartbroken. Deeply heartbroken, and I truthfully didn't know how to deal with it. I had never felt anything like this before. The ache in my chest was a relentless and continuous stabbing of my heart. Not the kind of stabs I felt when Robbie made nasty remarks about me. Those were nothing in comparison to what I felt now. My eyes quickly welled up as I sniffled in an attempt to hold it together. A heavy tear trickled down the side of my left cheek. I swiftly wiped it away as I didn't want Sonya to see. I didn't want her to worry more than I knew she already did. But it was too late. I felt her hand on my right shoulder as I braved another sip of the punch.

The sip departed my mouth, down my throat, as I tried to suppress the coughing. The hand persistently glued to my shoulder. My eyes looked over to Sonya. She was still standing next to me, watching the crowd on the dance floor - while her glass was cushioned between her hands. Both her hands. Wait, *both* hands? So whose hand was on my shoulder if it wasn't Sonya's? I slowly and anxiously turned around, afraid but curious. As Sonya felt my movements, she looked over and gravely inhaled, gasping for air. "Oh!" she exclaimed. My eyes swiped hers while my head turned the other way, with the rest of my body following. The expression on Sonya's face gave me nothing but a look of surprise, her eyes moving around left and right, and right and left, like ping pong balls. She didn't know where to look and almost dropped her glass.

Everything went so quickly, in a matter of seconds, milliseconds even. Milliseconds that couldn't usually hold this kind of suspense, this kind of captivating sensation. My body continued to turn towards the hand that still rested on my shoulder. My head impatiently hurried ahead of my body as the disco ball lights suddenly flooded my eyes. I awkwardly tried to blink away the irritation of the glare, calling to my arms for help. With my hands shielding the lights, my twitching eyes started to recover and my vision became clearer, until it fully sharpened. My eyes found the hand on my shoulder. Its wrist was covered by a smooth green pattern that extended to the rest of the jacket. As my gaze climbed the arm to reach its broad shoulder, the realisation set in but I was afraid to believe it. I denied myself to believe it. I hesitated and looked down where I saw black Converse shoes pointing in my direction. The realisation crystallised, pushing me to believe it. But I resisted. I started panting as if I had just run a half marathon. My body was trembling, my stomach was electrified. That electrifying feeling. How familiar it was! How scary it was! How exhilarating it was! My feet were anchored to the ground, my eyes still fixed on the black Chucks. I stood frozen, trying to free myself from the chains of anxiety. I closed my eyes for a moment and took a deep, satisfying breath after which I eventually moved my eyes away from the ground, away from the shoes, up along the black jeans that were hugged by a white belt around the hips. The sight of the familiar smooth green fabric of the jacket led my eyes to the chest, to the broad shoulders, to the neck until - finally - I was met with a face that had a soft dimply smirk painted on it. Sven! "Hi," he said as he brushed his hand off my shoulder.

I couldn't believe what I saw. I couldn't believe that Sven stood in front of me. Bedazzled by what just happened, I looked over to Sonya, her mouth half open as she casually tried to hide her surprise by lifting the punch to her lips and taking a sip. She cleared her throat. As a reaction to the punch but also to acknowledge the jaw-dropping moment of Sven's sudden appearance. Both her and I did not see this coming. "I, umm, I will give you guys a minute," she said, stroking my back as she walked behind me, vanishing into the dark alcove near the bar. My eyes followed her every step until I couldn't see her anymore.

Once she disappeared from my sight, I knew I couldn't avoid Sven's piercing green eyes anymore. I had to face them, I had to face him. And I *wanted* to. I was just so astounded, so knocked over the head surprised to see him. My eyes met his, his dimply smile still lighting up his face. "Sorry, I am late," he said. "Umm, uh, no...umm," I stuttered nervously, "It's fine. Uh, well, I... I didn't expect to see you. Well, I did... but then I didn't." I looked at Sven, unsure if he understood what I meant, if he knew how I felt and how I thought. "I mean, of course I wanted to expect you here but I didn't know if I *could* expect you." I realised that I was rambling. "I... I don't know if this makes sense. I... I just..." Sven tenderly put his index finger on my lips. It not only made me shut up but it also made my body tremble even more. A single touch, so slight but so impactful. I felt tingles emerging from the touch of my lips and moving unwaveringly through the rest of my body. "Shhh," he softly and reassuringly hushed, "It makes perfect sense." He slowly moved away his finger from my mouth. "Always expect the unexpected, right?" he stated. The conversant catch phrase transported me back to the time when he said that to me in the national park, ironically just before our lives, our friendship changed with the unexpected revelation of my magic freckles.

"Yeah." I licked my lips as if to taste the residue of his touch. "Shall we go somewhere quiet?" he asked. "Ah, yeah," I answered before Sven led the way through the crowd standing at the side of the dance floor. I stayed close behind him as we bolted through the mass of people, my eyes gliding through the room, sweeping by the bar where mum and Mrs Anderson were busy handing out drinks. As my eyes moved passed them, I caught the sight of Sonya who had been watching me from the corner, still hugging her glass of punch. She pressed her lips together and gravely nodded at me as Sven and I reached the main door, leading us to the stairs outside where I had waited for Sven at the beginning of the evening.

The air was fresh and pleasant, serving a welcome relief to the stuffiness of the moment. "Ahhh," Sven exhaled, "what a beautiful night." He peered at the stars above us. "Yeah, it is." I looked up, paying the sky a visit with a brief gaze, my feet entertaining some slight seesawing, until I decided to address the elephant in the room. I turned to Sven, about to express the words that needed to be said, that I needed to get off my chest, words that Sven deserved to hear. He whipped towards me in the same moment and beat me to it. "I'm sorry," he said, the exact words that I wanted to say. "That's what I was going to say. No. No, Sven! *I* am sorry!" I said, a faint smile appearing on both our faces. "No, Spence. *I* am sorry," Sven said as we started to walk down the stairs. "I am sorry I was such a jerk," he continued. "You were not. You were not a jerk," I opposed, "You were just..." I stopped to find the right way to end that sentence.

"Hurt," Sven interjected, "I was hurt." Even though this was something I knew, it was painful to hear from his mouth. The last thing I wanted was to hurt him, to subject him to the unpleasantries of agony. Still, I did. I did subject him to that. I hurt him. "And I am so sorry for that, Sven." My eyes began to water upon the thought of the pain I inflicted on him. "I know you are, Spence. I know you are," he said. "You tried to apologise and explain, and I wouldn't hear it. I didn't want to hear it because all I could think of, all I could see was my disappointment. What I didn't want to see was that you wanted to reconcile. What I didn't want to see was that you are only human too... I think?" He winked at me, playfully addressing my magic powers. "Yes," I awkwardly said, "I am still human but sometimes I wish that I wasn't, so that I didn't have to feel like this." A heavy shrug pulled at my shoulders. "I know what you mean. I don't want to feel like this either. But this is all part of the beautiful adventure we call life. There will always be sadness and darkness, but there will also always be happiness and light. You have to risk one thing in order to have the chance to experience the other," Sven said profoundly. "Yes, that's true," I said, letting his words sink in. "And you did exactly that, Spence. You took a risk. You took a risk to open up to me, and I shut you down. And for that, I am truly sorry, and I hope that you can forgive me." Sven took my hand into the comfort of both of his palms. "I just want you to understand where I was coming from, too." He gently stroked my hand with his thumbs. "I... I don't know. I am a mess really..." He let go of my hand and skittishly started playing with his chin-long hair. "No. No!" I objected, "If anything, I am the mess here." He smiled at me while still fiddling with his hair. "Maybe we both are." He took back my hand and held it tight.

"I... Spencer..." he resumed, attempting to find the right words. "Look, when I met you, I was immediately drawn to you. We started to talk. We started to hang out. We started to develop... something. Something special. Something that I cherished and couldn't wait to see where it would go, where it would take us. We were similar in many respects and yet so different, in a way that was exciting for me. We had a connection. Undoubtably. You were a friend that I always wanted, especially after going through a tough time at my previous school. You understood. You knew. And I loved that." He looked deep into my eyes as he went on. "Expect the unexpected. An advice I gave you once, yet I couldn't take it on board myself. I could have never expected this. I could have never expected that I would find someone like you. Sure, I always hoped but I truly never ever expected it. I could have never expected to meet someone as great and special as you. And..." He paused and sighed. "I could have never expected to meet someone with magical powers." I pulled his hand placidly. "I know, Sven. I... I didn't ex—" I hastily said. "I know, Spence," he stopped me. "You didn't expect this either." Sven knew exactly what I wanted to say and how I felt about it. He understood that it was just as much of a shock to me as it was for him - to find out that I was a witch.

"It was a difficult pill to swallow, Spencer. I... I struggled with it a lot. I started questioning everything. Everything that we had experienced. Everything that we had built. I started wondering 'Was any of it real?'. I asked myself this over and over again. Was it real or was it magic? My world was turned upside down when I met you. And then it was turned upside down once again when I found out about your freckles. I was just so... so overwhelmed. I was consumed with doubt and too focused on my pain, too obsessed to figure out what was real in the past when I should have looked at the present, at what was right in front of me. You. And you were real. You *are* real. And you have always been real with me. But I didn't see that. I was too busy examining the past that I completely forgot to pave a way for the future. To take a risk. To let go and let be." His words were hitting the core of my soul. All this time, I had wondered what he was going through, what he was thinking, why he withdrew from me for so long. It brought a wave of release over me, of contentment, of hope, as my eyes, my heart, my soul embraced every syllable of Sven's words.

"And then you came to my house." He squeezed my hand and shook it from side to side, a gesture of appreciation and awakening. "I did," I said, looking down uncomfortably as I felt my cheeks burning. "Ummm, maybe that was a bit much," I reflected. "No!" Sven threw his hands in the air in disagreement. "No! It was not too much. It was... perfect. It was so thoughtful. It was so you. It was so... real." He came a step closer to me as his hands found mine again. "It made me realise that everything was always real. You were always real. And while it all was real, it was also magic. A magic that I had never known, never felt. A magic that came out of your song, out of your words, out of your actions. A magic I didn't know how to deal with. But a magic I knew I wanted to explore. Together. With you." My eyes were locked on his mouth.

A moment of silence arose. I didn't know what to say. Instead, I was still staring at Sven's luscious lips. I wanted them to spit out more words, more revelations, I wanted more of the emotions that they made me feel. I stood motionlessly in front of Sven who still held my hands. He suddenly pulled them and shifted my body weight towards him. His lips started to come closer, and closer, and closer - until they hit mine. His lips touched mine. His lips kissed mine. My eyes closed intuitively, sending me into a realm of fireworks. That feeling. That electrifying feeling that I experienced with Sven reached new heights, a climax of enchantment. Sven's lips were so soft, like two comforting pillows, satisfyingly taking care of my deepest needs and desires. Our lips turned into a playground that hauled our minds into the unchartered waters of wants, leading to a merry-go-round of emotions that were overwhelming but fulfilling, unknown but exciting. I didn't want to move. My body was happily settled in that position. I didn't want it to end. I didn't want to open my eyes. I wanted to stay in this moment, in this world I was transported to. This moment, this world with Sven - I wanted it to last forever.

As our lips slowly parted, our eyes opened and met immediately - unflinching and direct. Sven smiled. I smiled. We stared at each other with the mutual gleam of happiness when Sven whispered, "I promise I will never doubt you again. I promise I will be there for you, with you. I promise." He leaned over and gave me another kiss. Gentle and meaningful. When Sven moved his head back, I pressed my lips together. Wanting to keep the feel of the kiss on my lips. Wanting to preserve it. "And I promise that I will not keep secrets from you anymore. I am so sorry that I hurt you, but I promise that I will never do that again." I put my hand on his cheek and caressingly moved my thumb across it before I flipped my arms over his head to hug him. My head rested on his shoulders while Sven put his chin on mine to lock our bodies in a tight embrace. His hands stroked my back while gently pressing against it. It felt good. To be in Sven's arms, to hold him, to feel him so close. That was all I ever wanted. A weight lifted off my shoulders. A weight I had carried with me for so long, but all the challenges, all the struggles, all the highs and lows of this path were worth it. They brought me here, exactly where I wanted to be, where I longed to be.

Sven's body continued to clinch to mine, its warmth counterbalancing the increasing chill in the air. "So," I heard Sven say over my shoulder, "umm, so what do you use your magic for? I mean, when you don't save bullying classmates." I chuckled as I released his neck from my hugging arms. "Well, uh, I don't know. I... I mean, I have used it a few times, but just to explore my possibilities. Or to have some fun." I told him about the spell I did on Mr Moore. "Ohh, the banana boxers! That was you?!" He snickered. I cheekily nodded. We burst out laughing at the thought of that image. "That was hilarious." Sven snorted, trying to catch his breath. "Well, he deserved it," he concluded.

The chuckle slowly dwindled. "Spencer?" Sven looked at me. "Can I ask you something?" I wondered what he wanted to know. "Of course. You can ask me anything?" I assured him. "Ahem," he cleared his throat, "would you... would you ever want to show me? I mean... only if you want..." I thought he was so sweet and thoughtful in that moment. He wanted to get to know the part of me that I had been hiding from him, that caused a rift between us. But now he wanted to see it. He invited it. He welcomed it. At the same time, he didn't want to pressure me to share it now and then. He was curious but also understanding and willing to give me the time that I needed for it. "Yes, of course!" There was no doubt for me. I wanted to show him. I had always wanted to show him. It felt like the final key to an unopened room that I invited him to step into, that I wished to share with him, fully, openly, proudly - of course, I wanted to do that. "Do you have anything in mind?" I asked to know if he wanted to see something specific. Maybe he wanted me to expose someone else's underwear? Or maybe I could have showed him how I fly among the stars? Or maybe... "Maybe," he interrupted my string of thoughts, "I don't know, maybe you could somehow use your magic to celebrate this?" Sven wiggled his finger in the air between us. I was a little muddled about his request at first, but I liked that he didn't want to see a random spell. He wanted to see my magic used in a relevant way to this very moment. I thought that was so romantic. Without much thinking, I quickly came up with the perfect answer, the perfect way to show him what he asked for.

I took his hand and led him to the side of the stairs. We walked underneath it where a hollow vault gave us shelter from any possible intruders. We stood on the threshold from where we faced the tree-lined area in front of the school hall. I kept his hand in the palm of mine. "Are you ready?" I looked at him for approval. "As ready as I'll ever be," he answered and smiled nervously. I squeezed his hand before I closed my eyes and took a deep breath. I felt his head turn and absorb my every move. Then I said, "Sparkle sparkle, day bestow. Sparkle sparkle, a night's rainbow."

Lights. Tingles. Whoosh.

The tingles in my body persisted as I opened my eyes. Tingles not just from my freckles, but rather from the excitement of having Sven next to me, of showing him what I could do with my sparkles, of evincing myself to him completely.

I smiled at Sven whose head was drawn to the sky. A night sky of a very different kind. A rainbow, its vibrant colours competing with the bright shine of the stars, yet perfectly aligning with each other to create the most beautiful feast for the eyes. Sven's mouth opened in astonishment, his eyes twinkling through the spectacle of light and colour. "Spence, this is amazing," Sven said and turned to me rapidly. "*You* are amazing." He kissed my hand before he moved back to his prior position as we marvelled at the glory in front of us. "I thought this was a good way to describe this moment, to describe us," I said as the corner of my eyes searched for Sven's silhouette. "A rainbow is the result of a tumultuous relationship between rain clouds and sunshine. A symbol of the struggle of being. A symbol of the joys of being. No matter how dark the clouds are, aspiration and perseverance can carry you back to the light, and it can create the most beautiful outcome. Something that means it was all worth it, just to see this, just to be here. To me, it's a symbol of beauty, and light, and hope. It's a symbol of you." I halted. My head slightly tilted towards Sven while my eyes begged to be reunited with his.

A second passed, and then I blurted out, "Oh my God, I'm so cringe!" I chuckled, embarrassed, as I leaned my forehead on

Sven's shoulder, wanting to bury my face in it. "Haha. No, Spence. You're not. You're sweet. But you're wrong, the rainbow is a symbol of *you*, not me," he said. I smiled at him and exhaled, the cold air transforming my warm breath into a misty cloud that conveyed my words into the atmosphere. "It's a symbol of… us." Sven pulled my hand, calmly swinging it while maintaining a tight grip. "A symbol of us," he said contently with a big grin on his face "We are both cringe," I concluded, the two of us snickering, as we continued to stare at the rainbow.

We stood in the niche under the stairs for a while longer. Enjoying the sky's celestial spectrum in comfortable silence. Nothing needed to be said, but everything needed to be felt. Everything needed to be taken in. Every moment, every breath, every heartbeat. The appreciation of the presence, even of the past that got us where we were. We stood still, and silent. And although we didn't talk, our hands said plenty, playfully communicating with each other. Our thumbs vivaciously wrestled while the other fingers competed to skim over the other one's palm. Our hands, our fingers, our whole bodies were full of life, nervous, excited to be standing next to each other.

I drew in some fresh air and exhaled with a grateful smile. As my eyes followed my hot breath ascending and seemingly becoming part of the rainbow, I turned to Sven. "Should we go back inside?" He smiled. "Yes, let's." We hunched out of the nook and started heading up the stairs. "Oh," I said, realising that the rainbow still accompanied the starry sky. "I should…" I pointed at the sky without finishing my sentence. We paused. "Sparkle sparkle, shiny glow. Sparkle sparkle, thanks rainbow."

Lights. Tingles. Whoosh.

Sven and I watched the rainbow bid us farewell, slowly and steadily fading away, until it completely vanished. We smiled, grabbed each other's hand and walked up the stairs and into the school hall. "Let's do this," Sven said, nudging his chin my way. "Let's do this," I repeated unanimously.

As we reached the entrance, the thunderous music greeted us, supported by an excited roar coming from the now busy dance floor. Everyone seemed pumped and full of adrenaline. I certainly was adrenalised as Sven and I stepped deeper into the hall, hand in hand. I spotted Sonya, still in the same corner. She waved at us and came walking towards us. The increasing crowd made it difficult to move but she managed to push through, until she was just a couple of metres away from us. That was when Mike bumped into her from the side, spilling his punch at her feet, only narrowly missing her Doc Martens. "You idiot," she hissed at him. "Get out of my way." I loved how she had no filter and gave it to him like that, intuitively. Once Mike stumbled away in submission, Sonya came over and looked at us. Together, reunited, and... hand in hand. She was happy for us, and we were happy to have her with us and share it with her. We clustered together and chatted about everything and nothing, naturally bantering as if we had never been apart at all. While Sonya was filling us in on all the prom gossip that we had missed, my eyes swept across the bar area where I saw my mum peer at me. She, too, had noticed Sven and I coming back to the hall, holding hands. She held a tea towel and scrunched it between her hands, like you would scrunch a stuffed toy. She held onto it tight as her look of love and pride filled my heart with joy and warmth. This was the first time that mum had seen me with a boy like this. It was the first time that she saw who I truly was. She always knew, deep inside her heart, but she never saw it with her own eyes. Until now. She could not only see who I truly was but also how happy I was being my true self. It was liberating to feel... whole.

As Sonya finished her update on the school crowd, we looked at the raging dance floor. "Sooo," Sven finally said, "wanna dance?"

He winked at me. "Umm, I don't know," I said hesitantly. I wanted to but I was still a bit taken back. I may have felt whole but I was still apprehensive about shouting it out into the universe. "Come on, Spence. Don't you wanna dance?" Sven said with a cheeky smile, referencing one of the prom poster slogans. Before I could say anything else, he swiftly took my hand and headed onto the floor. He kept walking further and further through the throng, gently pulling me with him. Where did he want to go? Where did he want to dance? Couldn't we just dance with all the other people? Yes, squished together like sardines but at least not so exposed. I would have been okay with that. But Sven kept walking, leading the way with my hand deeply imbedded in his. He eventually stopped at the steps leading up to the stage. He looked at me suggestively. "No!" I exclaimed. I shook my head vigorously and took a small step back, tugging Sven with me. "Let's stay down here, Sven. We can have a dance here." I gestured to a spot amidst the dancing mass where we could have easily joined. "Why do you want to go up there and have everyone look at us and judge us?" I asked, trying to make a point. "Spencer!" He took both of my hands, as if he was going to propose. "We both know what it's like to be looked at, to be judged, to be bullied. We didn't have any say in that. It was out of our power, out of our control. We were just being who we were, and we were judged for it without consent. So now, we have the opportunity to take back control, take back our power and give them something to look at, give them something to judge. But at least it would be something that we allowed them to see. It would be on our terms. And Spence..." He brushed his thumbs over my fingers. "I don't want to hide what we have here. I don't want to keep this a secret. I don't care what people think or say. I only care that I am with you. Sooner or later, they will find out about us. And don't you think it's better to call the shots on your own life, to come out, rather than them doing that for us? It should be up to us to do that, and this is our chance to do that. We can take the wind out of their sails," Sven concluded as his piercing green eyes looked at me intensively.

Sven had always been more confident than me despite his bullying past at his old school. His energy was inspiring. He delivered his point intently and convincingly. His mission was clear. He didn't want to be handcuffed by what other people did, or thought, or said. He wanted to be the master of his own life. He wanted to be free, to feel free. And he wanted to do that with me, together, on stage, in front of everybody. It was a scary thought. Scarier than anything I ever had to deal with before. It was scary but exhilarating. Like a rollercoaster ride that amped up your adrenaline levels but consequently gave you a feeling of pride and accomplishment. Something you did even though you were afraid. Something that made you break out of your comfort zone. Something that ultimately made you grow. Something that made you feel capable and inspired. Something that simply made you feel… free. This was that situation. This was that moment. Quite fittingly, Sven took me on the rollercoaster ride from his very first day at my school. And though there were many ups and downs, I always stayed on, and I had no intention of getting off now. I was there for the whole ride. No matter if up or down. As long as Sven was by my side, I knew I was going to be alright. I turned to him, his words still echoing in my head. "Okay," I said eventually, initially still with a grain of tentativeness, "let's take that wind out of their sails!" I looked at Sven with a smile that expressed rising certainty. "And let's blow their fucking minds," I added with absolute conviction of what we were about to do. Sven pulled me into his arms. He put his right hand around my hip, which not only gave me a sense of comfort but also reignited the inner fireworks.

A situation like this, walking towards something challenging or confronting, had always been daunting in the past, with a feeling of dread accompanying my every step. Now, however, it was the complete opposite. While still challenging and confronting, going up those stage steps was empowering. With every step in the arms of Sven, I felt my anxiety fade away and my true self take over. His words resonated with me like nothing else before, making me realise that I had given people the power that wasn't theirs to take in the first place. The power that was mine, and only mine. Much like my magic freckles, but this was the power over my life, over who I am, over who I want to be. And Sven made me see another thing: People will judge you. People have done so in the past and they will do so in the future. They will judge you if you did something right in their eyes, and they will judge you if you didn't. So if the result was always going to be judgement, no matter how I acted or what I did, then I should as well just be me, the *truest* me. As a result, this would made me feel more at peace, taking the pressure off myself to be the person that I was expected to be, and instead embracing who I wanted to be.

Electrified by both the newly found awareness and Sven's lingering hand on my hip, we reached the stage. We were the only ones there, everyone else was busting moves on the dance floor below. As more and more people started to wonder what the hell we were doing on stage, I put my entire focus on Sven and his piercing green eyes. He stood in front of me, his eyes on mine, he smiled gently, just enough to reveal his cute dimples. That was when the next song started to play. A gentle pop song, not too slow and not too dancy, that naturally drew our bodies to move. The disco ball shone light reflections across the room which looked like a thousand fireflies, a thousand stars. Like a thousand... sparkles, calling the ones within ourselves to break free. Those sparkles that were always there inside of us but afraid to come out, suppressed by bullies and anxiety. Sparkles that were finally allowed to roam and show their special magic, dancing all around us in a joyous celebration of light as Sven and I emerged deeper into the sphere of just us and nobody else. They shone right around us and supported every move we took as we danced in complete alignment, swept away in each other's arms. It was a moment so beautiful, it made my heart want to burst. I was filled with the purity of happiness, with so much joy, with so much life.

"Oh, by the way, thank you for my present," Sven suddenly said. "You mean the song?" I asked to clarify, a little confused because he had already thanked me for it, but maybe he just wanted to acknowledge it more? "Oh yes, I mean the song was beautiful, and I loved every bit of it." He paused and smiled. "But I meant the black box you gave me." He took a step back to give a full view of his body. "Oh that!" I said with an excited smile on my face. "You like it?" I asked. "No, I don't like it, Spence," he said with a straight face, transcending me into a brief state of shock, until he relieved me from it a second later. "I love it," he emphasised as he pointed at his chest while he opened his suit jacket to reveal what the black box held within. A t-shirt. And not just a t-shirt. It was a t-shirt of a swan, pictured sideways, with its majestic white body and its long, gracious neck, slightly tilted backwards with its head pointed forward to the right side. He looked at his shirt. "I love that you gave me a shirt with a swan. It's so awesome," he chirped enthusiastically. "Well," I said, "I thought it's not only a nice motive but also a way to show pride. Like you said, we should take our power back. You've been called awful things in the past, at your old school, but you can take that and turn it around, make it your own." I affirmed passionately. "I love that you think that way, Spence. You're adorable," he whispered. A shy, content smile appeared on my face.

"And also," I finally said, "those swans we saw in the park reminded me of us." The swans had what I wanted. A connection. A bond. And I felt this bond with Sven. So this was my way to express that bond, and how happy I was to have found it with him. "They did?" Sven asked with a cheeky smirk. "Yes, they did," I said confidently before I took a small step back, too. I slowly moved my hands to the buttons on my suit jacket, eventually opening it and uncovering what was underneath. Yes, a t-shirt. And yes, a t-shirt with a swan. A sideways swan with the same majestic white body and the long, gracious neck with its tilted head pointed at the left side.

Sven chuckled at the sight of my shirt and he immediately moved towards me to give me a hug. I was so happy that he loved the shirts and the fact that we both wore them. The shirts, the hug, his sheer presence made me feel united. When Sven released me from his strong arms, his gaze drifted from my swan shirt up to my eyes, tracing over me with quiet heat, before he moved forward to land his lips on mine. A soft touch that caused more electrifying tingles in my belly. As our lips intertwined, our upper bodies were pushed close together. And with that, so were the swans on our shirts. As Sven and I touched, so did the swans. Sven's swan touched the forehead and beak of my swan. They, too, shared an intimate and delicate moment as the unity of their heads and necks formed the shape of a heart. The ultimate symbol of love. Two swans, separately and individually beautiful and magical in their own way. And when they came together, they joined their individual beautiful personalities, they joined forces and created a bond of a team that understood, respected and loved each other in a way that was so magical that magic itself was 'outmagiced'.

As Sven and I, and the swans on our shirts, continued to sway to the ongoing music, my eyes surveyed the school hall. Some people on the dance floor looked at us bewildered, some whispered to each other, but many people actually just kept dancing without giving us much notice. Others turned to us with a tenderhearted disposition, like Angie and Angelica, smiling, bouncing slightly on their heels. People seemed… happy for us?! In the comfort of Sven's arms, I knew that any reaction from them would have been made more bearable, lighter and easier. While I was prepared for just about anything regardless, what I experienced was monumental. People didn't seem to care. Or if they did, it wasn't negative. The general reaction was a lot more uplifting than I could have imagined. Maybe nobody really cared after all about two boys dancing together? Maybe it was all in my head? Maybe I was just too scared, too anxious, too prepared for another bullying attack. Maybe I just didn't want to believe that people could be kind and understanding, supportive even.

While I was still digesting the sympathetic vibe coming from the dance floor, my eyes kept drifting around. I could see my mum and Mrs Anderson at the bar, standing still, both of them looking at us. Their faces were engraved with delight, while my mum's eyes were tearing up. I knew when my mum got emotional. She would get a slight nervous twitch which was her attempt to shake it off in situations where she didn't necessarily want to show it. But she never succeeded. Any attempts to hide her emotions actually resulted in a heightening of them. Mum only ever wanted the best for me. She wanted me to be happy. And in this exact moment, she could see it for herself. I was happy! As mum wiped away endless tears, Mrs Anderson warmly put her arm around her as they both continued to watch Sven and I enjoy our dance.

Sonya stood in front of the stage, nodding at us with a big, full smile, displaying her set of perfect teeth. A smile that almost felt misplaced on her usually so stern-looking face, yet suited her perfectly. It showed her soft side. A facet that she only showed with people she trusted. While she may have physically stood in front of the stage, her emotional presence on stage with us was undeniable. She was with us, she was cheering for us, she was celebrating us.

As Sonya and I exchanged smiles, my eye was drawn to a sight that made me shake my head in disbelief. For a moment, I didn't know if I was dreaming or not. "Do... do you see that?" I mumbled into Sven's ear while I stared at the corner of the room where Adrian stood before. Well, Adrian still stood there but not alone. He was in a deep conversation… with Robbie. Their heads were in a huddle, almost touching each other. Their arms were flying around in gestures, suggesting anger and disappointment, all the while talking calmly and respectfully. The longer I watched them talk, the more I grasped what appeared to be happening. They were making amends. *Robbie* was making amends. After all this time that he had ignored Adrian, he finally came to his senses. As I stayed fixated on them, Robbie's eyes unanticipatedly aligned with mine with his familiar look of emptiness. But the emptiness in his eyes suddenly changed. An unexpected light filled the darkness of his pupils that pointed right at me. He turned away from Adrian, giving me his full attention in a way that felt so distinct, so intense, like he had never done before. His mouth opened slightly as the inaudibility of his words felt deafening, daunting. "Thank you. I am sorry." Those were the words that travelled from his corner of the room, across the school hall, to the stage where Sven held me tight supportively as he, too, followed the word deposit coming from Robbie's lips. Those were words I had gotten from Robbie before. They were insincere then, sarcastic remarks on his apparent endeavour of becoming the biggest bully of all time. However, this was different now. Robbie seemed genuine. As genuine as he appeared with Adrian in that moment, he was genuine with me, too. He was so earnest that it almost freaked me out. It was unlike anything else that I had experienced with him. "He realised at last, did he?" Sven finally said. "Y-Yeah," I stuttered, blinking my eyes, still not 100% certain that this wasn't a dream, "I guess so."

But Sven was right. Robbie did realise. Not only how out of line he was with me, and with Adrian, but also how things could have been a lot more dire in the national park if they had played out differently. He finally realised, or rather *Sonya* made him realise. I was convinced that her words to him opened his eyes and conjured this epiphany that made him think over his actions in the past, and his actions for the future. I nodded back to Robbie, a slight acknowledgment of his apparent remorse. He reciprocated the nod which caught Adrian's attention. He glanced over at me and smiled approvingly before he and Robbie emerged themselves back into the deep conversation they were in. They had a lot to catch up on, and I was so happy for Adrian. All he wanted was to be friends with Robbie, and he was a great friend to him, until Robbie rejected him. But now, Adrian seemed to be getting the happy ending he deserved.

"Expect the unexpected," I quietly said to myself as my eyes finished wandering around the school hall and returned back to Sven. He gently kissed my forehead. And then again. Forehead kisses. The familiarity of what those kisses arose in me. A feeling telling me that I was in good hands, that I was safe and understood, and that I could just be. Filled with appreciation and fuzzy warmth, I laid my hand on his cheek and stroked it softly. As the song slowly came to an end, I intently pressed my lips against Sven's. My body quivered, full of euphoria while my head was vibrating, full of gratitude. This night at the prom was compelling. Intense. Mind-blowing. A revelation. It changed the way that I wanted to think, how I wanted to act, how I wanted to be and how I wanted to… believe. This night at the prom was a promise that I made to myself. A promise to always keep going, to always keep hoping, to always stay true to myself. Even with all the tough times I went through, all the bullying, all the nastiness - in the end, it made *this* all worthwhile. This moment with Sven, our bodies interwoven in proud and open unison. This moment was worth fighting for.

Lights. Tingles. Whoosh.

No, this wasn't a magic trick. There was no magic spell. It was a different kind of spell though, still magical but different nonetheless. It was the spell I was under in this very moment. I

238

felt the *lights* of happiness coming from deep within us. I felt the *tingles* all throughout my body. It was an unbelievable sensation. A sensation that made me feel swept away. '*Whoosh*!' - that sensation. That spell. That magic. I was thankful for what it gave me, for what it showed me, for it opened my eyes that I always had powers, I always had magic, even before my sparkles came along. I just didn't see it. I didn't believe it. I didn't *want* to believe it. But here I was now, in the arms of my broad-shouldered Sven, touching his lips with mine, our eyes closed and our souls lost in the rhythms of our heartbeats. The music echoed faintly through the space of time, and it complemented this moment so well. The kiss continued. It seemed endless. I *wanted* it to be endless. I felt Sven's hands travel across my back and to my waist, squeezing me affectionately. My hands in return moved to his waist, squeezing, wanting more. We were in sync. We were in the same universe. We were we. Unapologetically.

Lights. Tingles. Whoosh.

THE END
(for now)

A special thanks goes to

Jakub

G

Sassy

for your valuable support!